Half Known Lives

OTHER BOOKS BY JOAN GIVNER

Katherine Anne Porter: A Life

Tentacles of Unreason SHORT FICTION

Katherine Anne Porter: Conversations

Unfortunate Incidents SHORT FICTION

Mazo de la Roche: The Hidden Life

Scenes from Provincial Life SHORT FICTION

The Self-Portrait of a Literary Biographer LIFE WRITING

In the Garden of Henry James SHORT FICTION

Thirty-Four Ways of Looking at Jane Eyre
SHORT FICTION & ESSAYS

HALF KNOWN LIVES

Joan Givner

NEW STAR BOOKS
VANCOUVER
2000

Copyright 2000 Joan Givner

All rights reserved. No part of this work may be reproduced or used in any form or by any means — graphic, electronic, or mechanical — without the prior written permission of the publisher. Any request for photocopying or other reprographic copying must be sent in writing to the Canadian Copyright Licensing Agency (CANCOPY), Suite 1900, 1 Yonge Street, Toronto, Ontario M5E 1E5.

Excerpts from "Her Kind" from *To Bedlam And Part Way Back* by Anne Sexton are reprinted by permission of Houghton Mifflin Company. Copyright 1960 by Anne Sexton, renewed 1988 by Linda G. Sexton. All rights reserved.

New Star Books Ltd.
107 - 3477 Commercial Street
Vancouver, BC V5N 4E8
www.NewStarBooks.com

Cover: Val Speidel
Typeset by New Star Books
Printed & bound in Canada by Transcontinental Printing & Graphics
1 2 3 4 5   04 03 02 01 00

Publication of this work is made possible by grants from the Canada Council, the British Columbia Arts Council, and the Department of Canadian Heritage Book Publishing Industry Development Program.

CANADIAN CATALOGUING IN PUBLICATION DATA

Givner, Joan, 1936–
  Half known lives

ISBN 0-921586-78-7

  Title.
PS8563.I86H34 2000   C813'.54   C00-910979-X
PR9199.3.G566H34 2000

For Emily Givner

The event on which this fiction is founded has been supposed ... as not of impossible occurrence. ... It was recommended by the novelty of the situations which it develops, and however impossible as a physical fact, affords a point of view to the imagination for the delineating of human passions more comprehensive and commanding than any which the ordinary relations of existing events can yield.

FROM THE PREFACE TO
MARY SHELLEY'S *Frankenstein*

The fetus, scientists are discovering, is self-sustaining. Hormonal fluctuations, breast development, and most side effects of pregnancy are caused by the fetus's influencing the mother and not by the mother controlling the fetus. Therefore, it seems to follow that if a man became an incubator for a fetus, the developing baby would give him weight gain, morning sickness, lactating breasts, and anything else a woman may experience. It would be like a tubal pregnancy and the man could face a risky delivery after carrying the baby for nine months.

FROM *Listen To Your Body*
BY NEILS H. LAUERSEN, MD
AND EILEEN STUKANE

Consider ... the universal cannibalism of the sea; all whose creatures prey upon each other, carrying on eternal war since the world began.

Consider all this; and then turn to this green, gentle, and most docile earth; consider them both, the sea and the land; and do you not find a strange analogy to something in yourself? For as this appalling ocean surrounds the verdant land, so in the soul of man there lies one insular Tahiti, full of peace and joy, but encompassed by all the horrors of the half known life. God keep thee! Push not off from that isle, thou never canst return.

FROM *Moby Dick*, CHAPTER LVIII. QUOTED BY
G.J. BARKER-BENFIELD IN *The Horrors Of
The Half-Known Life: Male Attitudes to Women
and Sexuality in Nineteenth Century America*

Half Known Lives

PROLOGUE

IT SEEMS LIKE a miracle, your travelling here in the dead of winter and finding me on this island, as if your coming is the fulfillment of a prophecy. Even the little flat below seems to have been waiting for you.

I built this place as a summer home, and when classes ended I made the long journey west across the prairies, through the mountains, over the sagebrush desert and on to the coastal plain. Then across the strait by ferry and up the island to this spot. Sometimes I was alone and sometimes with a companion. I yearned for a lifelong partner, and sometimes I believed I'd found one, but they all came and went, appeared and disappeared.

The lower floor was a "granny-flat" though it never housed a granny. Usually it was rented by a schoolteacher or a nurse when I wasn't here. It was a convenient arrangement, but it's been a long time since anyone occupied it and I'm afraid it must be full of dust. I haven't been down there myself, since I can't manage the stairs. But you can clean it up, air it out, and nothing, after all, can spoil the view.

I like sitting here in the window watching the tides, the changing skies and seasons, but it was even more lovely before. There were seals in the water then. We all had binoculars and watched them on the rocks. At high tide their heads bobbed on the water and sometimes a killer whale sent them fleeing into the shallow waters. And there were birds too — seagulls and crows, but nobody paid any attention to them. They were scavengers, nuisances. Back then we exclaimed over herons and eagles as we do now at the odd surviving sparrow or crow.

4

There were deer here, too. They were a nuisance, like the crows, because they ate the vegetables people planted, but we valued the deer because they were graceful. Also, their existence confirmed that some past era was not really past — that wild life still roamed about. The first year I made this place my permanent home, a bear appeared. It walked into the garden in the late afternoon of a sodden November day and shook the apple trees to bring down the apples that hadn't been collected.

I'm astonished to think that you travelled so far and found me. Grateful too, though I realize you haven't come just to look after me. Perhaps you don't even want to do that. My dear, we must be honest with each other. You need something and I need something and surely we can pass the days in mutual assistance — not burdened by obligations, trading one favour for another.

I have so much to say to you. When my own mother was dying she lived in a fantastic world of her own creation. The ward and the wheelchair in which she was imprisoned weren't confining to her because she transformed them in her mind to the familiar places she'd known before — her house in its little circle of cottages in the seaside town. When I appeared, she told me, "I couldn't believe it when I saw you walking down the road." And when I was a whole continent away, they told me she believed I was still nearby, perhaps in the other ward beyond the doorway she never crossed. If a nurse dropped a tray, she complained, "Lucy's always dropping things. She's so clumsy." She and a fellow patient sat always side by side in their wheelchairs, her companion believing my mother was her daughter.

And so she hovered like a late summer butterfly in that no man's land between consciousness and unconsciousness, life and death, until one day, easily and painlessly, she floated over the privet hedge to the other side and never came back.

At first I was upset to see my mother so diminished, her mind gone, and my own future prefigured in her pathetic state. Then I realized that nature was merciful, that all losses were restored and all breaches healed. She asked about her parents and I told her truthfully what they were doing when last I saw them. Of my father, whose loss had been the severe blow that reduced her to this state, she remembered nothing. I came to see that her substitutions had their own kind of poetic truth.

And so if I confuse you with someone else, don't be dismayed. The mind in its lapsed and less vigilant state detects kinships which do in truth exist. You had a mother whom I knew, and you have come to me to learn of her. "I need to know who I am." I hope you don't suddenly vanish. I hope you aren't a mere figment of my imagination.

"Find Lucy, without delay," she wrote. "Without delay" underlined for, even then, there was the danger that it would be too late. But I hung on against all reason, as if I were waiting for you to find her message. And now I really am on what can only be described as my deathbed. I was older than the others — well, you can see that from the pictures. There I am on the right. There we all are — Julia, Lena, Monica, Max in the middle, Simone, and I. She's looking directly at the camera, Simone, as if she knew that one day after she was dead you would follow her instructions and carry these things to me to be explained. That's what you want me to do isn't it, bring all these pictures to life? Just beyond the frame of every picture hovers a whole life and history. The blind field. And it is for this you are here.

You know what's been the most wonderful thing? I was thinking of this as I waited for you to wake up and come upstairs, all the time fearing that you might have been a dream-person. But I thought, I felt sure from the moment you arrived, that you liked me. I saw in your smile a certain eagerness, though perhaps it was just relief at finding me alive and being at the end of your search. I mustn't let my great need suggest what isn't there.

It seems that what you need is so simple, the answers to some simple questions. Who am I? What am I? Where did I come from? If the answers turn out to be slow in coming you must bear with me, not think I'm deliberately spinning out the tales just to keep you here.

6

The story's difficult in itself, even if my memory were good. It isn't gone altogether, I don't want to suggest that, and in any case, there's plenty of material to fill out the dark spots. This place is a warehouse, you can see that, full of boxes of papers and letters and clippings. Some of it you can sift through on your own. I was always a hoarder, so that paper accumulated around me like snowdrifts wherever I was. Visitors murmured about fire hazard and spring cleaning, but I held on to everything and now my life-long habit is justified.

Am I comfortable with this machine?

It doesn't faze me in the slightest. It reminds me of the classroom, when students would come forward and put little portable tape-recorders beside the podium. Sometimes there'd be two or three sitting there in front of me as I lectured, whirring like crickets in the grass. They always asked your same question — courteously, curiously — would I mind?

To tell the truth, it did give me pause because my lecture method was at best a haphazard process — an extemporaneous commentary on the text we were studying, with some questions and quotations on three-by-five cards to jog my memory. I conducted my lectures as conversations with various members of the class — digressions, jokes, all kinds of irrelevancies and red herrings.

I fantasized sometimes about the fate of those tapes, for those who used them were usually the foreign students. I knew that mostly they were taped over in subsequent classes. But I thought that one or two must escape the process of elimination and that in some different country, in a hot climate, in a future time, a person no longer a student, casting about for a tape on which to record a piece of music, would slip one into the machine and be surprised.

Out would come my disembodied voice reciting a poem — "I am a miner, the light burns blue" — or delivering fragments of a commentary on palimpsest in *Wuthering Heights,* and the classroom in that frozen waste would come floating back like something preserved in a little globe of snow.

So that's how the time you want to hear about comes back to

me . . . as if someone had accidentally pressed a button and been ambushed by a memory — clear and fresh as the day it happened over twenty years ago in that same frozen wasteland. It's an odd exercise you're inviting me to make — like excavating Pompeii, or uncovering the Pharaoh's tomb.

What exists for me outside the frame is a whole world, an entire lost civilization. The figures you peer at so curiously have their own histories, their familiar voices. Their phrases float out on the air even as I look at them. Like a puppeteer I place my finger a certain way in a certain place and hope that they will spring to life — Lena, Monica, Julia, Max, Simone, and my younger self.

Am I wasting your time and your tapes? Unfortunately, I've always been garrulous . . . the habits of the classroom, the habits of a lifetime, die hard.

"Lucy, you're too fond of your own voice," they used to say.

Beginnings are the hardest. Where does anything begin? Which thread, when we give it a slight tug, will lead us to the centre of the labyrinth? When I think about the beginning, I see us all in my mind's eye like the fairy godmothers in the story of Sleeping Beauty, grouped around the crib at the christening, bestowing good wishes. Of course, there was no christening, at least not when we were there. And if there was a crib, we were none of us present and none of us knew about it. But it began a long time before the crib . . .

Oh yes. By all means test to see if the machine is working.

And make sure the batteries aren't dead. You'll need lots of batteries . . .

I

IN THE BEGINNING I was a different person, not young, but tremulous, and I was looking for a remote place in which to hide after the shambles I'd made of my life. There had been too much turbulence and I wanted to sit out the next two years. That was how long I gauged it would take before I was ready to join the world again. I'd planned it as time-out, a convalescence, after which I hoped I would be able to start out again, and maybe find a new partner and have children.

My first glimpse of the place was a shock. I thought I had come to the end of the earth. In those days the daily train from the east arrived early in the morning. I descended from it tentatively, stepping onto the footstool that the porter placed under the steep drop from the last step. All the other passengers bustled away, but there was no one to meet me, and I stood for a long time in a daze, looking after the train as it roared away to the other end of the continent.

It was like the end of an ocean voyage, and I was cast adrift with two suitcases and a ticket bearing the words SURRENDER TO TICKET MASTER ON ARRIVAL, which I threw away. I felt unnerved after the days of cosseting by waiters and attendants, the cozy roomette, the formal meals with starched napery and reservations for the first or second sitting. I'd even had a suitor of sorts who bought me drinks in the lounge car after dinner and told me alarming stories of what life would be like in this arctic region. He warned of stringent liquor laws that outlawed drinking on Sundays, made it illegal to drink while standing up, and forbade women from entering bars without male escorts. He explained the dangers of frostbite, snow blindness, whiteouts, and plummeting wind chill factors.

But there was no sign of winter that late summer morning. It was dry and dusty, the promise of heat in the air, and the faint smell of something burning. "It's going to be a hot one," people shouted to each other, and so I thought the warnings of frostbite and blizzard were just travellers' tales.

For the first day or two I was outside the life of the little prairie city as I never would be again. I walked the streets, observing in a detached way the people and the customs, noting the unusual features, which soon and ever afterwards I would accept as normal. The people were drab and faded, like a populace beaten down by years of war. I thought that shopping would be a problem, for the stores were badly stocked, with one exception. Where in the Lancashire villages of my childhood every other shop was a toffee-shop, here every other shop sold furs. I'd never seen so many fur coats. There were furs from all kinds of animals, fur hats and fur gloves, furs for men, women, children, and babies. So the travellers' tales were true, I thought, everyone needs a fur coat. It is a climate of extremes.

The city was the provincial capital, with a handsome parliament building set in acres of parkland, looking out across a lake, surrounded by paths and trees and rolling grassy hillocks. None of that was natural. The lake was artificial, the islands in it were created by hauling the earth, and every tree was planted by hand. It was all designed according to plans drawn up by architects and landscape gardeners. Its creation was an act of faith, a monument to the determination to make something out of nothing and in the most unpromising of circumstances. The first explorers had declared the place to be "uninhabitable," but the settlers had raised their fists and said defiantly, "We *will* have a city," as the Mormons said when they arrived at their destination: THIS IS THE PLACE.

Later I worried that a place established against such odds might suddenly disappear, as a garden, laboriously planted in poor soil, risks being swept away by a sudden storm or a drought. Were its foundations strong enough?

I began to have misgivings about this place I'd chosen without inspecting it. I'd done the interview at the Modern Language Association meetings in Chicago, been offered the job, and accepted it because it seemed to provide the best chance for a clean break with my previous life: another country and a different climate. What better way to erase the failures of the past, the disastrous marriage, the disastrous friendship, and another loss too painful to think about? It had seemed like a big adventure, this exploration of new territory.

At the end of the first week, I was plotting a swift retreat, wondering how soon I could extricate myself. Too many job changes look bad on a C.V., yet the climate might provide the excuse I needed. I was learning early that a climate of extremes can excuse many behavioural excesses. I resolved to give no hint of my plans but to settle in as if for the duration.

Finding an apartment was easy because there were few to choose from. The city grew rapidly in the next decade, but before that it was small and underdeveloped, the fledgling university divided into two campuses. One was a crumbling assortment of Gothic buildings that had formed the old teachers college; the other was two squares of concrete designed by a Japanese architect and set on a patch of gumbo, not yet landscaped. My apartment was in an old building on the edge of the park in the centre of the town. It was flanked by the palatial CPR hotel and two of the big churches — the First Baptist and a denomination new to me — the United Church of Canada.

The latter was to figure largely in my destiny because it precipitated me into something I had not planned: the acquisition of a house. One evening in early December I returned to my apartment to find it flooded with the sound of Christmas carols. These were being magnified by loudspeakers arranged like Christmas bells in pairs along the side of the church opposite and aimed at my house. I made a few hasty phone calls and learned that the Annual Rotary

Carol Festival was in progress. All my waking hours between then and the new year would be enlivened by music, as choir after choir from all over the city and the surrounding small towns performed their repertoire. I tried sealing the windows, plugging my ears, but nothing could shut out the bombardment as each song taunted me with its dreadful irony. "Hark! The Herald Angels Sing," "God Rest Ye Merry Gentlemen," "Good Christian Men Rejoy-oy-oice." All those bossy masculine commands assailed me, their imperatives balanced, point counterpoint, by the obsequious piety of "Silent Night! Holy Night!" "Away in a Manger," and "O Little Town of Bethlehem."

Even when I was out of earshot, the carols had so infiltrated my brain that I found myself humming the tunes as I walked along, or singing to myself, "Lo, he ab-ho-ors not the virgin's womb."

After my colleagues' amusement at my predicament subsided into helpfulness, I was guided into shopping for a house. I was out of the apartment in a week, breaking the lease, and happy to forfeit the deposit. Thus, by divine intervention, I acquired the large house that would be my home for many years. It was on a pleasant street in an old neighbourhood, lined by those same hand-planted trees I mentioned a moment ago. They met overhead, forming a shady tunnel in the prairie summers. And they all wore bands of yellow or gold, in varying widths. "My god," I thought, "even the trees are married." Then someone explained that armies of caterpillars attacked the Dutch elms, and the plastic bands prevented their procreation. Soon, banding my trees became part of my own seasonal observance.

It was a mixed neighbourhood, which in that largely Caucasian community meant that it housed both rich and not-rich. There were big old mansions, which had been there from the beginning, and squeezed in among them were small bungalows and two-storey frame houses with front porches. They were crammed together, as if for mutual protection, without regard for class or stature or affluence. There was a vast, empty plain enclosing the city like a sea, but on the streets the houses jostled each other so closely that anyone could look through the kitchen window and see what the neighbours were having for breakfast.

On the same street in their various houses lived Simone, Julia, and Monica and Sam Werner, but when I moved in I knew none of them, and so my coming among them went unheralded. I must have passed them on the street, and I've often tried to summon up my first image of each — of Julia walking gracefully along, her skirt swirling; of Simone playing hopscotch or jumping rope; of Monica looking distraught, with her unkempt, neglected children and her wayward husband. I try to decide if those visions contained any hint of our future association. Did I pat Simone on her golden head? Did Julia flash me a smile or a wink? Did I shrink from contact with Monica or she from me?

My ownership of the house signalled my willingness to adapt to the place. I even acquired a fur coat; not one of the fashionable synthetic fun furs, but the real thing. I chose one made from the hind legs of male minks. I no longer plotted escape or wondered if the civility of my colleagues would turn sour when I revealed my plans. I put down roots, which spread invisibly and thickened month by month. It was my first act of surrender. My second one came soon afterwards.

There was a complicated process by which newcomers were absorbed into the twin communities of town and gown. New members of the university were scrutinized closely for their alignments because they could cause shifts in the balance of power. At first glance there seemed to be a clear dichotomy between The Elect, born and bred in the region, and The Heathens transplanted from alien cultures — from the United States, England, France, Greece, or India. But sometimes those from elsewhere were drawn by sympathy and inclination into the group of The Elect. (Naturally I was not among them.) Eventually other factions developed between those united by political convictions or academic interests. And always there were those who stood alone, like non-aligned nations — recluses, misanthropes, oddballs. It was to this last category that I belonged — the unattached woman, neither a plausible faculty member nor a faculty wife, an anomaly.

I began to gain a measure of acceptance, however, by being conscientious and useful. I took whatever classes were assigned, gave them at undesirable times without fuss, caused no student complaints by over-rigorous grading, published a respectable number of articles, and attended scholarly conferences.

I was also establishing a reputation as a biographer because of a slender book I'd written about a nineteenth-century writer from the American South. It had given me a taste of the pleasure of living someone else's life vicariously and had paved the way for a more ambitious work.

I was now engaged on the life of the sister of Henry James, not an original project, although my approach was new. Where other female scholars had seen Alice James as a prism through which to view the constricted lives of nineteenth-century women, I saw her as a victim of sexual abuse at the hands of her brother William. Parts of the book I'd delivered as conference papers were already causing waves, but I persisted in defending my thesis, even at the risk of being dubbed a crank. I was less confident in delivering papers to my own colleagues, who were alert with suspicion, trying to catch me out and find flaws in my arguments.

The main intellectual forum was the Philosophy Department's History of Science Seminar. It was conducted in the Faculty Club, where a podium was set up in the lounge beside the bar. While it was open to all departments, few took advantage of the invitation, reluctant to appear amateurish beside the practitioners of the Master Discourse. I had the temerity to appear regularly, both in the audience and at the podium. On one memorable occasion, the fact that I had delivered the paper at the Modern Language Association meetings gave me the courage to present it to this intimidating group. It was an account of the literary detective work by which I assembled my lives of minor artists. I'd watered it down so that it was light on textual analysis and heavy on the kind of sensational discoveries that go over well in public forums. I was nervous naturally, but with the pleasant frisson of dread and anticipation that actors feel before a performance. It was a letdown, therefore, when on the appointed evening a great storm blew up with blizzard warnings and alarming weather reports.

I turned up, knowing full well that if the short journey there was hazardous, the return might be impossible. Yet I didn't want my absence to be interpreted as a failure of nerve. I thought it quite likely I'd give the paper to the three or four stalwarts and then spend the night in my office grading student essays. But even this plan failed, for the two or three stalwarts were heavy drinkers, already beyond the point of rational discourse and at the clamorous and noisy stage. To prolong my series of misjudgments, I joined them, let them press glasses of Scotch on me, and went along with their mood of revelry, smiling at their capers.

I was in a slightly disembodied state when I noticed the figure of a man leaning against the doorframe. He was tall and dark with very bright eyes, and in sock feet, with one foot raised and rubbing the ankle of the other leg. It was Sam Werner. Although he was a neighbour as well as a member of the Philosophy Department, he and I had never actually been introduced. He appeared to be making a signal with his eyebrow, which I interpreted as an invitation to get up and go over to him. Carrying my drink very carefully so as not to spill it, I went over curiously to see what he wanted.

"You shouldn't let Dunc give you that stuff, you silly girl," he said. "You've had too much already, you'll get a terrific hangover and not be able to teach tomorrow." He took the drink away from me, sniffed at it suspiciously, and then, holding me by the elbow, guided me down one corridor and another, round a corner, up an elevator, down another corridor, and into his office.

It was astonishingly unlike an office, for he'd turned it into a snug nest with every domestic comfort. There was a rug on the floor, a pot of hyacinths on the desk, an armchair, and a tray with glasses, bottles, and a refillable soda siphon. He had obviously been working because a piece of paper was sticking out of his typewriter. He took it out, covered the machine, poured my drink into the hyacinths, and handed me a glass of fizzy water.

"There's no question of you leaving the building tonight," he said, "so you may as well settle down here."

Outside, the blizzard raged louder than ever and the snow drove against the window. At one point, footsteps came down the hall and a voice cried out "Release that woman." Sam Werner put his finger to his lips, and eventually the knocking on the door stopped and Dunc went away singing an off-key version of "Hello, young lovers, wherever you are."

When I woke the next morning, the sun was streaming through the closed curtains and I was alone in the room. I lay for a while thinking how comfortable Sam Werner was in his own skin, how like a satyr, so hairy that even without clothes he didn't seem naked. Then a bell rang and brought me to my senses. My clothes were hanging over the open drawer of a filing cabinet, and I hurried to put them on, tidy up my hair, and rush over to my own office.

It was an odd beginning. At first I dismissed the night merely as an unfortunate incident, like a drunken encounter at a party. Sam Werner seemed inclined to do the same, for when I passed him in the hall he barely looked at me and went by without greeting me. But a few nights later, at midnight, I was reading in bed when I heard a light tap at the back door. Rather recklessly I went down and opened it on its chain, and there he was, standing in the snow. And so, these midnight meetings became a pattern. We steered clear of each other during the day, and if our paths happened to cross, we showed no sign of knowing each other.

Social events were a different matter, and ours was a very social community. In the absence of any professional entertainment — few restaurants as yet, and no theatres or symphonies — this was a culture of parties. They took place every weekend and there was no question of avoiding them. To have done so would have consigned one completely to outer darkness.

The ambience of the parties varied according to the day of the week or the season of the year. Friday gatherings were tentative and disorganized for we were listless and yet feeling a sense of release. You could sit in a corner and chat quietly with someone, watching the ashtray fill up, unembarrassed by long silences, shrugging off the fracas going on elsewhere. You could discuss work or family problems. I was usually on the receiving end of complaints about husbands and wives. The wives spoke for hours about teenagers and then said, standing up and smoothing out their dresses, "So good to talk to you. Lucky for you, you don't have kids."

That wouldn't do at a Saturday party. It was too gloomy and serious. People came in laughing and hallooing and went out laughing and hallooing even more. In the interim, many witty remarks were made, bons mots exchanged. A Sunday party was subdued and decorous with a sense in the air of an imminent call to duty.

Sometimes winter parties took place during blizzards, and the company was drawn into a precious intimacy. We came in shuddering from the cold and added our boots and overshoes to the pile accumulating by the door. At intervals guests dashed out to their cars, starting them and running the engine to make sure it didn't freeze up. Partying, like all other human activities, was a triumph over nature. From these parties we went home late and reluctantly, drifting off into the intense and deadly cold.

Summer gatherings had a carnival atmosphere as we reclaimed the outdoors, sitting on screened porches under lights strung from trees, or clustering around containers of burning insect repellent. The dinner parties were formal affairs around a table or carrying plates from the buffet into the den or the library. Open houses were anarchic and, with strangers rambling all over the house, an ordeal for the hostess. But they were all ordeals for me, all left me with a deep sense of unease.

Always there were insolent jokes, risqué remarks, and innuendoes. They were a subtle form of degradation, reminders that the jokers were the predators and I the prey. They were also tests. If you didn't laugh, you were puritanical, probably physically frigid as well. If you roared, you were hard-nosed, probably game for anything.

"Is that a mosquito zapper I see before me? What's the difference, Lucy, between a zapper and a zipper? Give up? One kills your fly, the other opens it!"

"Is that a Ukrainian Easter egg? Do you collect them? I don't collect them myself, I lay them. Are you a Ukrainian Easter egg, Lucy?"

"Have you heard the dentist joke, Lucy?"

The smoke and noise and alcohol fumes clouded the brain, and I had to be vigilant at all times in order to avoid drinking too much and being drawn into unwelcome intimacies. The next morning I'd wake to a keen anxiety. What had I done? Had I said something in an unguarded moment that might arouse suspicions or get passed along via the office grapevine?

It was one thing to be discussing the English Department curriculum in a meeting, making notes on a pad of white paper, and quite another to be standing so close to the lecherous Dean of Arts that his jacket brushed mine, my nose catching the scent of his aftershave lotion and the faint odour of his perspiration underneath. It was one thing to discuss a student paper in an office with the chairman of the department and another to find him sitting on the arm of my chair, the flannel of his trousers brushing against my stockings. The difficulty was in knowing whether the pressure of the leg, the meaningful look in the eye, was deliberate and what it could possibly mean. And then how did one act in professional encounters? As if the improprieties had never happened or as if there were a residual intimacy? I, in my lowly position, was not the one to decide but I had to be alert for cues.

By such means I was inducted into the community of scholars, offending some, puzzling others, and endearing myself to none. When I felt it incumbent on myself to give a party, I chose Sunday and spring or fall, a betwixt and between time, and approached the occasion with fear — my one horror being the predatory male, the lingerer who hangs back when the last ones leave, or who comes back soon afterwards on the pretext of looking for gloves or hat, and sits down and requests, glancing towards the stairway, one for the road ...

And now there was Sam Werner to complicate things, watching from a distance, circling while he seemed not to, jealous, proprietary, for I had become his property. His presence made me tense for it was at the same time flattering, disturbing, and dangerous. Of course there were rumours about my past and speculations about my present, as there were bound to be. Was I or wasn't I? Did I or didn't I? Had I or hadn't I? But when we finally betrayed ourselves, it was by the merest careless gesture.

The occasion was a departmental open house, Friday, a group of stragglers in a circle around the fire, reluctant to leave the warmth and go out into the cold. Sam Werner was sitting in an armless ladder-back chair beside my armchair. My right hand was holding a wine glass, my left arm was lying along the arm of the chair. Sam Werner, turning slightly to the person in the chair on the other side of him, absent-mindedly dropped his right arm along my arm, his hand covering mine. I might have gasped and drawn my hand away, removed it instantly, so that it looked like an accident. But I hesitated, and that hesitation was fatal. It made an image that lasted only a moment, like a sudden flicker of light. But in that moment everything was revealed as clearly as if we'd stood in the middle of the room and embraced.

I withdrew my arm, he withdrew his. There was a long silence, of the kind often described as "pregnant." No one said anything. No one needed to. The logs in the hearth stirred and fell, a flame flickered, someone took up the poker. The circle included the Dean of Arts, the head of the English Department, and a scattering of faculty members. Shortly afterwards, someone made the first move to leave, and we all got up and followed. It was Sam Werner that night who said, "I'll see you home, Lucy."

After that there seemed little need for discretion. We lost our cover and gained a new freedom. He came in and out whenever he wished, arriving by the front door in broad daylight. And he started a gradual transfer of his belongings — first books, then clothes — until eventually he had taken up residence in my house.

Thus started a different sort of isolation for me. I was not only a woman of easy virtue, but a home-breaker. Also, because of my unprepossessing appearance, I was considered deceitful. I'd represented myself as something other than I was, pretending to be demure. The jokers and jesters felt betrayed to discover how ripe I was for the picking. If they had known, they'd have done it themselves. Since they'd missed the chance, their righteous indignation knew no bounds.

As for me, life was not without its compensations. I had Sam Werner and I had my work on Alice James.

II

AND SO IT HAPPENED that, one summer long ago, I became the mother of two small children. No, they were not mine, though I pretended they were, and they even for a time called me "Mom." Their father, my lover, left them with me while he went to work in the British Library. He was not only working, as it turned out, but that's another story. Yet I, far from feeling put upon, relished this all-too-brief fling at motherhood. I think I was a good mother — a boast to which I have some testimony. They remained fond of me and evoked those months with me as a happy time of their lives. That's another story too, but the significant part is that during this interlude Simone became a member of my household. She ran in and out constantly, ate meals with us, went home only to sleep, and not even then if she could help it. I sensed that she found a refuge with us because she was in flight from her own family. That was a situation to which I had my own key, for it replicated exactly the configuration of my own childhood, when I attached myself to another family.

Schoolteachers back then were mostly unmarried. The 1914-1918 war had robbed many of their chance of marriage and motherhood. Also there was an unspoken rule that children repay parents for the cost of their education. By the time women had turned over enough paycheques to buy their way out of the family home, it was too late for them to marry. So spinster pairs — sisters or friends, one the breadwinner, the other the housekeeper — were pretty common. Occasionally two sisters, both teachers, lived together, but it was unusual enough to educate one daughter, let alone two, and so that was rare. Mostly the working partner assumed the role of man of the house, deferred to by all, and the other the role of subservient wife.

They were often the butt of jokes because the men resented their independence and the women envied it. I was not inclined to join in the ridicule for I was informally adopted by such a pair, returning to the battlefield of my own home only for the necessities of eating and sleeping. It was a kind of novitiate.

So Simone's desire to join my household was not without precedent for me. She was older than my two and lorded it over them a bit, and at the same time was slightly in awe of them. The deviousness, so much a part of Simone's character, was in evidence even then.

"Don't tell your mom," she'd warn them, but they, unable to keep secrets, as children often are, would immediately run and tell me. I supposed then that her secretiveness was the usual kind of defence mechanism found in children who are too closely supervised.

This experience of motherhood was painful for me only in its ending. My lover returned, took his children away, and the episode was sealed off like so many chambers in my fragmented past. But the friendship with Simone held firm.

It's impossible to speak of Simone without placing her in the context of her family, because she was caught up in them like a dragonfly in a spider web. She could and did escape, but only with great damage and not as a whole person. A part of her always remained in their clutches.

The driving force behind the family was Fern, her mother, whose size relative to her diminutive husband was an accurate gauge of the balance of power between them. She was a woman of considerable heft and solidity, so the cosmetic treatments she lavished on her person had an effect more comic than beautiful. This was the era of the bouffant hairdo, and Fern had perfected the art of whipping her hair into a miraculous superstructure, like a warrior's helmet. Sometimes when I returned home she would materialize on the path beside my house, wielding a broom, her hair — a work in progress — full of metal pins and rollers.

At first meeting I tagged her as negligible, but how wrong I was. It was tempting to underestimate her because of her ungrammatical speech and the banality of her mind, yet both were symptoms not of educational or mental deficiency but of stubbornness, a stolid resistance to hearing or learning from anyone else. "I come from plain-speaking people and we're morally superior. This is my way and it's best," she seemed to say. Her verbal awkwardness might have made her hesitant to speak out and voice an opinion, but instead it fuelled her confidence.

She and Wally were a mismatched couple, that common phenomenon resulting from bad judgment, which conventional wisdom tries to explain with a theory of opposites exerting a magnetic attraction on each other. She with her passionate intensity, he with his lack of all conviction. He (and Simone was his daughter in this) was intelligent, but his intelligence was no match for Fern's . . . not stupidity — but for her unshakable belief in her own infallibility.

I had moved in the middle of winter and met them for the first time during the spring thaw, when water was dripping from roofs and eavestroughs, and children were hunting for lost treasures in the melting slush. I stepped out of my side door to inspect more closely what had recently become my property. They, who had hitherto limited their contact to watching me and my effects through windows at the side of the house or from the front porch, emerged to greet me. I had been aware of their scrutiny, for whenever I or a visitor walked up the path, they would raise their heads like turtles to peer out of the windows. Far from being offended, I thought such vigilance might well protect me against burglars and that I could counteract the nuisance value by keeping my distance.

When they approached with outstretched hands and welcoming expressions on their faces, however, I had a quick suspicion that keeping my distance might not be entirely easy. They begged me to call on them in the event of what they referred to vaguely as my "needing anything." And this, with matching vagueness, I promised to do. Before they returned to their lookout posts on the front porch, Fern said to me, "You'll love this neighbourhood. None of the women work."

Evidently her sideline of peddling cosmetics was not classified as work. Perhaps in view of the cosmetic company's creed — God first, family second, business third — it qualified as a vocation, a means by which she insinuated herself into homes with the dual purpose of physical improvement and religious conversion.

Since I was unmarried, my occupation was not the liability it might have been. My attitude to religious observance was. In the tepid Church of England atmosphere of my childhood, God inhabited the old Norman church, where we visited him on Sunday, spruced up and subdued, as if he were an elderly housebound relative. How different were the practices of my neighbours, for whom God was a familiar spirit, a member of the extended family like rich Uncle Fred from Prince Albert, his name dropped into every conversation at the slightest pretext. On the rare occasions when I returned an invitation for coffee, I silently added, "and bring God along too if he happens to be free."

Conversations were foreclosed by the invocation of God's name or words. When a mentally deranged neighbour was charged with shoplifting, an offhand remark about her needing help brought the rejoinder: "It's not a psychiatrist she needs, but God."

"He'd certainly be cheaper," I couldn't help adding, a response which put a strain on the developing neighbourliness.

These details are relevant because they explain one important factor in my story. It is this: when Simone spent time under my roof, it was for her a foray into dangerous enemy territory. There must, I feel sure, have been summit meetings to discuss what constituted a family crisis when Simone developed a friendship with my little girls. Who knows why in the beginning it was permitted?

Was she allowed to risk contamination because her faith was

perceived to be unwavering? Or because I was English, did I give the surface impression of a conventional respectability that made my irregular life seem like a lapse from which I might be rescued? Perhaps she was being conditioned even at that early age for missionary work — to be sent out to some unmapped part of the world where the natives had their own culture, and to try to eradicate it? And was her mission similarly to try to save my girls, to tell them about God, to establish an exemplary Christian presence in my home?

From the start I had been the object of proselytizing activity, and their not-so-subtle invitations were intended to expose me to the Christian way of life. When I failed to extricate myself from an invitation to supper, I sensed the unspoken admonitions as the food was blessed and God was thanked (somewhat optimistically) for the gift of friendship. As my glass was filled with fruit juice, I saw an invisible banner floating over our heads. "We don't need alcohol in order to enjoy ourselves around this table."

This then was the atmosphere in which Simone floated, swam, and eventually sank. All the activities for which she joined us were subject to the strictest scrutiny and censorship. If we went to a movie, a catechism preceded the excursion. What was the movie about? Would it contain bad language or people having sex? Were we coming directly home? If we intended to have lunch afterwards, would it be in a restaurant where people were having alcoholic beverages?

"Well, probably not in the middle of the afternoon, I shouldn't think."

"No, but our church don't believe in drinking at all, and we wouldn't want her going in a place LIKE THAT."

"Oh, alright, we'll have an ice cream at The Bay."

And so ice cream would be consumed in an alcohol-free environment.

Normally I wouldn't have put up with such nonsense, but my two pleaded for Simone's company. And even more persuasive was Simone herself. During my interrogation she stood, silent, fingers invisibly crossed, eyes expressing a mute appeal, yearning for permission to go.

I developed a sixth sense for what would cause trouble for Simone. She liked to browse along the shelves of children's books that had been escape routes during my own unhappy childhood. I had never brought myself to part with them but had carried them along, rarely used before that summer. Invariably her small hand reached for fiction rather than non-fiction, and for risky titles suggesting those dubious subjects — demons, devils, ghosts, and other supernatural beings — disapproved of by her mother. Since the staples of my childhood were Enid Blyton and Edith Nesbit, there were a fair number of these. I'd warn her "better not take that home, Simone," and she would understand. Often, when the others were running around outside, I'd find her quietly curled up in a chair, avidly reading a book with a picture of a heathen deity on the cover.

When, at the end of the summer, their father removed his books, his furniture, and his daughters, I felt I was providing for my neighbours confirmation of the instability, misery, and loneliness of a non-Christian home, for I was incapable of disguising my despair. And when Fern came over and invited me to go with them to church, I, who had been so proud and arrogant, was humbled. I felt that I had reached rock bottom and become an object of pity, and one that confirmed their creed. For a time I no longer wished to live.

In all this there was one saving grace. Misery, as we know, does not love company, and so I became even more isolated from my colleagues at the university. I was an outcast, a rejected lover, an abandoned woman. But Simone, aware of my unhappiness, and also sharing it, for she too was bereft after the abduction of my daughters, slipped in when she could to visit me. I think she was motivated by affection and sympathy, though the lure of my library was stronger than either of those emotions. Whenever she came in, shyly bearing a muffin she had made or a poem she had written, her eyes ranged hungrily over my shelves of children's books.

Years passed, my pain lessened, my work began to thrive, and Simone followed her sister Andrea from grade school to high school. In the natural order of things, the bond between Simone and me might have weakened as she became more involved with friends, and I with the rewards and compensations of my changing career. But against all those odds, it strengthened, and the unlikely crucial factor in its endurance was that it had Fern's blessing.

For one thing, I was not only a neighbour, but also a dependable purchaser of beauty products. Although I turned down invitations to the "parties" at which she demonstrated her wares, I submitted myself every few months to a ritual visit. At these times Fern set out on the coffee table before me a dazzling array of tubes and bottles. This was accompanied by a sermon, the gist of which was that even I could look attractive if only I would make the effort. At its conclusion I went through the motions of examining eyebrow pencils, lash curlers, eyeliners, mascara, eye shadow, and pancake base. All these I rejected, finally settling for some bath oil, hand cream, and often a tube of lipstick — Cherries in the Snow, Where's the Fire, or Snow Rose. Fern then departed, discharged of any further responsibility for the pathetic nakedness of my face. The lipsticks either accumulated in the back of a drawer or ended up with Julia.

Besides the commercial transaction, another happy accident favoured Simone's continued association with me. Fern had been advised by Simone's teachers that if she were to do well in school, she needed to read more. Fern herself had wanted to become a schoolteacher, a job that would have provided a gratifying sense of power to one of her controlling disposition. But growing up during the Depression put education out of reach, and she didn't even finish high school. The only position of authority she achieved was over preschoolers in Sunday school. Thus thwarted in her own early ambitions, she was rabid with ambition for her girls, and she knew that for all my moral defects, as a professor of

English I could help with her goals. She not only permitted but actively encouraged Simone to come and borrow my books and enlist my help with her English assignments.

In this matter, expediency overrode the teachings of her church and her own misgivings. The president of the Board of Education, a deacon in her church, insisted that his daughters avoid contamination by absenting themselves from the classes in which certain books, such as the novels of Thomas Hardy, were being taught. His example was followed by many parents, but Fern, to her credit, would have none of this. Perhaps she sought the help of God, and He and she together decided that Simone should get all the help she could from the English professor, whose presence next door seemed providential.

I was careful to lend only exemplary Christian texts — *Little Women*, *Little Men*, *Black Beauty*, Helen Keller's autobiography. I noted with approval that Simone's taste did not run to these standard, blameless works. She preferred the fantastic, but she was always mindful of how the wind was blowing at home. She distinguished between the books to be read there, and those to be read only in the privacy of my house. When she sought help with homework, I made copious notations on her essays so that Fern would have tangible evidence of the benefits of our friendship. So we became collaborators, members of an underground resistance movement.

At first I cherished Simone for her connection with my lost daughters, but inevitably, we established a bond that was strengthened by our shared need for secrecy. As her antennae became ever more attuned to what was approved and what might result in the termination of her visits, she was slowly but surely at this early age being nudged into a double life. We were two adjacent houses on the same street, close enough that if the windows were open and we were sitting at our kitchen tables, we could have passed the cream and sugar back and forth. We shared a fence, a narrow walkway between the two houses, side doors so close that it was almost necessary to close one before opening the other.

And yet the gulf between the houses was as deep as it could be, and if Simone was to pass back and forth with impunity, camouflage and subterfuge were necessary. She was experiencing the seduction of the forbidden fruit, learning the lure of the banned book. She did not articulate back then why certain books — the fantasy and fiction that she loved — were disapproved of, but she was being conditioned to take pleasure in what was illegal, and to practise deceit in order to get that pleasure. She was also growing more alert to what was not spoken, for often it was without words or in and around them that she and I communicated about books and about everything else. She was undergoing a metamorphosis into someone who dwelled in a no man's land, for she belonged neither to my household nor to her own.

She knew that if I was drinking or entertaining certain people, it was not to be mentioned. And she knew that she had to prove the benefits of reading my books and writing essays under my tutelage by getting the highest grades in her class. Here began her fierce competitiveness, her ruthless determination to be the best at every subject she studied, at every sport she practised.

And Simone, did she ever worry about which was the real world, the more substantial? Did my influence foster a vestigial duplicity that had always been there? But, of course, the split existed long before my presence on the scene. I noticed with some amusement that when Fern and the two girls went to visit an aunt, the tenor of the house was suddenly changed. I saw Wally carrying in six-packs of beer. I saw that the car remained in the driveway all Sunday morning. Minor details, but enough to suggest that Wally, so temperamentally akin to Simone, was also leading a double life. I thought how often they both must have listened to Fern's clear-cut, indisputable arguments and nodded in agreement, while beneath that surface acquiescence they were forming counterarguments.

During all those years, my door key lay under a plant pot in the garage so that cleaners and workmen could enter the house when I was away. Simone had permission to use it at any time. It was a privilege and a sacred trust, and she never once abused it. She never made mischief, never brought in a friend, as a child might, to show what the secret precinct was like. She never even helped herself to food from the refrigerator, though I invited her to. She was cautious, wary, politic, single-minded. It was the books she came for, and they were transgression enough.

I occasionally bought books that were suitable to be carried back to her house — non-fiction, informative books full of historical or geographical information. I wondered at myself and, looking back, I wonder at myself again that all this was taking place without my developing any real fondness for Simone. At the same time, I didn't use her as a vent for my didactic instincts. At least, I don't think I did.

Typically, I would come home from school in the late afternoon and find her curled up in the half-light in a corner of the sofa or a deep armchair.

"Why, Simone," I'd exclaim, in my mother's scolding voice, "sitting in the dark. Bad for the eyes." And she'd blink like a barn owl as I flicked the switch and flooded the place with light. Then she'd look at me, torn between the need to be polite and the absorption in the book. At other times she'd want to talk about what she was reading or thinking. I'd get a drink — a glass of wine or a Scotch and soda. She must have noted this fact, registered it as something not to let slip out at home. I never knew how she truly thought of it — with interest, disapproval, or wonder. Her most persistent question about the books she read was "Is it true?" "Could it be true?" "Could such things really happen?" She was wrestling at a young age with the nature of fiction and truth, and I tried to help her as best I could. It came up constantly because of the books she chose.

Did she, I wondered, ask the same question of what she was learning at home and at her church? And what answers did she receive? "You have to have faith"? Did she compare the subjects that provoked the questions, and the answers she got in various places?

When as a child she'd read Nesbit's *Five Children and It*, she became obsessed by the psammead. Was there such a thing as a psammead? Could there be? Then why had the writer used it, described it? I tried to explain that this furry creature with eyes on the end of stalks might stand for something — a being from another world than ours, a different time and place.

"Like the girls?" she said surprisingly. She was always invoking my erstwhile daughters.

"Have you stopped being sad about them?" she asked, giving me a quick, sidelong look.

"I'm not so sad as I was," I said.

"Me either," she said, "but I think about them all the time and miss them. Do you think they miss us?"

"Maybe."

"Why didn't they write back when I wrote to them?"

"Too busy perhaps."

"They probably have a lot of new friends."

"Yes."

"Did you like Renny best or Suzy?"

"Suzy, I think. And you?"

"Oh, Suzy too. She was so funny."

Simone was a model of control and responsibility. I never had to remind her that it was time to go home, that she shouldn't be late for the five o'clock supper.

"Why did you go to university? Did your mom want you to be a teacher?" she asked once.

"Not really," I said, and then corrected myself. "At least not for all my life. She wanted me to get married and have children. Teaching was something you could always fall back on in case anything happened to your husband. An education could also help you to find a successful husband. Preferably a doctor or a vicar."

"What's a vicar?"

"That was what we called our preachers. A vicar was supposed to be a representative of God."

"Did you want to marry a vicar?"

"No, I wanted to *be* the vicar. I used to get the other kids lined up so I could play vicar."

"The way Suzy liked to play school!"

"Yes. I'd dress up in a bedspread because our Church of England vicars wore elaborate vestments. I'd get a prayer book, read the service, deliver a sermon, and have them singing hymns. Sometimes if we found dead birds I'd conduct the funeral."

"But now you don't go to church at all."

"No."

"Are you an atheist?"

The word lay between us like an undetonated bomb. I sensed that discussions at home about my conspicuous non-attendance at church must have worried her. *Lolita* was fresh in my mind, and I recalled Nabokov's words that the strongest taboo is the story of the total atheist who lives a happy and useful life and dies in his sleep at an advanced age. I couldn't bring myself to reply simply and truthfully "yes." I rationalized my cowardice as a refusal to define myself by something I was not.

She was young then, and I had no wish to appear monstrous in her eyes. Later, when she was older and taking philosophy in university, we argued back and forth honestly and with mutual respect. But at that early time I thought it best to say I was an agnostic, explain it to her as a matter of uncertainty, and leave it at that. She brooded a great deal on theological subjects, in a childlike way, wondering how a benign deity could have created cats to torture mice.

I had to fight a spirit of mischief that urged me to put notions in her head, paraphrasing David Hume to suggest that this world might only be the first clumsy effort of an infant deity who abandoned it halfway through, ashamed of his lame performance; or that it might be the work of a stupid deity, laughed at by his colleagues; or it might be the production of a deity in his old age or dotage . . .

Sometimes she fell upon a book that transfigured her with excitement. This happened when she read *Frankenstein*. She was about fifteen and it was a set text in one of my classes. She found it on my coffee table, picked it up to examine my scribbles, and became riveted by it, peppering me with questions.

"How do you teach it in your classes?"

"I tell them about Mary Shelley and her times and how she came to write the book. Then the students discuss what it means."

"Tell me about Mary Shelley."

"She was only a few years older than you are now when she wrote that book."

I told her about Mary Shelley's life, her mother's death in childbirth, her own loss of three of her children, her marriage to Percy Bysshe Shelley, and her connection with Byron.

"Could it really happen?" she asked.

"Happen?"

"Could someone make a person in a laboratory?"

It was not long afterwards that she picked up, again from my coffee table, an illustrated history of gynecology and obstetrics. Since it contained much lurid information about cauterizing, gouging, and leeching, I worried that it might give her nightmares. Young girls have a tendency to be preoccupied with childbirth as a fearful experience that lies ahead, but it grew into an obsession with her.

"I don't want to have a baby," she said. "It's too scary."

I explained that childbearing was a whole lot different in our day and that it was usually safe and often painless.

"When did it start being safe?" she asked.

I said that it had not been safe for very long and I couldn't resist adding that more women had died in childbirth than men had died on the battlefield. I feared that her interest might bubble over and cause trouble for her at home.

At this time, whenever I came home she was waiting for me

with a long list of questions. Tired from teaching, I almost resented working overtime. My drinks got stronger — more gin than tonic, more Scotch than soda — as I tiredly embarked on this last seminar of the day. I looked surreptitiously at the clock, longing to kick off my shoes and surrender myself to the bland comfort of a television news program.

Her questions were wide-ranging, clear evidence of her intelligence, and my respect for her mind grew. She asked about the virgin birth, the rise and fall of midwifery, the history of contraception and abortion.

"Do you believe in abortion?" she asked, as she had earlier asked if I believed in God, perhaps dreading that my reply would place me among those destined for hellfire.

She became obsessed with the abortion issue, a subject that must have highlighted the split between our two households. On the one side was her own, firmly grounded in God's authority as interpreted by Fern. On the other was mine, floundering on the shoals of ambivalence and ambiguity.

She must have carried the arguments back and forth like a dog carrying a bone. I guessed that she took mine back home to be demolished. I could see Fern listening reasonably, going through the motions of considering them fairly, and giving the final verdict: Life begins at conception, destroying life is murder, it can't be right to destroy a life. Then Simone would turn around and bring that back to me. And we'd talk about where life begins — at conception or at birth — and I'd tell her I believed that a foetus is no more a person than an acorn is an oak tree.

She managed eventually to see the propaganda films, which pit the rational male voice against the dark, unfathomable female; the male foetus against the murderous mother.

And all the time I suppose she was thinking — there's a way between the two, one doesn't have to be right and one wrong. And she must have thought of *Frankenstein* and wondered if there could be a way for a woman to have a baby without harbouring the foetus in the stretching womb and expelling it for the terrible journey down the birth canal.

In another era she might have tried to resolve her conflicts by working with evangelical fervour to improve methods of birth control. Instead, she went into medicine, though the motives behind her choice of that prestigious and lucrative profession were by no means simple. They could be understood only within the context of the family dynamics.

Given the difference between Wally and Fern, cracks in their united front could be expected, and no doubt there was a deep undertow of tension. But from the outside there was little evidence of it because Wally had caved in long ago. It took more energy, more unwavering confidence and willpower than he had to oppose the steamroller effect of Fern's certitude.

The fissure that did finally open beneath their feet developed because the parents' temperaments were replicated in the children. Andrea, the older one, was Fern's spiritual daughter — self-righteous, full of conviction, and impervious to all counterarguments. Simone, with her acute mind, was Wally's child — vulnerable, accommodating, ambivalent. Accordingly, she was always the loser, disarmed by her intelligence, doomed by her imagination. Also, being the younger created its own pattern of oppression so that she developed childhood grudges and wrongs that she spent a lifetime trying to redress.

One result of the family division was that an implacable, lifelong hatred and rivalry developed between Andy and Simone. In spite of Simone's success, or perhaps because of it, nothing she ever achieved was completely acceptable to Fern, and it was her judgment that counted. In Fern's eyes, only Andy was above reproach. And so, in the close-knit family circle, it was she who triumphed, who could do no wrong, who was her mother's darling.

Another result of Fern's dominance was more sinister and concealed. Under the influence of his wife's repressiveness, Wally developed a furtive, dislocated sexuality. This I discovered not from Simone but from my neighbour, Julia, whose daughter was Andy's friend and provided the only window on what actually went on in the house. She told me it was an open secret among the kids in the neighbourhood that Wally had a cache of pornographic magazines and photographs, in the words of the children, of "ladies in their underwear with boots and whips." "Those are no ladies," Julia had said, laughing, but all the same, permissive as she was, she had issued a rare edict forbidding her daughter to enter that house.

"Why?" I once asked Julia. "What did you think might happen?"

"Oh, nothing really," she said. "He isn't a rapist or anything like that. It's more a lot of peeping. The children dressing up and Wally hanging around. Anyway I didn't want her going to slumber parties over there. More of a gut feeling than anything else." I must say Julia's words gave me pause, because my girls had often been invited for sleepovers, and I'd raised no objection. And then I thought of Simone.

"She must have been aware of what was going on?"

"Who knows? Who knows?"

Was she conscious of her father's prurient sexuality, and did she weigh it against Fern's habit of demonizing the neighbours? All of us were somehow socially irresponsible, immoral, wicked. The persistent face that both of them showed to the world was one of despair at its delinquencies.

A crisis arose in the family when Wally suddenly and prematurely retired from his job as a television salesman. Rumours flew about that he had been fired, had been accused of finagling expense accounts, but I suspected something of a different nature. It was all covered up after the minister of his church intervened, and Wally's early retirement was turned into a personal sacrifice in the interests of church work and public service.

Then Fern, always resilient, always energetic, stepped forward as the breadwinner. She became — either through the intervention of the same minister or of an even Higher Power, director of the cosmetics firm for the whole province. She was now the owner of a pink car, in which she zigzagged all over her territory, supervising her minions.

One can only guess what Simone made of it all. But she was very loyal to the family and never gave a hint to me of anything untoward. Was that what I resented — the loyalty that prevented her from weeping on my shoulder and confiding her troubles, instead of leaving me to draw my own conclusions?

What would it have taken to turn Simone into an open rebel? She might have developed unsuitable boyfriends, left the church, flirted with drugs, run away from home. But she didn't. Fern's control held. All Simone's anger, all her desire for escape, was turned inward and underground. She stuck to her church attendance all through university and medical school, in the face of mockery by her friends and classmates.

I often wonder, if I had made a strenuous effort at conversion would things have turned out differently? Or if I had taken her into my heart . . . That was what Simone said later, "You never took me in . . . " She meant that I never took her into my heart. Why not? I enjoyed her company, and the warmth sometimes flared and flickered, but it always went out. I rejoiced in her successes and held out the hope that she would change, but then something would happen and it was the same old Simone, in thrall to the family, spouting the party line.

The main reason that I kept her at arm's length, emotionally speaking, was that she never lost that streak of dishonesty. It appeared at first in small matters and would have gone unnoticed if it hadn't been so persistent. In the early days it showed itself in grade school exams taken with multiplication tables written on fingernails. Later it was false insurance claims for stolen bicycles, various shady transactions with shopkeepers — returning as faulty merchandise that was worn or undesirable for some reason. Later, in college, there was plagiarism, essays written by other people, sources unacknowledged. She was clever enough to succeed honestly and without help from anyone else, but she was afraid to risk failure. She had to make sure that everything she did was perfect.

If by chance I learned about these transactions, I always called her on them, and she always had ready answers.

"But the insurance companies charge us too much anyway..."

"But, Simone, it's no excuse that the people robbed are rich. You could say the same about shoplifting. It's still stealing. It's no different from breaking and entering."

"Suppose the stolen stuff is given to poor people so they can feed their children. It would be alright then, wouldn't it?" I can still see the earnest expression on her face as she said that. I did honestly try to like her more, often imposing the task on myself as a kind of exercise. I forced myself to remember images of her younger, more vulnerable self — the little figure sitting on the steps, waiting for us to come back when I took my young charges on an outing. The rap on the door, on her birthday, as we were having breakfast. My two had tantalized her with the promise of a gift and she couldn't wait to see what it was. There she was in the doorway, the morning sun shining behind her, illuminating her in her thin summer dress, her hair not yet brushed and braided.

Always beleaguered at home, she developed strategies of subversion and survival, means of doing what she wanted to do in a hidden roundabout way. And her life's work developed from this festering lifelong sore. She became hailed as a secular nun for her missionary work among the poor and afflicted. And finally she got the whip hand over Andy by gaining absolute control of Andy's husband, her family life, and her children.

It wasn't easy to adopt children back then, and Kenny was unemployed. But doctors and lawyers had ways of arranging informal adoptions, especially if the kids were native. And Simone could well afford to pay for the kids, buy off the birth parents, do whatever she wished. And so, sacrificially, she supported them. It was easy, you know. There was a brief tug-of-war at first, with Andy trying to gain the moral high ground. Kenny became a deacon in the church and Andy tried to put over on Simone the line about "It's not me you're doing it for but God and the church."

But Simone wasn't going to have any of that. She was quick to turn it around and make clear who supported and controlled everything and who could make it all disappear in an instant. It was a power play, and she'd become an expert at it. This happened a lot later, when she was more of a fighter and not the old acquiescent Simone.

It's funny how our memories of her, yours and mine, have placed her there, framed in the doorway, always on the threshold of our lives, trying to come in, be taken in and welcomed, but never quite succeeding.

III

YOU SEEM CONFUSED, as if I've left out too much and jumped into the middle of things. But I'm not sure where the beginning is or where to start. With a series of begats? A list of the *dramatis personae*? A voice on the waters, the growing of light, the separation of night and day? Certainly I would have to go back to a time long before the pictures.

I grew up in England which, like most countries, has yielded to the universal urge to dichotomize and is marked by a Great Divide. It is divided by climate, industry, economy, education, politics, manners, and speech into two regions — the advantaged and the disadvantaged, the heartland and the hinterland. We, the have-nots of the North, had multiple liabilities that made us the subject of music hall jokes. Even in a damp rainy country, the climate was wretchedly so.

"I spent the summer in Manchester."

"You did? What day did it fall on this year?"

It was an industrial region with dark Satanic mills and collieries, supplying the rest of the country with cotton and coal and our lungs with poisonous vapours long before the effects of such pollution were recognized. Our speech had the sounds and cadences of an earlier era, marking us as primitive. Since no Faulkner or Brontë romanticized our roughness in novels, we were regarded by ourselves and others as an inferior breed. Our only salvation lay in getting out of there as fast as possible, even fleeing to the New World.

I've never had cause to return, but I've heard that the mines and mills have closed, the once flourishing market towns have declined, and it is a place of urban decay — its problems exacerbated by the opening of monstrous shopping centres. My ancestral village, with its Norman church and the graves of my forebears, has faded into oblivion. And so the prairie city I found in its place became my new Jerusalem — gleaming, white, prosperous, and surrounded by fields of waving corn.

And that was where we came together, living within walking distance of each other on the same street — Julia, Monica, Simone, and I. Books were the catalyst, for we were readers, at a time when books were losing their potency. My house became a drop-in centre, and everyone who liked reading came to use my library. I was like the child on the block who develops a spurious popularity because she has the best toys. The reason I had so many books was that one of my sidelines was book reviewing, so books multiplied like mice in my house. And the people who came to borrow them didn't just want to read them. They came by afterwards to talk about them with me and with each other.

With the exception of Monica Werner, of course. She was Julia's friend, and it was Julia who later brought her into the group so that she got involved with Max. Before that, she and I avoided each other. In different circumstances we might have been friends, for we were similar in age, education, and nationality. On the other hand, if a man hadn't come between us, the insidious divisions of our native land would probably have followed us across the ocean and set us against each other. Her manners, even in her ravaged condition, were the legacy of teachers and clergymen who had held forth for generations in cultured voices in England and her dominions. Even if she hadn't scorned my grammar school, my Johnny-come-lately redbrick university, my traces of Lancashire dialect, I would have imagined she did. Then there was the natural hostility of housewife for career woman to come between us.

Although I lent books freely, I asked people to make a list of what they borrowed and leave it on the front of the fridge. Where other people had lists of groceries held up by magnets, I had lists of book titles:

    THIS SEX WHICH IS NOT ONE
    THE GUERRILLAS
    THE SECOND SEX
    THE MERMAID AND THE MINOTAUR
    THE LAUGH OF THE MEDUSA
    SEXUAL POLITICS
    THE HORRORS OF THE HALF-KNOWN LIFE
    DESIRE IN LANGUAGE

I was always amused by my visitors' habit of standing in front of my fridge and commenting on each other's choices.

"Is she *still* reading that?"

"She doesn't know French so she probably doesn't understand a word of it."

"Now why is *she* reading *that*?" Lena would say, scrutinizing Julia's choice. "*Of Woman Born*. Fat lot of good it will do her." (Or "will do *her*").

Between Lena and Julia there was a curious antagonism. Of course division and enmity between women is the norm rather than the exception, but it was odd in this case because Julia was so amiable that it was hard to quarrel with her. Lena, in contrast, was a pulsating mass of anger, and for some inexplicable reason Julia bore the brunt of it. She had a natural aristocratic courtesy and elegance, and these very qualities repelled Lena. Julia had the habit of pulling a tube of lipstick out of her pocket and applying it absent-mindedly but quite accurately without the help of a mirror, a skill that astonished me. Lena watched this performance with repugnance, as if Julia's beauty, and desire to enhance it, was a personal insult. If Julia reached out a slender beringed finger, the nail tinted as delicately as a seashell, Lena looked at it as if it were a poisonous spider.

It was on account of Julia that I kept track of books because she treated them like Gideon Bibles. She had a tendency to take them on picnics and lose them, or pass them along to friends she thought might profit from them. This attitude to books was absolutely symptomatic of her character. It wasn't that she was careless so much as casual, and unconcerned about material property. It was this generous and endearing trait that accounted for her popularity. You could make free with any of her belongings (her liquor, her car, her house, her clothes, whatever she had), and you could also *say* anything. How many people, however generous with tangible things, allow that kind of verbal leeway? "Judgmental" was a buzzword then, and Julia was the most nonjudgmental person in the world. Sometimes when I was going on about the horrible neighbours, she reproached me. "Since when is it alright to laugh at the disadvantaged?"

But to the others.

Simone was the youngest, but I'd known her the longest. From the time I'd moved in she'd lived in that wood-frame house, jammed up against mine with a narrow walkway between us. But that story you've already heard.

Lena was the one I saw most often just then. She would have liked to move in with me, but I wisely resisted, so she kept her own small apartment above a gift shop in the shadow of the cathedral.

I should tell you what I knew about Lena at that time. I found out a great deal about her eventually, but that was much later, after the Max thing was over. She fell into my orbit because she was interested in feminism and someone must have said, the way people did, "The person you should meet is Lucy Heathcote." I was an evangelist in those days, always directing women to the university, as if their salvation lay in getting degrees. So she sat in on one class, and then attached herself to me, and we fell into a friendship, or perhaps it was a mutual dependency. She was a good photographer, and I had a half-finished bathroom in my basement, which she used as a darkroom. In turn, she took photographs of me, which I used on my book jackets. I'm not photogenic, but she did tricks with lighting and an airbrush that made me look quite presentable, even attractive. She had a little car and helped me with errands, and then became my regular chauffeur, driving me to my classes and back every day.

One day we'd gone for a drink after class and she tentatively showed me a page of something she'd written. It was very short, the mere beginning of a story, but it was the first time I'd seen anything other than a class assignment. The plot was something of a cliché, a tale I'd often heard from descendants of those who fled the pogroms — an account of families with small children hiding in a cellar while the Cossacks ransack the town. When a baby starts to cry, it has to be murdered for the common good. Although the story was not original, she told it with such a distinctive tone, such a clear and original voice, that I exclaimed in surprise. "Why Lena, you're a writer."

She looked gratified, but it was a long time before anything came of the promise of that tentative start. She often suggested that she had a story but it was too scandalous and incendiary to tell. I paid little attention because that is a fantasy common among beginning writers. All the same, I did believe there was some monster lurking in her past. Because she had an almost imperceptible foreign accent, I assumed she was haunted by terrible memories. I imagined midnight flights across mined borders, possibly torture and rape, and later speculated that it might be something closer to home, brutal treatment by her brothers. These conjectures grew exponentially during the time we were taking care of Max.

So that was who we were.

As for me, by this time, I was teaching Women's Studies, a convert to a new field from an old one. I'd drifted through the groves of academe wherever the current took me, propelled forward by a series of accidents. I went to university because I was assigned in grammar school to a stream of people headed in that direction. Once there I chose to study Old English and Chaucer because these writers spoke the language of my own people. Only after I arrived in North America did I understand how strongly the blood of the

Angles and the Saxons ran through my veins, and that studying their language and literature was a means of hanging on to my identity. Eventually I assimilated, changed course, and turned to American literature, finding a mirror there too. I saw, in the early period, immigrants like myself, released from the straitjacket of class, custom, and church. But instead of becoming free, they were like rickety buildings with the scaffolding removed, desperate to grasp anything that would prevent collapse. I tried to breathe life into those wax Thanksgiving centrepiece figures with their tall hats and drab colours, calling them not Puritans, but radicals.

And then suddenly new vistas opened. The day came when every woman was a feminist and we found a new religion to unite us and replace the old ones that had failed us. There was so much to gain — maternity leave, pay equity, equal opportunity — that not even the skeptics rejected the label outright. They became "clapping feminists" and "but feminists." They applauded the activism of others, reaped all the benefits, and did nothing themselves. Then they bolstered their position by dissociating themselves from an imaginary lunatic fringe (not easy in a reasonable and non-violent movement). "I'm a feminist, BUT I don't believe in bra-burning." "I'm a feminist, BUT not a man-hater." "I'm a feminist, BUT not one of those flaming radicals." The opposition tried to inflict death by slogans, but these only fuelled our resistance and proved our case. We busily mimeographed the insults and circulated them as pamphlets, along with lists of misogynist quotations by Milton and Swift.

1972: IS WOMEN'S LIB A PASSING FAD? *The New York Times*
1973: WOMEN'S LIB IS DEAD *Educational Digest*
1975: THE WOMEN'S MOVEMENT TOO MUCH OF A GOOD THING? *Mademoiselle*
1976: REQUIEM FOR THE WOMEN'S MOVEMENT *Harper's*

1977: WHY WOMEN'S LIB IS IN TROUBLE *US News & World Report*
1978: IS THE WOMEN'S MOVEMENT STUMBLING TO A HALT? *Glamour*

Eventually we lost the slogan game, for it didn't take our detractors long to regroup, change tactics, and find strategies to divide us. But for a brief shining hour we flourished, holding sway in the leafless groves and corridors. We rejected the description of our discipline that appeared in university calendars:

WHY STUDY ENGLISH?
By doing so we share the experience of all men and are therefore better able to understand ourselves. Literature's aim "is not a restatement of what our eyes see," as Christopher Collins has said, "but an exploration of that uncharted world of man's thoughts and impulses, his desires and fears, that all-important inner world out of which flow all his actions, his arts of peace and his arts of war, his acts of love and his acts of savagery, his total history and his unquestionable future.

We countered with a manifesto by a feminist critic:

Women are estranged from their own experience and unable to perceive its shape and authenticity ... they are expected to identify as readers with a masculine experience and perspective, which is presented as a human one ... Since they have no faith in the validity of their own perceptions and experiences, rarely seeing them confirmed in literature, or accepted in criticism, can we wonder that women students are so often timid, cautious, and insecure when we exhort them to "think for themselves."

Suddenly personal and professional lives underwent a sea change. Whatever had been a liability, overnight became an asset. A failed marriage became a credential; being an abandoned woman was like a battle-scar from Agincourt. Having a consuming interest in the lives of so-called minor women writers no longer confined one to a literary backwater. The non-canonical status of such writers constituted a critical blind spot. And those who sneered at the elevation of minor figures, in this looking glass world where everything was reversed, simply looked like dinosaurs.

These were heady times and we were exhilarated and overconfident, thinking our ascendancy would last forever, forgetting that every dark age begins as a new dawn. In the hierarchic world of the academy we moved from being servants to being an order of nuns to being the new priesthood with our sacred texts, our austerity of dress, our acolytes and disciples.

Resistance and ridicule only added to our aura, giving us a heightened sense of bravado, strengthening the bond between teacher and student. Insidiously, our anger turned into righteous indignation.

Graffiti flourished in the corridors of academe, where the office doors sprouted cartoons and jokes alongside class lists and examination results. The notices on the office doors of female professors were routinely defaced. A terse notice that read

OFFICE HOURS
Monday, Tuesday, Thursday, Friday 2-4
and by appointment
L. Heathcote

would attract an inventive array of obscenities — "blows goats" or, absurdly, "fuck the queen." Sometimes these were clearly inspired, if not executed, by learned colleagues.

LOST

One merkin of good quality vinyl and camel hair in the vicinity of room 293 in the English Department. Substantial reward offered.

They became badges of honour, proof of our embattled state, and grist for our classes, which came to resemble group therapy sessions. They were large classes, made up of women of all stripes — the tentative, the curious, the skeptical, and the already converted.

The semester that led up to the insemination of Max was, for me, more potentially explosive than most. It was dominated by Marion and Jinny, both vocal and ebullient, but entirely different, at least at the beginning. Because they were polar opposites, they magnetized each other, at first engaging in confrontation for our entertainment. Then they lost sight of us, performed exclusively for themselves, and became locked in a struggle so exhilarating that they couldn't release each other.

Marion was one of many women who, at a time when so many doors were opening, aspired to the ministry in their various churches. Being Catholic, she knew that it was an unattainable goal for her, but she came as close to it as she could. She was the chaplain in a small Catholic college, a singular honour, as she loved to explain to the uninitiated, because such a position was rarely filled by a layperson, and even more rarely by a woman. She was allowed to give homilies and enjoyed (or imagined) a privileged relationship with the priests, with whom she was daringly familiar and flirtatious. She had a hearty disdain for the nuns, whom she called "nunny-poos." I never knew if this contempt developed independently or if she picked it up from one of her priestly comrades. Either way, it was the woman-for-woman hatred that is dangerously close to self-loathing.

I worried about Marion and her role as counsellor, she who so clearly needed counselling herself, caught as she was in her own irreconcilable conflict. She upheld the standard of traditional womanhood with the same energy that she fled from it herself, so that observing her was like watching two trains hurtling towards certain collision, and it made me uneasy. How long would it be before the crash, when and where would she be, and would she survive? And what form would her self-destruction take?

She needed the status of widow — that perfect alibi for those who crave autonomy without the defiance of conventions for female behaviour that is necessary to gain that autonomy. A true love killed in a war would have done as well, or a lover who became a priest. (We'd all recently read *The Thornbirds*.)

Jinny's lapses into depression were almost a refreshing contrast to Marion's euphoria. That semester Jinny did an awful lot of talking in my office, and I did a lot of listening. Well, that's not entirely true. I'd tune in and tune out, not from indifference or heartlessness but because there was so much repetition. The same records were played over and over until their impact diminished — therapeutic to the speaker, but tedious to the counsellor.

"I'm supposed to be teaching literary criticism, not running a drop-in centre for the lovelorn."

"How will I ever find anyone?" she'd ask plaintively. "What are the chances when only one in ten is like me?"

"You might just have to fall back on men, *faute de mieux*."

"Yuck."

"One of these days I'll probably run into you coming across the Victoria bridge with a buggy-load of snot-nosed babies."

"Well, they won't be mine."

It did sometimes happen that after all the heartache and the confidences, the temptation to go straight for a while was too great, the fear of pariahdom too strong, and I'd run into a former student like Jinny with a boyfriend or children, looking at me, faintly sheepish. Then later it would all fall apart — the divorce, the lapse into madness — dreadful things happened.

But, on the whole, I thought Jinny was safe because she was so sure about herself, so comfortable in her own skin, so accepting of herself. She was often buoyant, but not with Marion's pumped-up, fake jollity. Jinny had a wonderful androgynous charm and half the class, I felt sure, was somewhat in love with her, enchanted by her. I'd find myself smiling at her distinctive boyish stride as she walked briskly across the parking lot on her way to class.

All the same, Jinny was suffering from a complexity of problems that semester when she spent so much time in my office. One was unrequited love, the other was coming out to her family, moving out of the family home, and living alone for the first time. And then there was the sub-theme of "The Dog." At one point or another in the ongoing narrative, Jinny would arrive at the scene that never failed to make her incoherent with grief. She had had a pet dog, and during the various upheavals of her life she forgot to look after it. She'd returned home one day to find it had been missing for several days. Nobody had even thought about it. She'd rushed outside and found it chained to a shed, frozen to death. Sometimes when she talked about it she'd sob so hard I'd find tears running down my own face. At other times, horrible as it was, I'd want to laugh. She said she'd never forgive herself or her parents for letting this happen, and I thought she was probably right. As a mark of respect I had a picture of this dog over my desk.

Because the tenets of our new discipline stressed the authority of experience and the continuum between the personal and the literary, the classes had an informal atmosphere, conducive to intimacy because teacher and student both felt free to offer personal testimony. The confessional mode of the classroom meant that students developed a support system for each other. As I walked along the corridor by the cafeteria I often saw them hunched in groups around a table, drinking coffee and talking with great animation.

The first time I saw Marion and Jinny together, I thought how nice that they'd effected a reconciliation. My office overlooked the parking lot, and while I didn't keep a constant vigil, I inevitably noticed the comings and goings as I lifted my eyes from the page. It amused me to think of Marion giving Jinny a lift in her car and continuing the sparring that began in class. Later, when I began to see them drinking coffee together on a regular basis, I felt some alarm. It wasn't difficult to imagine a scenario: Marion, the trained counsellor, getting Jinny alone and making a play for her soul, trying to lure her away from her wicked, ungodly ways. I had little concern for Jinny, who was the least lureable person I knew. I thought only Marion would be obtuse enough to try to convert her. But it seemed sinister, like a Victorian clergyman finding a prurient satisfaction in rescuing a fallen woman. I didn't like it.

In the middle of the semester we had the break we called "suicide week" because the desperate climate was supposed to induce despair and lead to bodies swinging from the rafters. Students could take a week off and go to a warmer place or stay home and prepare for the mid-term exams. Marion was always talking about retreats, and she intended to make one at a monastery in the middle of the province.

When Jinny came in with a paper after the break, she apologized because it was late. She'd been away, she said, in a tone that invited me to ask more. I refused to be led on, so she volunteered that she'd made a retreat, then threw back her head and laughed.

Soon afterwards, I was sitting in my office when the telephone rang. It was Jinny, her voice full of muted amusement. I suspected and dreaded that it had something to do with Marion, and for a moment thought she might say, "Guess who I'm moving in with?"

"Are you in your office?" she asked.

"No. This is just a person they've hired to staff the women-in-crisis hotline we seem to be running here."

"Seriously," she said.

"Alright then, seriously," I said, "I confess. It's me and I'm here."

"I'll be right over. There's someone I want you to meet."

I waited in trepidation, but when she rapped on the door and walked in, it wasn't a person who accompanied her but a staggering puppy of no recognizable breed. Jinny was grinning like a proud mother displaying a baby to the grandparents.

"You get to name it," she said.

"Is *it* a he or a she?"

"What a shocking first question coming from you. Honestly, Professor, I wonder sometimes if your principles go very deep at all, or if they aren't merely a veneer, designed to keep you in these opulent surroundings and on this huge salary."

"Alright, alright, touché. You caught me off guard. I'm honoured to help in this matter of nomenclature. How about Orlando, Flush, Basket, Keeper? I've got it. Let's call it Dogwood, out of respect for the late Woody. You can call it Dog for short. And what would be a suitable christening gift. A flea-and-tick dog collar?"

Then the phone rang and a sombre voice wanted to make an

appointment, not about a class assignment but about "something personal," and Jinny went off cheerfully with the now-named cur. I saw them to the door and couldn't help noticing, as I looked down the corridor, that Marion was turning the corner at the far end. Jinny went off in the opposite direction, and I wondered if Marion was stalking her, bent on conversion or bent on something else.

Jinny's visits to the office continued, but she never spoke of her relationship with Marion. Once or twice I thought she was on the point of confiding something to me but, as often happened, the phone rang or someone came to the door and we were interrupted.

It was not long afterwards that I received in the office mail a large envelope with my name on it in Jinny's hand, clearly not a class assignment. I weighed the envelope in my hand, thought better of opening it, and put it in a drawer. Jinny said nothing for a week or two and then brought up the subject.

"That letter I sent. Did you get it?"

"I did," I said. "I didn't open it and it's still here somewhere." I ferretted about and found it. "Do you still want me to open it?"

"I guess not. It was pretty stupid."

"I somehow thought you might have second thoughts," I said as I handed back the envelope.

Finally, the long semester ended. The women in the class, reluctant to drift apart, suggested a class picnic. They announced that they were going to hold it in my garden.

"The hell you will," I said. "It's a tarpaper shack and I don't want any more holes put in the walls. The wind already whistles through the place." In spite of my protests, they arrived anyway on the appointed day, carrying hampers of food and wine. It turned out to be one of those heavenly Saskatchewan days you get in late spring and early summer, neither too hot nor too cold. They trooped into the house exclaiming. "It's a mansion!" "It's a baronial manor!" "It's Thornfield Hall!" I said it was just your average lumber baron's home from the time when the logging industry throve on these plains. It did rather resemble such West Coast mansions — on a small scale.

It was a golden afternoon. The women were not just relieved that classes were over, but a large number of them, like Jinny, had negotiated some tricky rites of passage. And so there was an air of "look we have come through." Perhaps the class had helped. Some of them thought so. Even Marion was in good form, her usual ebullience toned down to a normal level of gaiety. They wandered through the garden and through the gate at the end that opened onto the public park, donated to the city by the Rotarians. I warned them about the creek, which was a sluggish stream full of algae and duckweed.

"Don't fall into the crick whatever you do, because the water's foul."

Jinny promptly fell in.

Later, back in the garden, she took off most of her clothes and the others hosed her down, and they all played about on the grass like the young virgins at Hanging Rock. At one point I looked up and saw Fern's disapproving face pressed against an upper window on the side of her house. For a brief moment I saw the scene through her eyes as one of debauchery — the bottles of wine and beer, a group of women hopping about like children, and Marion training the hose on an almost naked Jinny.

But there was no other sour note, certainly no hint of tragedy, only good fellowship and good feeling all round. After the picnic they grew sleepy and lay about saying, "Tell us a story, teacher," mocking my habit of beginning my lectures with stories (a carry-over from the Church of England sermons of my youth). I went along with the mockery.

"Once there was a convent in which the nuns wove a fine linen intended for the bridal sheets of royal houses of the kingdom . . . "

"Oh, not that again," they shrieked and pelted me with missiles of balled-up plastic wrap and orange peel.

"Very well then. Once there was a Chinese emperor who wanted to make all the women in his harem into soldiers . . . "

Another shower of protests and missiles.

"Alright, you lot. Tell your own stories from now on."

"No, come on, teacher, we need stories. But we need *new* stories. If we continue to tell the same old stories, we shall continue to lead the same blighted lives blah, blah, blah . . . "

"Yeah. Womanhood must be reinvented by women who can imagine blah, blah, blah . . . "

It was too early and too bright a sunny day for the ghost stories I wrote for light entertainment, but after they drifted into the house I picked up a chapter I was working on and tried to read some parts I thought they might find amusing. It was enough to get them yawning and on the road. They went off waving and laughing, Jinny shouting neighbour-shocking profanities.

After they left, I suddenly felt let down and unhappy. I have a strong morbid streak in my nature. Why else would I think when something wonderful happens — a prize, a success, a magical social occasion when everyone's in harmony — that the thunder-clouds are gathering as if the gods have been taunted? Perhaps because it had happened to me so often. Well it wasn't the next day or even the next week that the frame was placed around that afternoon, sealing it off as a memory of something perfect and absolutely irretrievable.

IV

WHAT HAPPENED TO IT was coupled with another summer day later in the month, in exactly the same place but with a different cast of characters. It was evening and Simone and Julia were sitting on my porch. Lena came by later. I can't recall if we met by chance or by arrangement. We met a great deal for both reasons that summer, for it was a gilded kind of season. We lingered on the porch after the air turned cool, and after the mosquitoes and gnats started to get in by ones and twos through the holes in the screens. Many more beat their wings on the outside, drawn by the candle flame.

"I should go home," Julia said, but instead of moving she reached for another cigarette.

She was an unapologetic smoker who never tried to quit, even though she had a persistent smoker's cough. If anyone mentioned health hazards, she would counter that lots of people who did all the right things got cancer, and how cheated she'd feel if she deprived herself of the pleasure of smoking and came down with a brain tumour anyway.

"Lung cancer more likely," Simone said.

"No more painful than any other way of going out," Julia said.

"What about cancer of the tongue or larynx?"

They'd had variations on this exchange so often, it had become ritualistic. But on this particular evening we were all too mellow for argument.

"I should go too," said Lena, yawning. "I've had too much to drink already. I'd better walk home and get the car in the morning."

"Oh shoot, I'm on call tomorrow," said Simone, still new enough to the profession to say it with pride.

But no one moved except to fill a glass or trim a dripping candle. One by one we watched the stars come out. And then the phone rang. It took that ring to dislodge us from our languor, but no one left that night. Julia, who was nearest the door, got up, went inside, and picked up the phone. When she didn't return immediately, I followed her, and as I approached she looked at me anxiously and assured the caller that I wouldn't be alone. She stood watching me while I talked.

"One of my students has killed herself," I said when I put down the phone.

We moved into the house from the patio, all suddenly chilled, blowing out candles, carrying glasses. I lay down on the living room couch, and Lena went upstairs and got a blanket to put over me because my teeth were rattling and my fingernails were blue. Someone passed brandy around and later on someone made tea. They no longer thought of leaving. Instead they started to talk, as if telling stories could shore up lives, establish a beachhead, and stave off chaos and death.

They crouched on the floor around the coffee table in front of the couch, keeping a kind of vigil. My grief eventually turned to anger, and that seemed to fuel the rage of the others and tap into a communal well of bitterness. When one story ended, another began so that the well seemed bottomless.

They barely knew Jinny, but they knew me. I didn't say much, but their voices washed over me, soothing me as I half listened to them. Because my eyes were closed, I was more aware of their voices than usual. Lena had a strange voice, as if she'd lost her mother tongue, adopted another, but never quite shed traces of the original. Julia's was deep and husky, like that of an androgynous film star of the forties. Simone's was incongruously meek and conciliatory for such an assertive person.

I was thinking of the letter from Jinny that I hadn't opened, wishing that it had remained in my desk so that I could go to my office the next day and find a last message. It was a long time before I stopped thinking about that unopened letter and the clue it might have contained to what had happened.

Lena's stories were strangely disjointed, as if they came from a battle-zone or an occupied country, where soldiers could come to the house and take whatever they wanted. She told of a gang of youths who brutalized her childhood. These stories turned our stomachs, ranging as they did from the savage to the bestial, from tormenting her to mutilating her pet kittens and rabbits. She described the destruction of a doll, its face melting in the flames. We sensed that these horrors masked something else and that there was one story back of everything that she couldn't tell and stay sane.

"There was this woman. None of the kids had shoes."

"What did they wear?" Julia asked. For a long time Lena didn't reply, as if the question had caused her to lose the thread. Then she went on.

"They wore what they could find — broken sneakers, shoes stuffed with paper and straw to make them fit, pairs that didn't match. In warm weather they went barefoot. It didn't matter because it was in the country. But the oldest girl was getting so she needed proper shoes.

"The mother goes into town one day. Where she always stands, on the opposite corner is a shoe shop. Men's and ladies'. She notices this big sign in the window: GET A PAIR FREE. She knows you never get anything free, and she thinks it must mean they'd give you an extra pair if you buy a pair. But something draws her across the street, hopefully. And it isn't what she expected. Turns out it's a game. There's a big jar full of beans, you have to guess how many, and if you guess right you get a pair of shoes. There's a display — shoes, boots, and sandals, all different styles and colours.

"She's very smart, this woman. She already has a jar, so all she has to do is buy a bag of beans. The hard kind you soak in water, navy beans, and she fills her jar with them. Then she dumps them out on the table. That night all the kids sit round the table, putting beans in piles, counting beans, till they get dead tired and fall asleep, numb from counting beans. Only the mother is still awake and the girl, counting every last bean, way into the night.

"The girl goes along the path to the outhouse, her head aching. It is a full moon and all the trees are bright as silver birches. Suddenly she knows it won't work, it's all been for nothing. The storekeeper won't sit up counting beans. They won't know how many there are. She feels bad, not for herself but for the mother, who has nothing and tries so hard.

"But she's wrong. They must know how many beans there are because when the mother puts the paper with the number on the counter, the man looks at it a long time. First he's amazed and then suspicious. Then he calls out 'Merna,' and a big well-fed woman comes out of the back, holding a dust rag. She looks at the piece of paper and then at the mother and the girl. They are all looking at each other, wondering what will happen next. Then the woman goes in the back and comes out with a brown paper bag and dumps it on the counter. There's shoes in the bag. The girl wants to cry out, but the mother's scared now and wants to hurry away as quick as possible. She's worried they might call the police. As they leave, she sees the woman taking the jar of beans and the notice out of the window.

"You wouldn't think anyone could be that mean, would you?" Lena said.

"What were they like, the shoes that were in the bag?" Julia asked, but all Lena would say was that they soaked the beans and made a soup with turnips.

Julia talked about her marriage and divorce. She'd been a beauty queen on her campus, she said.

"You were a beauty queen?" Lena said, incredulously. She had come out of her trance and returned to her old self.

"This was back when," said Julia. "It wasn't so unusual at the time. There were these competitions and we all entered them."

"Did you wear a bikini?" Simone asked.

"No, no," Julia said, "it wasn't like that. Just photographs and people voted. The guys put money in boxes, it was a kind of fundraising thing." But that was how she met her husband. He saw the picture and asked her out. The guys in his fraternity had bets that she wouldn't accept. But she did. Three months later she dropped out of school because she was pregnant.

"Did he want a date with you, or was it just a dare?" Simone asked.

"Was it rape?" Lena asked.

"No, of course it wasn't," Julia said. "It just happened, a no-fault pregnancy." She got a job in a dress shop to put her husband through school, and her mother looked after the kid. There were more children and everything went well until he took up with someone else. She tried to sue for child support, for alimony, but didn't get much. He was a prominent figure in local politics by this time, and she didn't stand a chance in the courts. So she resigned herself, accepted a "settlement" on his terms, and got along as best she could. It was what they call "an amicable divorce."

"A no-fault divorce," Julia said. "It wasn't his fault the girl he'd married turned out to be a mother, which he didn't need because he already had one. So naturally he found himself another young girl."

Simone talked of the humiliations of medical school — the insults of elderly professors, her fellow students with their girlfriends and wives, the patients who looked at her and said they wanted to see a real doctor.

"So what?" said Lena contemptuously.

When her injuries didn't provoke much of a reaction, Simone went on to regale us with horror stories from the history of gynecology. She said the practice of medicine hadn't changed much over the years, over the centuries.

"Oh come on now, Simone," Julia said.

But Simone insisted that it hadn't. Experiments with knives were outlawed now, she said, but the attitudes were the same. Unnecessary surgery, unnecessary pain, women still having too many children, too close together, painkillers withheld on a whim ... There were too many hysterectomies and Caesarean sections performed, too many experimental drugs dispensed in disproportionately high numbers to women; menopause pathologized as menstruation once was. She recited a litany of its supposed effects — hair loss, bone loss, tooth loss, memory loss — all of which could be remedied by taking drugs.

"You think clitoridectomies happen in backward places? Well, they began in England and started in America in the middle of the nineteenth century. And they were done for sixty years."

"That's true," said Lena, who had also spent hours immersed in my copy of Barker-Benfield's *The Horrors of the Half-Known Life*. "They were used as treatment for psychological disorders. Women had their ovaries removed for the same reason."

"The great doctors," said Simone, "competed in inventing instruments and experimenting on women. They used slaves when they couldn't find white women to mutilate. They'd try anything in order to increase fertility. One even tried splitting up the neck of the uterus to help the menstrual flow out and the sperm flow in."

"Marion Sims, the Architect of the Vagina," said Lena. "He also invented the 'uterine guillotine' for the amputation of the cervix. There's someone you should have written about, Lucy, instead of Alice James."

I thought of Alice James. Her psychological disorder would have made her prime candidate for such treatments. Would we ever know what happened to her in those clinics in New York? The medical records didn't exist, and modesty would have kept anyone in the family from mentioning anything done to her sexual organs.

Even as a child Simone had been preoccupied with physical torture and I wondered how much that strange taste had factored into her decision to study medicine. As she went on with her grisly anecdotes, I had no means of knowing whether they were a part of her medical training or whether she did her research independently, out of some morbid obsession with the subject. It struck me as warped in her, a motivation somehow different from that behind the personal testaments of Lena and Julia.

In grade school, when the other kids would be doing reports on whales and butterflies, she'd be researching medieval instruments of torture or the Spanish Inquisition. I had a sudden flash of Simone as a child, sitting at my kitchen table with a rapt expression on her little face, talking about walking on hot coals, about tearing lumps of flesh out of the breast for a paper on the Sun Dance. What strange imperative lay behind this obsession? Had religious indoctrination conditioned her to see the world in primary colours, in stark contrasts of black and white, to dwell on the Inquisition, the witch trials, satanism, and demons of all stripes? Once after the family took a packaged tour to England she'd come home excited not by the changing of the guard or the crown jewels, but by seeing the rack on which Guy Fawkes was tortured at the Tower of London and by the Chamber of Horrors at Madame Tussaud's. I really wondered about her taste for blood and gore — was it congenital or was it acquired? And what had brought it out on this particular evening?

Does suicide always cause anger and resentment to rise to the surface, and the need to blame someone? I felt grief for Jinny but also guilt. So much of what I believed was coded within the covers of books. I'd always thought that phrases like "living in an ivory tower" and "being out of touch with the real world" came from envy and suspicion of book learning. But there was another side.

I felt shame that for all my preaching, all my theory, it was Jinny who tried to live the rebellion, live the subversion that I only theorized. I hadn't done a single thing to make the world a safer place for Jinny. I might even have pushed her into danger, into death. I armed the students with information and ideas that only made them reckless and vulnerable. I sent them out to expose themselves, like those old generals of the First World War who stayed behind the lines but ordered the young men into the trenches as cannon fodder. I was one of the General Haigs of the feminist movement and Jinny's death brought this home to me. I didn't even turn out to pro-choice rallies, excusing myself on the grounds that my weapon was my pen, my medium the printed word. So it wasn't just grief with me but guilt and shame.

When I came out of my reverie and listened again, Julia was describing an abortion insisted on by her husband. Lena, in her vague disconnected way, began to yammer on about women who died in childbirth.

"No woman who died a cruel death in childbirth was ever considered a martyr. No one who gave birth to twelve children was ever canonized. Funny isn't it, considering the so-called reverence for life, motherhood, and childbirth? And nobody ever romanticized death in childbirth in a poem."

We'd played around with this idea once in class. It was the kind of thing we did then, reversing the gender of characters in fiction, supposing Bartelby or Oliver Twist had been a woman. Quite a literary industry grew up around it. We'd made a game of writing sonnets that Mary Wollstonecraft and Charlotte Brontë might have written, variations on such poems as

I have a rendezvous with death
Spreadeagled on those snowy sheets

If I should die, think only this of me
That there's some boy will take my place
To fight for king and country in a foreign field

When I have fears that I may cease to be
Somewhere upon a bed of blood
Before my pen has gleaned my teeming brain

"The trouble with the movement is it's been too passive and non-violent."

"You can tell that when the yardstick for extremism is bra-burning."

Even in my semi-comatose state, I couldn't help rousing myself to gloss that phrase, as I had so often done in class. "And that didn't really happen. A few women tossed bras into garbage cans to protest a beauty contest in Atlantic City. The whole thing was blown up by the media."

"We should fight for reproductive rights like the militant suffragettes fought for the vote."

"But they were a small percentage of the female population. And not many were militant. How many chained themselves to railings and threw themselves under horses? Or ended up in prison and went on hunger strikes? Very few."

"Well, they didn't know how to make bombs or get guns."

"We do. But we won't use them. When the extremists mount attacks on abortion clinics and doctors in the States, they have absolutely no fear of reprisal. The so-called right-to-lifers feel perfectly safe to go on harassing the clinics, quite confident their lives will be safe. No one's going to take revenge. They won't be the ones buying bulletproof vests. Funny that, isn't it?"

"The only equalizer," said Lena, "would be if the motherfuckers were forced to bear children themselves. Give 'em a chance to prove their reverence for LIFE."

"But it isn't a men versus women thing. Most of those doctors who put their lives on the line are men. And the anti-choice ranks have plenty of women." That must have been Julia.

When I replay in my mind the conversations of that night, I'm never sure who said what. That remark about bearing children — it came back to me in Lena's rough voice, but it could have been Simone.

We tossed around various scenarios — seizing the right-to-lifers, taking them inside the clinics they were harassing and simply impregnating them with the embryos they were desperate to save. It seemed a reasonable, fitting, non-violent, unvengeful solution.

"Unless they're outright hypocrites, they should feel like voluntary kidney donors. They'd shake hands at the door when they leave and say what a privilege it was to save a life. What a wonderful experience and how soon could they do it again . . . "

"It would be useful, too, for gay couples who want children. And for heterosexual couples where the wife has a health problem . . . "

"Or drinks or smokes . . . "

"Or simply isn't very brave about labour pains. A loving husband might want to relieve her of the burden . . . "

"And think of transsexuals. Many of them would like to have babies."

"Too bad it couldn't be done."

"It could be done," said Simone without a moment's pause. "The uterus isn't absolutely necessary for a pregnancy. There have been several cases of women giving birth after they've had hysterectomies. As a matter of fact, abdominal pregnancies happen all the time — about one in every 10,000 pregnancies. It would be pretty easy to insert an embryo into a man's abdominal cavity. With a bit of luck — the kind needed in any pregnancy — the egg would attach itself to the fatty tissue of the omentum, the placenta would start to develop, and the pregnancy would be established."

"There's a precedent in nature," Julia said.

"There is?"

"The sea horse, of all the species, is known for monogamy and male pregnancy. The female lays her eggs in the male's abdominal pouch. They're bright red and the filled pouch glows with them. And every morning during the pregnancy, the partners dance together just after sunrise. The pregnancy lasts ten days."

"It's funny that the sea horse has never caught on as a symbol like those mythical beasts — unicorns, phoenixes, centaurs — when the sea horse is far more beautiful and more wonderful."

"It must be a relic of a time when childbirth wasn't divided so unequally between male and female, don't you think? Biological roles must have become artificially divided through evolution just as gender roles did. Could the biological balance be restored?"

"It's been tried in animals," said Simone. "A fertilized egg from a female baboon was transferred to the abdominal cavity of a male baboon in the mid-sixties. That was at the George Washington University Medical School."

"What happened?"

"Human intervention happened. The pregnancy was terminated after four months. Gestation takes seven months in baboons so that's well over halfway along. It was proceeding very well, the dangers were just ethical ones."

"They tamper with all kinds of things surgically and pharmaceutically, but modifications in gender roles scare people to death."

"Male pregnancy would be risky though, wouldn't it, in humans?"

"Not excessively so. Especially not if the bearer were young and healthy. And certainly no more risky than for many women who have health complications."

I often thought later about Simone's lack of hesitation and wondered if the automatic nature of her responses meant that the idea had been in her mind long before it entered ours.

"Could we?"

"Yes, we could."

They began to talk as if correcting this one biological imbalance would be a first step toward eradicating a great divide and subsequently all the other inequalities in the world.

At first I only half listened to the talk going to and fro, to speculation giving way to certainty, to hypothetical situations. Then I began to pay attention as a thought took shape in all our minds and we recognized a chance to do something for once instead of talking and theorizing and pleading for justice. Eventually a kind of commitment was made by each to the others. We had a lot of anger, little power, and few means of protest, so this seemed as reasonable a gesture of defiance as any other.

As dawn broke we made coffee and toast, and they prepared for their days. I assured them that I'd be fine and sat at my kitchen table marking a pile of essays. Mechanical routines are the only solace for grief, and it was supremely comforting to work through the papers, automatically making the proofreader's signs — arrows and circles and parallel lines — restoring order and clarity by eliminating dangling participles, faulty antecedents, and ambiguities.

Only Julia came with me to the funeral in a little rundown church on the edge of town. I found it moving — the organ music, the sparse choir, the liturgy, the soberly dressed mourners, and even the sickly smell of incense. Aromatherapy goes back a long way. It was strange I hadn't realized that Jinny was Catholic. She'd mentioned the United Church and I'd assumed she was a dissident daughter of it, as I was of the Church of England. But I saw now that she was a lapsed Catholic who had been bereft of a spiritual home. I grieved not only because I hadn't understood she was Catholic but because I'd underestimated the whole religious dimension in her life, and ignored her great need. I, of all people, should have known that when you remove the props, take down the walls that imprison people, they don't just walk free. They need halfway houses, rehab centres, something to help them make the transition to freedom. Again, I yearned for that letter I hadn't read.

We sat at the back of the church, latecomers, and Julia was eager to get outside so that she could light up as soon as possible. But we weren't the only ones to arrive last and get away first. As we came down the steps, someone came rushing after us a little breathlessly. It was Marion, and, incongruously, she had a grin on her face like the Cheshire cat.

"I wanted to tell you something," she said, the bearer of glad tidings. "Jinny came back to God at the end."

Julia grabbed my arm before I could say anything and marched me firmly to the car. "That was the one, wasn't it?" she said as she started up the engine. I didn't understand what she meant, and she said, "Don't you remember, when you got the phone call, you said a student had killed herself and it was the wrong one?"

I hadn't remembered, but without a doubt, if I said that, it was Marion I had meant.

"She's a drinker, that one," Julia said. "Didn't you notice? The smell nearly knocked me over."

And so, if there was a beginning, I think that was probably it. If you want to construct your genealogy, it would have to begin with Jinny.

Oh, I forgot to mention that I inherited Dog.

V

I'LL DO MY BEST to describe Max as he was then. But each of us would have told you a different story about Max because he showed a different facet of himself to each one of us. I suppose most of us present different faces to our various friends, and maybe there was nothing calculated in Max's doing so. I've read the correspondence of prolific letter writers who tell the same event to several people, modifying it according to the recipient. Deceitful? Schizophrenic? Who knows? So you have to understand that when I tell you about Max, it's simply as I knew him, which is probably not how Lena, Julia, Simone, or even Monica knew him.

I have to admit that I thought Max and I had a special relationship, that we met as equals. I thought of him as I would one of my colleagues at the university, and when he was in our custody, as it were, I imagined that I was the one whose period of duty he waited for, looked forward to all day long. I might have suspected otherwise if I'd been more alert, but I wasn't.

Julia was the one who suggested him in the first place, and we assumed it was a random choice, a kind of wild shot that hit the bull's eye. But let me tell you about how we did choose him. You'd want to know that, wouldn't you?

After that first long night and its intimacies, we fell into the habit of meeting more regularly. I would invite Julia and Simone together, and Julia would invite Simone and me, and somehow Lena trailed along with me. We always reverted to the same topic and it became a game — suggesting names of authority figures for our possible vessels. That was what we called them, vessels. So-and-so would make a good vessel. There were numerous candidates.

For a long time I'd kept a Blithering Idiot file. It began as a way of counteracting the steady acid drips of misogyny and homophobia that came across my desk in newspaper and journal articles. I tossed the clippings into this black folder, as if I were consigning the offenders to outer darkness. I needed little urging to bring out this file, dip into it, and read whatever I randomly came up with. These readings became a feature of our meetings:

> Many men in Parliament seem to have a real problem with women's body parts. Clare Short, the secretary for international development, told a recent television program about women in Parliament that some of her male opponents begin giggling when, for instance, the subject of cervical cancer programs comes up.
>
> "They're very public-schoolboy primitive," Ms. Short said. "Breasts, of course, just finish them off completely."
>
> So, apparently, does any reference to birds, which, in British slang, means what "chicks" means in American slang. "The speaker had to intervene the other day when a woman stood up during an agriculture debate on wild birds . . . they thought it was hilarious that a woman was asking about birds."

> Closets are designed to hide unsightly reminders of our work-a-day world. That sexually "disoriented" people have emerged from their closets speaks well of society's tolerance and compassion, but does not justify or legitimize behaviour that is an affront to the natural sense of decency and human purpose of most people.

That last was a typical drop of venom from one local preacher whose manifestos appeared as paid advertisements in the newspaper. The editor claimed it was not his job to censor the advertisements that people paid for, even if they incited hatred and violence. He trusted the good sense of his readers to evaluate what was published. Every week I'd clip and read the latest column, and one of us would say, "This has got to be the man." Someone else would say, "Why don't we nab the editor of the paper? He allows it and he should know better." But somehow there was never a consensus on either of these two. There were practical problems because we knew very little about their personal habits and so no plan of action suggested itself. If we agreed that one might do, it never went any further. I kept thinking of academics and, in fact, when we finally picked Max on the evening of the fall convocation, I was ready to push for one of the deans. I couldn't stand the way those who left the classroom for the richer rewards of administration were constantly pontificating on the importance of teaching. My outrage at the hypocrisy increased every time I saw their spacious suites of offices and compared them with the airless, windowless cells in which I conducted most of my classes.

Here's what happened.

After the convocation ceremonies I went along to Julia's place, where the group was gathered. Julia's house had once been the large family home of a banker, and it functioned both as her home and workplace. She ran a little kindergarten school on the lower floor, and her own living quarters fitted haphazardly in and around the schoolrooms. It was a sprawling house, with so many additions and irregularities that it was impossible to keep track of all the rooms and cubbyholes. In England it would have been set in acres of parkland, and in another century it might have harboured a priest, a smuggler, or some other person on the run or in hiding. For that reason it was perfectly suited to the enterprise we had in mind. It was the ideal safe house and without it we couldn't have done what we did.

There was a long pleasant living room on two levels — a sunken conversation pit with a fireplace, and an upper level with French windows opening onto a shady garden full of evergreens. Her bedrooms were somewhere on the third level, with the school sandwiched between the two. I was rarely there on weekdays to see the school in progress, but I supposed that it wasn't then much different from any other time. It was characteristic of Julia's place that there was a constant shifting population of family, visitors, and friends who happened to be out of luck or suffering from emotional difficulties.

When I got back from convocation I helped myself to a glass of wine, intending to settle down in front of the television set in Julia's den. The faculty can never see the ceremony from where they sit, sweltering under arc lights at the back of the platform, and I wanted to see the woman who got an honorary degree. For once, someone had made an inspired choice and bypassed the usual affluent businessman in order to honour a local writer who celebrated the lives of rural women.

When I walked in, I was shocked to see Monica Werner lying on the couch. It was years since she and I had been in the same room, and I wondered furiously if Julia had any sense of discretion at all or if she was just stupid. She knew we'd all been hoping that tonight we could settle the vessel question once and for all. Julia came in behind me and said she hadn't invited her but that Monica just drifted in and out. She was going through an especially bad time at the moment. It was a neutral comment with no overtones of accusation.

Bad times had been Monica's natural element long before I came on the scene, but they intensified after Sam left. Suzy had eventually disappeared and hadn't been heard of again, and Renny had little contact with her mother. Monica had been arrested for shoplifting, had nearly died several times from drug overdoses, and had become a hopeless alcoholic. So it was hard to see, in view of her past history, how her current bad time could constitute a crisis. Julia said, "She won't get in the way of anything."

We watched the ceremony together and then went to get some food. By that time Monica had passed out completely, and I could see what Julia meant when she said she wouldn't interfere with anything. So we talked vessel and I let the others toss various ideas around while I waited for the strategic moment to make my pitch for the dean. Lena went on about a certain preacher, and Simone read a newspaper column. And then Julia, leaning with her arm along the mantelpiece, said nonchalantly, "Max Hoffman."

"Hey, I think we got the dawg," Lena said.

And you know, we had. The recognition and the rightness of it struck us all at the same time. We felt as if enlightenment had somehow descended from above like a dove and settled on Julia's head. Our mood became quite festive, and we opened more bottles of wine so that we could toast the choice that buoyed us on our course.

It was not to be a long evening, and soon afterwards we left and went out into the October night. Julia said she'd bed Monica down and look after her, and Simone and I walked Lena back to her apartment. It was no longer safe to walk the streets alone after dark, even for short distances. We walked slowly because it was a fine crisp night and the leaves, still thick on the ground, crackled and rustled as we waded through them. Before we parted, Simone and I lingered briefly at the side doors of our adjacent houses.

Sobered by the chilly night air I asked, "Is this really going to be possible?" And again without hesitation she said, "Of course. No doubt about it. None whatsoever. Stop worrying about it, oh you of little faith."

∽

I was the one designated to capture Max. Perhaps "capture" is too colourful a word, suggesting a kind of cloak-and-dagger operation. There was actually none of that, only a certain amount of subterfuge of a kind I was quite practised at. In writing biographies and biographical profiles, I'd had plenty of experience insinuating myself into people's homes, interviewing them, drawing them out, playing on their fears and vanities in order to win their confidence.

Also, I had a slight acquaintance with Max. We'd recently been together on committees and literary juries, had acted as judges for debating tournaments, and had a fairly cordial relationship, in spite of political differences. We attacked each other occasionally in meetings, but usually it was all charm and civility.

We were friendly enough for me to be able to call him and ask if I might come and see him privately and know that he would agree to see me. He would expect to be consulted on some matter concerning the arts, the university, or the debating clubs. I looked forward to the prospect because it had been a long time since I'd done an interview, and I missed worming my way into the homes of "witnesses," getting them to open up and tell me more than they really intended. There's a skill involved in this, and I didn't want to lose it.

There was that, and also the fact that Max was a somewhat fascinating and mysterious character. Rumours circulated, as they do about prominent people in small communities. These concerned his past, his childhood, his political associations, his wealth, and, naturally, his wife. Since she was flamboyantly beautiful and he was slightly built and ordinary looking, it might have been assumed that she married him for money. But the word was that they were childhood sweethearts. All the same, there was much talk in town about her constant travels. Speculation about her destinations ranged from expensive health spas where she would lose weight, dry out, or have cosmetic surgery to liaisons with international crooks for shady business transactions. There were even reported sightings of Francine in international resorts of the rich and famous, being escorted by famous actors or young gigolos. These were more indicators of people's glamorous perceptions of Max and Francine than reliable reports of their lives.

And then there was the house, which was an extension of Max himself, the visible symbol of his position, an impregnable fortress defended against all comers. It loomed behind him as the Vatican looms behind the Pope, Buckingham Palace behind the Queen. In our time it was "the Hoffman place," but it had its own distinguished, though checkered, past. It was a historic house and we all loved going through it whenever it was thrown open to the public for some charitable cause.

In an earlier era it had been "the old Gursky house," the home of bootleggers in the second decade of the century and modelled on an English baronial manor. Harry Gursky himself built it when he moved from Yorkton to the big city and started to make a fortune during the Prohibition era. It was the first emblem of his success, but as everyone knows, he had ambitions beyond being the Merchant Prince of a dusty little prairie city. He went off east to Montreal and to greater glory and empire building, while his house remained for those who craved and could afford an ancestral mansion. It was even haunted by its own ghost, because a subsequent owner had shot his wife in the garage.

Like many of the old houses in the city it featured a motley combination of styles. The exterior was the standard beam-and-stucco banker's Tudor. The inside was mostly medieval, with a minstrel gallery, and there were oriel windows, porticos, and tyndalstone terraces. Max used the third-floor ballroom as an art gallery. The former stables had been converted into a garage, and the room above it into a reading and map room, connected to the second-floor library of the main building by a panelled walkway. With all its nooks and crannies, it was a bit like Julia's house, only on a much grander scale and impeccably maintained where hers was shabby.

It was on the main boulevard, and I entered through big wrought-iron gates and walked up a long driveway, bounded by statues imported from Italy. As I stood on the steps after ringing the bell, I looked out towards the legislative building, with its formal gardens and the lake beyond.

I wasn't the least bit nervous because I'd had a brilliant idea. With the recent convocation in mind, I'd simply called him at his office and said that I wanted to put his name forward for a special honour, that it was highly confidential, but that I needed certain information about his career.

Lena hooted at the irony of that "special honour" because he was always going on in his public speeches and statements about the great privilege, the great honour, the great responsibility that it was to bear a child. But, of course, he assumed that I meant an honorary degree — nominees were not supposed to be informed so that they wouldn't feel slighted if the committee didn't approve them. He, predictably, was flattered. He seemed very vain, as if he really craved glory, loved having things named after him, hearing his praises sung from platforms and engraved on plaques as a great civic leader and patron of the arts.

When I called, he asked if I wished to have lunch with him at his club. I didn't want a crowd of witnesses to this meeting, so I said that evening was better for me. He checked his calendar and I pretended to check mine, we settled on an evening and a time, and it all worked out better than I could have dreamed.

I arrived at his house around seven and had to wait a while before he answered the doorbell. In fact, I was beginning to grow anxious when the door opened and he appeared, looking quite ruffled. He said he'd had an unusually busy day and confessed he'd forgotten our appointment and was just about to eat. "But come in anyway," he said distractedly.

He explained that Francine was away for a few days and he was fending for himself. There was no sign of the housekeeper, and I was delighted that Francine was out of town. I knew the chances were good that she'd be out for the evening, but this way he might not even remember to mention my visit when she got back. Her absence seemed like a godsend.

I followed him through to the kitchen, where the only sign of dinner was a small tenderloin steak recently extracted from the freezer and thawing out on the counter. No other preparations were evident, and he said he'd leave the steak and just get some cheese and crackers. I reacted in a very housewifely fashion. I guess I was disarmed by the pathetic look of that steak and offered to cook it for him. The others hailed this as a stroke of genius when they heard about it, and rolled about laughing.

It occurred to me that he really was an isolated, lonely kind of person. I mean, most men in similar circumstances would call up a friend or drop in on someone and join their dinner table. But here he was faced with this hopeless bit of meat. I might add that after that day I could never again look dispassionately at a tenderloin steak or eat it with any pleasure.

He seemed a little skeptical about my competence as a cook, as people tend to be with career women, but I guess he was hungry enough to agree, and with his permission I took a look inside the fridge — not a promising prospect. I took off my suit jacket, hung it on the back of a chair, tucked a tea towel into my waistband, and went to work. He told me there was a wine rack in the basement and invited me to make a selection.

From the showy collection of expensive imports I gathered either he or Francine was a wine snob. There were some German Schloss Lederhosens, a few California reds, but not a Canadian label in sight. Perhaps he shared Sam's opinion of Canadian winemaking: it was like women preaching – "not well done but you were surprised to find it done at all." Being faced with an impressive wine cellar and the prospect of concocting a meal inevitably made me think of Sam. He would have whisked out his vintage card and made a careful selection. I tried to remember what he liked and finally chose a 1961 Richebourg.

Max nodded absent-mindedly when I showed him what I'd picked. I poured myself a glass and drank it while I put together a salad with some tomatoes, olives, and olive oil. He stood with his back against the counter, watching me and drinking a Scotch and soda. I seem to recall that I did something with a stick of bread I found in the freezer. There was a spice rack, well stocked and fairly exotic, but it appeared to be there for decorative purposes.

It was really very convivial. I seared the steak and made a deglazing sauce, pouring half a cup of the Richebourg a bit guiltily into the pan. He was pleased with the result, and surprised that a so-called bluestocking could cook well. I told him how I'd learned to cook from an old beau, and I wondered if he'd heard rumours about Sam and me. We finished off the wine as he ate and I talked. Then, seeming very cheered up, he lit a cigar and insisted on opening another bottle of wine. This time he went to get it himself and returned with a good but fairly ordinary bottle of Côtes du Rhône.

My biographer's training has conditioned me on these occasions to drink less than the interviewee, so I kept on filling his glass, not drinking too much myself, and keeping my wits about me. After he finished eating, I wanted to wash the dishes, but he wouldn't hear of it, saying he had someone coming in in the morning. He had, it was said, an army of loyal retainers, bound to him by gratitude for his legal services. The jaundiced view was that these people were forced to work for him for years to pay off their fees.

And so we moved into the living room and sat in front of the fireplace. He put a match to the fire, and while the logs burned up I asked about the antiquarian books and the antiques, deliberately fanning his suspicions that I was coveting them for the university art gallery.

What was so useful was that there was no question of our doing the interview that night, and I was able to lay the groundwork for another meeting. He was perfectly acquiescent to meeting elsewhere, wherever I could find some recording equipment that I would be comfortable with. It all unrolled in the most plausible manner.

When I said the acoustics would be fine at Julia's house, he expressed surprise that she was my friend. He'd been one of the lawyers involved in her divorce case, and from his sudden alertness at the mention of her name I sensed a more than casual interest in her. I had never until that moment wondered what was behind Julia's suggesting him when she did. We all thought it was so appropriate that no one suspected she might have a specific personal motive.

Of course, the mention of Julia always had the same effect on men who, even if they didn't know her, knew of her and wanted to know more. Francine was beautiful, but so expensively packaged that her looks seemed contrived, as if they resulted from hours of consultation, treatment, and mirror gazing. Julia had the kind of bone structure and natural, understated beauty that makes other women seem overripe and blowsy, no matter how attractive and well groomed they are. Perhaps it's a matter of class more than money. That's what everyone said about Julia, "She has class." So it was perfectly natural that he was interested in Julia, as who wouldn't be?

When it was all arranged, he was still reluctant for me to leave and I was struck again by his loneliness. He delayed my departure by taking me upstairs to look at some first editions he'd recently acquired. Once we were in his study, he found other treasures to show me so that it was near midnight when I eventually got away.

We shook hands warmly at the door and he said he looked forward to the interview. (I actually did conduct it during what you might call his confinement). Then he made a heavy-handed joke about my culinary expertise. He said my talents were wasted as an English professor and he should set me up with a restaurant because my true calling was as a chef. I bridled at the words "set you up." You could always count on Max to say something belittling just when you were warming towards him. But the evening had been such a success that nothing interfered with my triumphant mood.

As soon as I got back to my house, I rushed to the phone to call Julia. The pattern of her life was such that you could call her at any hour of the day or night and she'd be awake and never resentful about being disturbed. I told her gleefully what had happened and she laughed and laughed.

"You're a genius, Lucy," she said, "no one would suspect it of you."

"You know, Julia," I said, "I believe he's interested in you."

"No doubt he is," she said.

I wanted to talk more, but then I heard a man's deep voice in the background.

"Look," she said, "I have to go now. Why don't you come around after school tomorrow?"

I wondered about Julia and her never being alone. What was her mind really on? And how safe would any secret or confidential arrangement ever be with her?

I had not switched on the light as I talked to her, and before doing so I went over to close the curtains at the side of the house. As I stood by the window, I looked down and saw Simone letting herself into her house by the side door. She was not alone, and she seemed to be making sure that neither of them made any sound. Her companion was not much taller than herself, and I could make out neither features or gender because they were both muffled against the cold night air.

At first I thought she was trying to get in without disturbing anyone on the inside. Then she looked up at my house and I realized with a start that I was the reason for all the stealth. Feeling hurt, I stepped back from the window and undressed in the dark. I lay awake for a long time wondering what kind of dubious relationship Simone had got herself into, and about the curious group of people I was involved with.

VI

I SOMETIMES THINK the clearest memory I own is of telling Max he was going to bear a child. It was an incandescent moment, frozen in time, all of us forming a tableau like David's painting of the death of Socrates. We were sitting around the white bed, in the white room, with the white landscape outside the window. Julia, Lena, Simone, Monica, and I, Lucy. And, of course, Max.

It was the day of the first snow. In that place it was an event like the first day of creation. All fall there were intermittent flurries and sometimes quite heavy snowstorms that left a few inches of snow on the ground. But they soon disappeared. And then you woke up one morning to a strange eerie light on the bedroom ceiling and a kind of muffled quiet. Looking out, you would see that it had snowed steadily all night and that everything was shrouded in snow and would remain so until spring. Sometimes the snow was still falling when you looked out and sometimes it had stopped, but you felt a kind of relief, as if something you had been waiting for had happened at last. If I were ever lecturing in another part of the continent around that time of the year, I worried that I would miss that moment.

You felt holy going out in the morning and being the first to walk on the clean snow, virginal, immaculate, out of all time and place. You trod carefully and thoughtfully on the snow and under the white laden branches of the evergreens, noting the muted, reverent sounds of cars and buses, all hushed and expectant, as if waiting for a wondrous event, a strange birth.

So you see, the first snow's coinciding with the annunciation seemed an almost supernatural confirmation, an approbation, a sign of divine approval. There was nothing messy about it, nothing unnatural, just a clean, pure event.

As for the whiteness of the room, that was Julia's doing. I hadn't been in on the operation at all, but Julia had prepared everything according to Simone's instructions. She'd transformed the upper storey of her house into a theatre for the implanting, and Simone had carried it out. I would guess that Simone had intended the room to be clinical, but in Julia's hands it looked more like a bridal chamber than a hospital room. The walls were white to begin with and there were white Venetian blinds, and Julia had put up white curtains and brought in her white leather sofa and some white wicker chairs from here and there. I remember a great glass vase of cascading white flowers that I stared at when I didn't want to keep staring at Max. Whenever I see arum lilies I think of that time. It was early afternoon when we all converged on the house. Simone was in her white lab coat, her long blond hair drawn back, and Julia was wearing a long Aran sweater, the wool bleached white, over an ivory corduroy skirt. She looked pale and beautiful, and, looking at her and Simone, I thought of angels. It was quiet and strange but peaceful. There were long pauses in the conversation but no one got up to leave. We sat and waited and tried to get used to the idea.

It took a long time, and we were patient in answering all Max's questions reasonably and calmly. I don't suppose I can recall everything that was said, but fragments of conversations came and went and repeated themselves, and sometimes we covered the same tracks again and again.

Quite naturally we expected Simone to do most of the explaining, as it was fairly technical, and her explanation was not just for Max but for all of us. She had a chalkboard from the schoolroom downstairs and she drew diagrams and figures very rapidly with chalk while she spoke. I remember I resented the schoolteacherish manner she adopted, as if she were warning us to behave ourselves and be responsible and conduct ourselves appropriately. It passed through my mind that she had taken over as head of the enterprise.

In the beginning, Max was befuddled by the anaesthetic and by the painkillers, but much more disoriented by the situation. He kept saying, "Where am I? How did I get here? What happened? Last thing I remember was being interviewed. I can't even remember getting into my car to drive home. Did I have an accident? Did I have a concussion? Is this a hospital?"

Simone talked in her crisp voice, saying that yes, there had been an accident if he cared to call it that. But it wasn't a car accident. In fact, it wasn't the kind of accident that usually happens to a man. It was more of a woman's kind of accident, familiar to everyone in that room at one time or another. At least to most of us, she said, perhaps remembering Lena or thinking of herself and her own chosen celibacy. She said, "An embryo has been implanted in the lining of your stomach, and as a consequence, you are pregnant."

Naturally, Max rejected the idea out of hand. But Simone went on in her calm, authoritative voice. "You'll notice the incision in your stomach, a slight sensation of discomfort, but this will pass. You will gain weight and possibly experience nausea, especially in the morning. These symptoms are quite normal. You will be well taken care of here during the next nine months."

He had already found the scar and he'd been fingering it, so Simone's explanation was beginning to seem only too plausible. Searching for someone to deny what he was starting to believe, he turned to me. "Lucy, this isn't true is it? What about the interview? What about the honorary degree?"

"I have to be honest at this point, Max. The interview was only a pretext, a means of getting you here. Perhaps I can nominate you for an honorary degree some time, but not at the moment. Meanwhile, you've been chosen, shall we say, for a higher calling, a more singular honour — that of incubating a foetus. You'll be the means by which human life itself will be perpetuated."

It sank in pretty quickly, and then Max began to marshal his objections. "You can't do this to me. It's illegal . . . it's a violation of . . . it's a criminal offense . . . I'm a lawyer, remember. I'll sue."

Simone took over on that one, telling Max that we had understood the risks from the beginning and had undertaken them willingly. She assured him that we all knew we were subject to severe penalties, but she reminded him that he would have to appear in court pregnant.

Lena hooted at this, derisive as a jaybird. "Imagine the pictures in the papers," she said. "Imagine the publicity, the headlines:

ABORTION FOE FINDS SELF PREGNANT
LAWYER'S LABOUR PAINS
MISSIONARY POSITION LEADS TO MAN'S PREGNANCY."

Simone rather angrily told Lena to shut up and then, turning to Max, explained that he wouldn't want the publicity.

"But what makes you think you can get away with this even if I consent?" he said. "Don't you think people will search for me — my friends, my law partners, my wife?"

"Not if you warn them off, they won't," we said.

You see, this was one of the reasons we'd chosen Max. If we'd just wanted any anti-abortion campaigner, there were plenty of candidates. We might have picked up one of the fundamentalist ministers, even old Meiskowski himself. But we picked Max partly for his notorious shady dealings, his reputation for getting away with anything, his skill at twisting the law to his own advantage. And as for his friends, we were pretty sure that he didn't have any really close ones, and his partners were more like partners-in-crime. When we pointed all this out, he said we made him sound like a criminal.

"Just a manipulator. Just your average holder of high office in government and politics. Someone above and beyond the law with a lot of people ready to cover your tracks."

"Including your wife," said Lena.

"You will have to call Francine and tell her to cover for you. That will be arranged later. Just keep putting money in her account and have her tell everyone you're working on a book. They'll all suspect the worst, but no one will dare say it." That was Julia. I remember because it was the first time she came into the conversation. She knew Francine.

"No one will suspect the truth. You can bank on that," said Lena.

"But what do I tell Francine?"

"Well," said Julia, "she does her own disappearing acts, doesn't she? Where does she go when she leaves for those long sojourns at health spas? Is she drying out or is she up to something else?"

"You make one phone call to her and tell her that you have to leave town and not to get in touch with you. She'll just think you're into deeper shit than usual."

"I'll get rid of this thing," Max said abruptly.

If the point of the exercise had been to make him eat a lifetime of words, how quickly we had succeeded. I think we were all disappointed because the victory had come too easily. We'd been looking forward to seeing his resistance cave in gradually, his position change slowly over the next months. But the shift in his thinking was instantaneous. It was gratifying in a way because it opened vistas of a changed world. If only we could have done the same thing to popes, presidents, prime ministers, religious leaders. All that was needed was to contrive similar accidents to people in powerful positions.

Again Simone went on, reasonably but relentlessly. "That feeling's quite natural, and we can all understand it, Max. You feel violated, encroached upon, and you want to be unviolated, cleared out, rendered unpregnant. Women frequently feel so when they discover that they are unexpectedly pregnant. You want it removed like an aching tooth. But no reputable gynecologist would undertake to remove that embryo. And no abortion clinic anywhere would accept someone as a patient who has spent his entire career being the bane of its existence."

"Yeah, imagine begging Dr. Morgentaler to overlook all past abuses and kindly perform the operation you've spent years trying to make illegal." That was Lena probably.

Max, even in a drugged state, was still the lawyer, the debater, the fighter, and he wasn't about to relinquish the moral high ground without putting up a fight. "This is different," he said. "It's grotesque . . . it's unnatural."

"Max, a great many pregnancies are unnatural. They happen to the most inappropriate people at the most inopportune times. Not to men very often, I admit, but to children of eleven, women of fifty-six, to the unmarried, the mother of twelve, the poverty-stricken, the destitute, the homeless, the ailing, the mentally handicapped, the physically disabled, the drug-addicted, the alcoholic. Compared with these cases, you are the most natural, plausible host in the world for a foetus."

"And there is a precedent in nature," said Julia, and told him about the sea horse.

We spoke with a single voice, all against poor Max.

"You're a healthy human being, Max, and you're in the prime of life. You're a person of means. You've reached the peak of your career as a lawyer. You can put it on hold for nine months and then resume it. The inconvenience will be minimal."

"But," said Max, "it's inconvenience I didn't bargain for. I wasn't consulted. I was forced . . . well, it's like rape. You girls all oppose rape, don't you?"

"Yes," said Lena, "we girls all do. But remember, you're the one who doesn't think rape is any justification for abortion. Abortion only compounds the crime."

"Let's not get off the point," I said. "There's no rape involved here. No sexual assault. No violence. You were merely chosen as the appropriate vessel for this foetus."

"Against my will."

"Many people harbour foetuses against their will."

"Out of carelessness most of the time."

"So, Max," said Lena, "you think of pregnancy as punishment? The woman gets her just deserts. She should have been more careful."

Max was not slow to put two and two together. "Punishment? Is that the point of all this? Am I being punished for my pro-life stance? And, if so, will I be excused as soon as I admit that I'm wrong?"

"There's no such thing as an unmixed motive, Max." Simone again, infinitely reasonable. "We needed someone to bear this child. As for being punitive, I prefer to think of the choice of you as convenient and instructional. It will be a learning experience for you. If, after bearing this child, you pursue your campaign against reproductive choice, you'll have earned the right to use the term "pro-life," and you'll have the authority of experience behind your claim. We'll respect you more. You might even find a convert among us to your way of thinking. But as far as removing the foetus, that's out. There's no point in arguing about it. It could not be removed and live and we want it to live."

"Well, supposing it doesn't live. Let it not live. I'll give ten thousand dollars to the food bank. I'll give it to the abortion cause and say I've changed my mind . . . "

"I don't believe my ears," said Julia. "All your convictions blown away in the space of a half-hour. Imagine the effect on the world of accidents like this."

"Why doesn't one of you host this thing?" said Max, trying another tack.

"I'm too far along in years now, Max," I said, "and still establishing my career."

"I've had my children," said Julia. "I was a good mother, too. Am a good mother, in fact." She looked at Simone, as we seemed to be taking turns.

"I still have my way to make in my profession. If I have children, I'll have them later, after my training's finished. I want to be a great doctor as well as a mother. I want the two to go together, each role making me more fit for the other one. That's reasonable enough, isn't it?"

"I wouldn't mind having a . . . kid," said Lena. "If I get one I'll have to adopt one because I can't carry one of my own. But I couldn't do it now. I don't have a job and my life's a mess. I want a kid after I get it all together."

"Am I allowed to know something of the parentage of this thing inside me?"

"If you knew," said Simone, "you would perhaps be willing to house it, willing to bear it. Imagine a girl whose life would be stunted, her chance at a fulfilling future with productive work ruined by a pregnancy at this time. Think of it as a gift to her. You're the one who said we live in a society that would silence Beethoven in the womb. Well, maybe you're carrying a brilliant musician. You could be making possible two Beethovens — the mother and the child."

"But why didn't you just care for the mother and put the kid up for adoption? Surely that's the obvious solution."

"Max," I said, " adoption isn't the answer to anything. To give up a child for adoption is like giving up a limb to be amputated. The pain keeps on throbbing and never stops. And half the adopted kids feel illegitimate."

"But I'm supposed to give up this thing after birth, aren't I?"

"No one said that."

"You're not expecting me to raise it after I've harboured it, are you?"

"Why not?"

"I couldn't impose that burden on my wife."

"Always one to think of others, aren't you, Max?" said Lena.

"And what about the paternity?"

"As so often happens — unknown."

"There you are — it's of degenerate origin. Suppose the thing has criminal tendencies and becomes a menace to society."

"Why assume that? Most child-abusers are trusted relatives, friends of the family, people in authoritative, responsible positions. Most rapists are known and trusted by their victims."

"Suppose it's deformed?"

"That," said Simone, "is a fear shared by every pregnant woman."

"I remember the dreams," said Julia. "I remember watching television, seeing thalidomide deformities and not being able to stop worrying, feeling terror. I dreamed that my child was a cyclops with one eye in the middle of its brow. But if you're one of the lucky ones, it turns out well and they hand you a perfect child. People talk of the ecstasy of the moment of birth. Mostly it's relief. In any case, however it turns out, you have the means for excellent child care."

For the first time, Max looked totally defeated. At that moment he must have thought beyond the pregnancy and realized that he might become the permanent guardian or parent of the child. This idea seemed to induce more panic than the idea of being its incubator. And again the idea of getting rid of it came up.

"Abortion is a punishment without a crime and a death sentence without a trial," Lena said. She was quoting the kind of thing Max had said in numerous editorials and courtroom cases. "Foetuses are nothing less than our country, our families, and our future. You carry our future there inside you, Max. Abortion denies foetuses the right to life, liberty, and security of the person . . . "

"Shut up, Lena," said Simone suddenly. "In case any of you entertain vengeful thoughts," she went on in a hectoring tone, "let me warn you this is not altogether a normal pregnancy. Shock and depression could be fatal for the baby and the . . . parent. If this baby isn't carried to full term, its life and Max's will be threatened. And so will our lives be too."

She had said all this before. "Whatever you're individually trying to prove or avenge, the next nine months will not be the time to do it. Torturing the victim is out." She looked coldly at Lena.

It was a warning that Lena never quite took to heart, perhaps couldn't take to heart. I don't think Lena believed there was any particular danger to parent and child, or perhaps she didn't much care. "I wish Simone would get off this doctor kick once and for all," she said to me later. "All this stuff about the mental well-being of the patient. It's too like the old school of thinking beautiful thoughts and having a beautiful baby. Stupid bitch. How many mothers on welfare have tranquil, undepressed pregnancies? The motherfucker needs a bit of mental turmoil to help him along."

The discord that eventually split the group began quite early.

"I'm scared of this thing growing inside me," Max said, and he did look genuinely terrified. I was sorry for him.

"There are risks," said Simone, "but these are no greater than those faced by most women who have Caesarean sections — the risk of hemorrhage, for example."

"Suppose I'm alone when it's ready to come out."

"You won't be alone," Simone said. "One of us will be with you at all times. You'll have much better care and support than most pregnant women do, of that I can assure you. I give you my word."

"Try to think positively, Max," I said. "You lead a high-pressure life. Look at this nine months . . . "

"Nine months! That's an eternity. Anything can happen to my law practice, to my marriage, to my . . . "

"Don't think of it that way. Think of it as a convalescent or sabbatical leave or a retreat. We'll bring you anything you need . . . books, music. We'll play chess with you. Provide anything you want to eat, as best we can."

"What I need now," he said, fumbling for his pockets, "is a cigarette."

"That, unfortunately, is out," said Simone. "You can't smoke during a pregnancy. It leads to low birth weight and all kinds of possible complications. So you'll have to get along without smoking."

"But I can't," he said. "I've smoked since I was twenty. I'm addicted to nicotine. I'll lose my mind without it."

"It's a small thing, Max, for a healthy baby."

"And think of it this way," I said. "You've probably wanted to give up smoking and said it's a nasty habit. Now's your chance. You'll end up after this experience healthier than before."

"It'll be as beneficial as one of Francine's health spas," said Julia, "and it won't cost as much."

"It'll cost plenty," said Max.

"Well, you can afford it," said Lena.

So it went on, gradually sinking into Max's consciousness that a pregnancy was a long project and that it would strip him of all the rights he generally took for granted — the right to plan his future, establish his own priorities. He was now, for the first time in his adult life, reduced to a state of dependence on others who would decide what was permitted and what was not. He was carrying something that had competing rights, which could take precedence over his rights. So he had plenty to think about.

He had fallen silent and then he looked around and said suddenly, "I need to go to the bathroom."

We all looked at Simone.

"Don't look at me," she said. "You'll all have to take turns doing the honours of the bedpan. You're not squeamish are you?"

"Can't I go to the bathroom?" asked Max.

"Not for the moment you can't," said Simone. "Being pregnant also means that you have to give up a certain amount of privacy."

And so there it ended.

After that day we were all changed, and the changes determined the rest of our lives. Of course the conception of a baby always changes many lives. Late in the afternoon most of us drifted away to our own homes. But in a sense we never separated; we had been drawn together into a cohesive group, united by our joint purpose. Perhaps we had become partners-in-crime.

VII

THE EVENT I THINK OF as "the annunciation" happened fairly close to Christmas, and that coincidence served to bind us together even more tightly and to ritualize the bonds among us. Normally Julia and Lena disappeared somewhere into the country for the holidays, but this year we all tacitly agreed that we would celebrate together. Simone's work always provided her with an excuse to do what she wanted, in this case to absent herself from her family's Christmas dinner. So we all converged on Julia's place early in the morning.

Julia had laid out a kind of Easter breakfast with braided bread and hot rolls and cinnamon buns, all in an uncharacteristic (for her) state of not-having-gone-wrong-or-stale. We drifted in carrying gifts, which we dumped under the tree that Julia had set up dangerously near the blazing fire. She had a habit of doing such careless things but, as it happened, nothing seemed able to go awry that day. Even the turkey that Julia was cooking by a special slow method turned out neither red at the bone nor dry, and already in the morning the house was redolent with its smell.

Julia was in the kitchen keeping an eye on the turkey and at the same time on Monica who, she explained, found Christmas depressing. "What else is new?" said Lena. Monica was sitting at the kitchen table with a drink in front of her and her head in her hands.

"Monica, you'll feel better if you eat something and don't drink Scotch on an empty stomach," Lena said and went off upstairs to do her stint of Max-duty.

I went in to watch the Queen on television and listen to the Pope, the Prime Minister, and the Governor-General all making speeches about helping the poor and destitute and keeping in mind the inspiration of Christmas as embodied in the story of the wondrous birth of the Christ-child. The words took on a special irony in the circumstances. But I couldn't help thinking later, as we sprawled around the living room opening presents like any other family on Christmas morning, that the miraculous birth we were awaiting did seem to have created its own special harmony among us.

Julia had given us all the same thing — little baskets with jars of caviar and miniature bottles of various brands of vodka. Simone had got rather lavish selections from the Belgian chocolate shop. I thought she probably had a secretary or someone call down an order for boxes already wrapped for everyone she knew. Lena's gifts were rather odd, because most of them were knives. Julia got a pen-knife and Simone an antique butter knife. I got a stiletto that turned out to be a paper knife. They made quite an array of weapons, all very sinister-looking. For Monica she'd got one of those shaped inflatable pillows that you can put behind your head when you snooze in the bathtub. We opened it and exclaimed over it, as Monica was in no state to do so. I thought the idea of Monica snoozing in the bathtub was very dangerous, rather like giving someone a special ashtray for smoking in bed. I gave everyone a book, a woman's biography or autobiography, and thought that, apart from Lena's, mine were the most thoughtfully chosen and individual gifts, even if they were review copies.

When we'd opened our presents and Monica's, there was a pile left for Max, so we trooped upstairs to give them to him. Julia took the turkey out before we went up, and got Monica to lie down on the couch.

Max, of course, had brought no clothes with him except what he was wearing when he came to us and had mostly worn pyjamas and a white terrycloth robe that Julia had given him. So now she gave him a pair of fine silk Japanese pyjamas and a robe. He seemed quite pleased with them, and very amicable. Again, looking back, I'm surprised at the sense of normalcy about the whole occasion. I gave him a book, not a review copy but one that I'd gone to a lot of trouble to find. It was a beautifully illustrated book about sea horses, which I'd found in an antiquarian bookstore. Simone offered the most lavish gift of all — an electronic chess game. Only Lena's gift seemed to strike a discordant, abrasive note. Normally her gifts were roughly packaged, but this time she had an elaborately gift-wrapped box, obviously done by the gift-wrapping desk at a department store, with baby-shower wrapping paper. As soon as I saw the storks with babies suspended from their beaks, I suspected something insulting or dangerous. It turned out to be a copy of Dr. Spock and some knitting needles, pink wool, and a pattern for a simple baby jacket. There was a brief moment of embarrassment when Max pulled the wool out and then everyone, Max included, laughed.

Gradually we made our way back downstairs to have some lunch in the catch-as-catch-can spirit of Julia's meals, carrying plates and perching about the house. Julia brought her own plate and Max's up on a tray, and I brought mine to eat with them. Lena and Simone were sitting in the kitchen, where Monica had come to and was working her way through the vodka miniatures. I thought that Lena would bully her into eating something. Julia and I had got a good bottle of burgundy with our lunch, and we gave Max a glass because it was a special occasion.

"I'm just thinking of the time you came to my house and cooked a steak for me," he said. I felt sheepish remembering how I'd insinuated myself into his house and what it had led to, but he didn't seem to be holding a grudge.

"That was a very good steak," he said. Then he sighed slightly, perhaps also thinking of what happened afterwards.

Like any other family we divided into those who sleep off a feast and those who walk it off in order to prepare for the next onslaught. Accordingly, Lena and I struggled into our boots and arctic parkas and set off to take Dog for a walk around the lake. It was easier at this time of the year when the lake, completely frozen by now, had undergone its seasonal transformation to a recreational facility. There were tracks along the shore for people like us, engaged merely in a *paseo*, another set for the cross-country skiers, a section for a hayride drawn on milder days by an old farm dray, like the brewers' drays of my English childhood. Over by the island, normally inaccessible except by ferry, was a skating rink. We headed towards the rink, where a speaker was blaring Viennese waltzes, the "Merry Widow Waltz" and the "Skaters' Waltz" — to which the bundled-up children and parents twirled. Our dinner having somewhat jogged down by this time, Lena and I bought large paper cups of hot chocolate to ward off the cold. We carried them to the island, where we found a perch and sat watching the skaters.

Christmas fell on Monday that year. The Sunday before Christmas I always had open house for students and former students. It was on the Sunday before Christmas because I wanted it to be an invariable day so that students in town for the holidays would always know, without calling and without invitation, that they could stop by.

This time it had fallen on Christmas Eve and been less well-attended than usual, but a group from the women's studies class had come over and stayed on after everyone else left. We had sat for a long time talking about Jinny and mourning her loss. Now again, watching the skaters twirl on the ice, I could imagine her darting among them, gliding up between two people, latching on to their shoulders, causing minor havoc and perhaps a total upset resulting in a confusion of arms and legs muddled together on the ice. One had to avoid crying outdoors in such a climate because the tears could freeze on your cheeks.

"I've been wondering," I said, "about the possibility of getting some exercise for Max."

"Yeah," she said, and I went on thinking about smuggling him out in disguise in our all-concealing winter parkas on a mild day for a walk around the lake. He hadn't expressed any desire to leave the house, but it didn't seem healthy to have him lying there inert for large parts of the day.

"He could do some housework," said Lena. "I don't see why we should work in shifts like hired help to keep his room dusted and polished. Let him scrub floors and crawl about dragging his belly along the floor while he polishes it."

"I doubt if he'd know how to go about cleaning up," I said mildly.

"The fucker could learn," said Lena. "He's the one that believes the woman's place is in the home and all that crap. Let him have nine months of it. If it's a confinement it might as well include bed and kitchen duty. Barefoot, pregnant, and in the kitchen. It would do him good to work on that floor with wax and a polisher."

Somehow the idea of Max doing forced labour was repugnant to me, like a form of torture. I let the matter of the exercise drop for the moment.

So far the day had been one of unusual harmony and I wanted to keep it that way. But suddenly I was overtaken by a wave of Scroogian common sense. It became clear that Christmas had gone on long enough and that it shouldn't last the whole day. I knew that Julia would have leftovers, drinks, music, and a roaring fire, and I worried about Max and who would be on duty. I felt I really ought to go up and read him to sleep like a child. But self-protectively I decided to disengage myself from the group. I said good-bye to Lena as we passed my house, turned in, and spent the evening alone.

I went upstairs into my library-study, which I had made by taking out the wall between two bedrooms that ran along the front of the house. There was always sanity and clarity in that ascetic atmosphere — the rows of book spines, the desk with its piles of white paper, the typewriter like a pet waiting to be stroked. Sometimes I turned it on merely to hear the purr. The gooseneck lamp leaned its neck over me and cast down a pool of light. Like moonlight it encircled the keyboard, my outstretched hands, and the white sheet waiting to receive my words. It was a little world complete in itself and full of the peace of the season.

I started to think of the child that was to be born and on which

I had begun to pin such hopes. I wondered why. I was like the mother of a lost daughter who desires a grandchild as a starting-again, a chance to do better, or simply yearns for another child with the slightest resemblance to that lost, loved one.

I was no longer young and was inexperienced in caring for babies, but I felt sure that I could manage one. There was plenty of room and I could easily afford to provide whatever was necessary. I'd seen a report recently reprinted from some august medical journal — *Lancet* or the *New England Journal of Medicine* — about the possibility of extending women's childbearing years indefinitely. A commentator had said that the disadvantages of an older woman having a baby were outweighed or at least balanced by the advantages of maturity, experience, financial stability. I thought that grandmothers made good mothers. I started to do calculations. When she was this age, I would be that. When she was in her thirties, I might be dead. But it wouldn't matter. She'd be out in the world and self-sufficient by then.

There was another thought too, that perhaps Monica could be pressed into service. It might make up for all her other losses. Maybe caring for another child would be her salvation, perhaps the one thing that could assuage her suffocating personal grief. Was that a romantic impractical idea and was Monica too far gone to be accessible to any kind of help except the oblivion contained in those endless bottles she consumed? I envisioned the child calling forth all our resources by its own need and helplessness. I wanted that child so badly. I wanted to spoon food into its mouth, wipe its face after meals, read stories, and make paper dolls. For it was going to be a girl named Virginia. We'd call her Jinny.

And which of the others would fit the role of mother? Simone with her stethoscope and her endless tests and gauges had only a clinical interest in the process. Lena was the one I worried about most of all, because the enterprise for her seemed more and more to have become a vengeful one. She was thinking of childbearing as men sometimes did, as a payback for frivolity, as an antidote to self-indulgence. Let the women stay pregnant, it's what they're made for, and it keeps them out of trouble. I couldn't erase that memory of her saying we should let Max scrub floors and crawl about with his belly dragging on the floor as he polished. It haunted me and made me fearful of leaving Max in her hands.

But what of Julia? She was the most successful at mothering. A neighbour once told me that her own children held Julia up to her as a shining example of what a mother should be. I told Julia and she laughed, dismissing the compliment. "Yes, totally permissive," she said. And she was. Yet her daughters liked her, always drifted back home with partners or alone, to visit, occupy the house and Julia's time for a few weeks, and then leave again. If I said that to Julia, she would dismiss that too. She would probably say, "Oh they come when they need something — a loan, a pad, a place to crash during a crisis." That was true too. But how many children seek such solace from their mothers? I began to think of Julia as my rival for possession of Virginia. Jinny.

VIII

THE PICTURES WERE TAKEN during the early months and so Max looks quite ordinary and unremarkable. We look happy and, astonishingly, we were happy. Most astonishing of all, Max was happy much of the time, in spite of his anxieties. Perhaps the anxieties receded and seemed unreal because the whole atmosphere was so unreal. It was as if this white cocoon existed out of all time and place and quite unrelated to our normal lives. Let me give you an example.

One day I came in for my shift of Max-sitting and found Lena reading aloud to him in much the same voice you might use for a very young child or a stupid person:

> Imagine this. You wake up in the morning and find yourself back to back in bed with an unconscious violinist. A famous unconscious violinist. He has been found to have a fatal kidney ailment, and the Society of Music Lovers has canvassed all the available medical records and found that you alone have the right blood type to help. They have therefore kidnapped you and last night the violinist's circulatory system was plugged into yours, so that your kidneys can be used to extract poisons from his blood as well as your own . . .

I sighed and stood listening myself and then said, "Alright, Lena, I'll take over . . . "

"I really want him to hear this," she said, showing no signs of leaving.

"I'll read it," I said and took the book and continued as long as it took her to gather up her things.

. . . the director of the hospital says, "Tough luck, but now you've got to stay in bed, with the violinist plugged into you, for the rest of your life. Because remember this. All persons have a right to life, and violinists are persons. Granted, you have a right to decide what happens to you and your body, but a person's right to life outweighs your right to decide what happens in and to your body.

As soon as she was out of the room I closed the book and said, "You don't really want to hear this do you?" And he smiled wanly and said, "It isn't a true story is it?"

I realized that he was at the point of thinking that if what had befallen him could happen, anything could.

"Look, Max," I said, "it isn't even a story. It's an example that a philosopher called Judith Jarvis Thompson dreamed up in defence of abortion. It's a colourful argument, a standard text in feminist philosophy."

He was quiet for a bit and then he said, "I really don't know much about abortion, do I? I'm a bit of an ignoramus." So I found him a collection of philosophical essays on abortion and some related legal, moral, and constitutional issues. It appealed to his legalistic mind, and this was the kind of thing he enjoyed during these months — reading books he'd never previously come across or had time for, and talking about them. He brought out a submerged didactic strain in Lena's personality and she turned him into a one-person class, lecturing him constantly, determined to indoctrinate him with all the feminist lore she'd absorbed and to get him to toe the party line. For the most part he didn't mind, because he was genuinely interested in new information and argument. Of course, Lena always had to carry things to extremes and get belligerent, so in the end what she was doing turned sour. But for a while it was fine.

It didn't take long for us all to realize that the job of Max-sitting would be far more demanding than we had anticipated. If we had thought that we could roll a television set into the room, bring in a radio, or get a few books from the library, it soon became apparent that we were wrong. Round-the-clock supervision was necessary for his mental as well as physical well-being.

Simone had shown us how to monitor his pulse, temperature, and blood pressure and administer the crucial hormone shots, and we did these chores routinely when we went in for our hours of duty. We all neatly recorded the results in the books Simone had provided. But we also had to occupy Max's mind, keep him alert, and not allow him to sink into apathy and despair. We all solved this problem in different ways. Julia liked to play games and brought in chess and scrabble and taught him some new card games when he lost interest in the old ones.

It was about this time that in spite of the anxiety and in spite of the bone-cracking hard work (we couldn't get help cleaning the place except for one all-purpose gardener, handyman, and heavy worker for the schoolrooms) I came to think of the white room as an oasis. It became a beacon of light to be looked forward to during the day. Whenever things were tense at work I rubbed my hands along the knotted places in my neck and shoulders and thought ahead to four o'clock, when I could hurry home and across the alleyway and enter the calm, clean, suspended animation of life there. I came to love its order, the sense of time being arrested, and, above all, the fragrant smell of the flowers and scents. There was nothing of the hospital smell of disinfectant. And there was Max, now in his Japanese robe, waiting for tea and books and conversation.

One of the unexpected side effects at this time was the improvement in Monica's condition. We rarely addressed each other directly, but exchanged stares guardedly from across the room. She seemed to be drunk less often. In fact, she was fairly sober and busy most of the time. I noticed that she was no longer drinking Scotch and lying about the place passed out or being covered up by Julia. Often when I arrived at the house she was sitting at the kitchen table with a glass of beer or white wine which she was drinking slowly. She always had a pile of newspaper clippings beside her and a pad of paper in front of her. Those clippings constituted most of her reading material, and I thought they could hardly be engrossing fare. I looked over her shoulder sometimes and saw that they were newspaper articles about runaway children, homeless people, and murders.

I spoke of this once to Julia and she said tersely, "She's writing again." So I gathered that Monica was collecting the clippings as plots for her stories. I recalled that years ago Monica had been an active member of the writing community and that she'd published a slender volume of stories with a local small press. They had been well received locally, and I think there was a prize somewhere along the way. I resolved to look up the story collection the next time I was in the library picking out books for Max.

Sometimes, too, Monica would be eating a sandwich which Julia gave her and which she would have ignored before. Food had previously lingered untouched in front of her until someone tossed it into the garbage. Once I came across her sitting with a small child on her lap — one of the children from the school, who was crying about something. Monica was stroking the child's hair and face carelessly and looking at her very sadly and tenderly, as if the child's grief for the lost toy or whatever it was were her own. She looked vulnerable, and somehow the little tableau bothered me.

And reading and writing weren't Monica's only occupations. I noticed that she'd got hold of the pink wool that Lena had given Max for Christmas and had either managed to read the pattern or had Julia show her how to make the jacket. Quite a recognizable garment was emerging. Simone said, "Hey, Monica, that's lovely," and she looked proud.

"For Maxine," she said, and I wondered how much she knew about what was going on. I had stopped worrying about her as a security risk because even if she had said anything to anyone outside the group, no one would have believed her. She was generally considered mad.

I'd noticed, too, that Monica was amassing books with titles such as *What To Name Your Baby*. I don't know where she got them from. Perhaps Julia had some left over from her childbearing days or perhaps Monica herself had, but these, along with the newspaper clippings, constituted her reading material.

One Sunday morning we were standing around the kitchen drinking coffee and waiting for some cinnamon buns that Julia had shoved into the oven. After the coffee, Lena and I planned to take one of our brisk walks with Dog around the lake. Monica was sitting at the kitchen table with a mug of coffee. She was actually sober, though looking out of the window and not paying much attention to our conversation. Suddenly she turned with a happy smile on her face and said, "Let's call her Desirée."

Julia responded quite spontaneously with a smile and said, "Why, Monica, that's a lovely name." I thought it was a ghastly name and sounded like the heroine of a costume gothic or a Harlequin romance, but it was so startling to see Monica sober and happy and wanting to make suggestions that I said, "So do I." Lena grunted and said nothing.

One day as I opened the door I was surprised to hear laughter and found Max and Lena in the midst of an animated and cheerful discussion.

"Lena tells me I'm a fallen man," he announced.

"Tell him about fallen women," she said.

"It's a persistent theme in literature," I said. "*Madame Bovary, Tess Of the D'Urbervilles, Anna Karenina,* and so on."

"It's a persistent theme in literature by men," Lena said. "They like slobbering over the corpses of ruined women."

"Well, that's not quite true," I said. "There are exceptions — *Adam Bede*, for example."

"But George Eliot wrote that early in her career," Lena said. "She wasn't writing as a woman."

"You always say that," said Max. "When a woman behaves or writes in a way that falls outside your narrow category of how a woman naturally acts, you label her an honorary man. That's what you say about Margaret Thatcher and Indira Gandhi."

"And when a man behaves in a way that falls outside the narrow definition of masculine behaviour you call him 'effeminate,' a much more derogatory term," I said.

"Lucy taught a course once on The Fallen Woman," Lena said.

"That was in the early days, when feminist criticism was primitive," I said, "and it was an extension course."

"Oh yeah," said Lena, "that was in another country and besides the wench is dead."

"Well, I admit it was fun," I said, "the enrollment was pretty high and it got a lot of attention."

"The student newspaper had a field day with it," said Lena. "Who could forget the headlines? ENGLISH PROF INSTRUCTS FALLEN WOMEN. WOMEN OF EASY VIRTUE SUBJECT OF COURSE."

"It was a serious course," I said, "and the full title was 'The Fallen Woman: The Death of a Genre.' I was showing how the theme has run out of steam in an age of single mothers. And also what happens to it in the hands of a woman writer like Willa Cather."

"When she's writing as a woman," Max said.

"That's something to consider," I said.

"But what about fallen men?" Max said. "I can think of several."

"So can I," said Lena, "and it's always the woman who gets the shit for it — Adam, John the Baptist . . ."

"Heloise and Abelard," I said, trying to help out. "But there the man comes to grief not at the hands of the woman, but at the hands of another man in a powerful position."

"Edward the Eighth," said Max.

"The case of Edward proves the point," I said. "He was ousted from the throne by the patriarchal political structure and the blame was fixed squarely on Wallis Simpson. She was supposed to be the one who led him into the highways and byways of Nazism and fascism. There were even rumours that she wasn't really a woman but some kind of genetic freak."

"There you are," said Lena. "And think of women being denied painkillers in childbirth because the pain was supposed to atone for the sins of Eve."

"Well, Queen Victoria put an end to that," I said, "so that shows that there's an advantage in having a female monarch, even if she doesn't altogether think as a woman."

The conversation was getting off topic at this point, and Max lost interest and began to look dejected. I think it was the mention of pain in childbirth that brought back certain anxieties. And Lena, seeing that the conversation was at an end, gathered up her things and left him to me.

"I'll be back in half an hour," she said, for Simone had called one of our rare meetings.

"I wish you wouldn't leave me alone with her," Max said.

"Her? Oh, you mean Lena. Don't worry. She's not as fierce as she sounds."

"I'm not sure of that," Max said. "There's so much anger I'm worried she might explode and attack me at any moment."

"I don't think so."

"I wonder if you really know Lena," Max said.

"As well as anyone does, I should think. I'm her closest friend."

"She isn't as loyal a friend as you imagine."

"I think you're wrong there, Max. I can imagine very well the extent and limits of her loyalty."

"She says very nasty things about you."

"I can not only imagine that, but I can imagine the exact form her nastiness takes," I said. "Remember, I've known her for some time."

"Not long enough," Max said. "You know that nobody can stand her but you, and everyone wonders how you can stand her."

"I get the innuendo," I said. "Max, you should have seen her when she first wandered across my path, and the change now . . . She may not be a joy to be around, but at least she's functioning. She's taken university courses and she supports herself in a way that isn't dehumanizing."

"I see. I suspected something of the sort. A reformed whore. Nice company of nurses I have."

"Max, that's uncalled for," I said feebly, filing away the subject as something to be taken up when there was more time.

"Just so long as she doesn't take out the anger on me."

"She can be very gentle," I said. "You should see her with the kids downstairs."

"And how would their mommies and daddies feel if they knew their dear ones were in the hands of a psychopath?"

"Max," I said, "I think that sometimes you haven't changed a bit, that none of this has been more than an unfortunate incident to you . . . an interlude that has no relation to the rest of your life."

We went no further on the subject that day because it was time for the meeting and Julia, Simone, and Lena all came in.

"Is there any special reason for this meeting?" Julia asked.

"The reason is this," Simone said. "I'm worried about him. His blood pressure's very high and I can't figure out the reason."

"I can," said Lena, looking pointedly at Julia.

"Oh can it, Lena," Julia said.

But Lena didn't, and she was obviously bursting to tell something. "I have a pretty good idea of what goes on here when everyone leaves and Julia's on the night shift."

"Dry up, Lena," Julia said. "You don't know anything about anything, so don't try to stir up trouble."

"Hasn't anyone but me noticed the strenuous efforts to air this place out — windows wide open on the windiest days, flowers always of the heavily scented variety?"

"This is a sick room. It's stuffy," Julia said.

"What is this?" I said.

"I thought you were sharp enough to guess, Lucy. It's drinking and smoking to beat anything."

"No," said Simone.

"As soon as the coast is clear," said Lena, "it's children's playtime up here. Did any of you ever check Julia's garbage cans?

They're full of bottles of Scotch and gin and wine. And that's not all Monica's garbage."

"Is this true, Julia?" Simone said.

"Not the way she makes it sound. We aren't having all-night orgies. Obviously, if this place turned into a saloon it would take more than a few hothouse lilies to cover up the smells. We have a nightcap. The odd cigarette. It was in moderation."

"I'll bet," said Lena. "We know your moderation in all things."

"Lena, you fucking shithead . . ."

"Alright, stop it you two," Simone said. "Oh Julia, how could you? And Max . . ."

"You'd think some concern for the child might have restrained him," Lena said. "With substance abuse combined with his genetic make-up, the only thing this kid's going to be good for is dwarf-tossing."

"You seem to forget this kid doesn't share my genetic make-up," said Max.

"From the look of you, I'd say you certainly qualify for next of kin," said Lena.

"Look," said Julia, "I know as much as the rest of you about fetal alcohol syndrome and this is out of all proportion."

"Truthfully, Julia," Simone said, "how much has he been drinking?"

"A nightcap. A sedative," Julia said.

"Then *you* must really be hitting the bottle," said Lena, and she marched over to one of the closets and dragged out a cardboard box with clothes on top, concealing a cache of empty liquor bottles.

"May I say a word on my own behalf?" asked Max.

"Go ahead," said Simone.

"I'm not a heavy drinker. I'm certainly not an alcoholic. Far from it. But since I've been here, I've been very tense. I'm worried about my work and the loss of income. I'm worried about my marriage and if I'll even have one when I return to . . . I'm worried about the outcome of this thing. Worried about the ordeal at the end of these nine months and if I'll survive. I can't get to sleep without a drink. It was I who persuaded Julia to get me something last thing at night. Is that so bad?"

"You bastard," Lena said. "What does it matter to you if the kid's slow or harmed or has learning problems? You don't give a shit, do you?"

"I didn't get myself into this situation voluntarily, remember. What happens to . . . this thing . . . is really your responsibility, not mine."

"You see he hates the baby," said Lena. "You bastard, oh, you fucking bastard."

"How could I not be antagonistic to something that's caused me so much trouble and that's threatening my life?" Max said. "You're all on its side, and you're all ranged against me. I can't do this and I can't do that because it'll harm the baby. Isn't it more than could be reasonably expected for me to cherish it?"

"We can all relate to that," I said. "We understand the phenomenon all too well. It's usually considered monstrous and unnatural. Not by us, I should add."

"Well, drinking and smoking's not the only thing," said Lena, "while we're on the subject of monstrous and unnatural. You know how Julia comes on to anything with pants on. So it won't take much imagination to understand what else goes on during the witching hours."

"Oh my god," I said involuntarily, "how could you, Julia?"

"How could I?" said Julia. "Sometimes I think I'm the only human being in this group, the only one who understands sex and sexual needs. You all have your own agendas here. Lucy — some vague feminist one. Simone — some idea of medical experimentation. Lena — god knows — some debt to pay off. You asked me to join this scheme and I slipped into it because it seemed like a good idea and I thought I was helping someone out. I guess I didn't think through this one. But from the start you've used me. You needed me because I had this place and you've taken it over. I had to make it safe for you, stop seeing anyone, arrange my whole life around the project. And from the start you've all treated me like some kind of imbecile. Frivolous Julia who cares about clothes, who's soft on men. I may be, but goddammit I feel like a human being isolated in a group of heartless, gutless ideologues."

"Good for you," said Max. "I might add to that that she's the only one who doesn't make me feel like a broodmare."

"This has got to stop," I said.

"It will stop," said Simone. "That's the reason I called this meeting. I thought I could deliver the child here in this room, but I no longer think I can do that. There are too many possible complications — toxemia, high blood pressure, and other things. I've decided that I'll take him down to the clinic in North Dakota."

"But that's an abortion clinic. He's not getting an abortion. He's going to have the baby, isn't he?"

"Of course he is, but he can hardly go through the delivery room and the ob-gyn ward in an ordinary hospital. North Dakota's the nearest place where secrecy will be guaranteed. I'll see to that."

"Don't you have to make arrangements?" I said.

"They've all been made," Simone said.

"But who will go with you?" I said. "Julia and I can't leave our teaching, and Lena . . . "

"Of course you can't. I've arranged for one of my medical colleagues to go along in case of an emergency."

"But what about secrecy?"

"There's no problem there," Simone said.

"How could there not be a problem? The more people involved, you said yourself."

"I've explained before," said Simone. "It's obvious. There's an abortion network in the medical profession. There has to be and there always has been. Doctors' wives and daughters, politicians' wives and daughters, anti-abortion crusaders' wives and daughters, for that matter, all need abortions. The men can't treat their own families and there's a convention of mutual support and secrecy. It's absolutely watertight because everyone has too much at stake."

"But what about the border crossing?"

"What I just said applies to the police and the immigration people. We have contacts there. There's nothing to worry about except the well-being of the child and Max."

And so there was nothing else to say. As usual we fell in with whatever Simone decided. What alternative did we have?

IX

SIMONE'S DECISION to take Max away happened well into the eighth month. I can still see her standing there in the silence that falls on a room where violence has taken place, even if it's only verbal violence. We were all quiet, all ashamed of the scene we'd participated in, all absorbing the knowledge and the implications of what had been going on. Only Simone seemed to be preoccupied with physical, medical matters.

"I don't like this," she said. "I don't like it one bit."

She had her stethoscope around her neck, her blood pressure equipment in her hand, and she looked every inch the clinician. She gave us instructions to keep him very quiet indeed. "I'm going to give him a mild sedative," she said. "No more tea or coffee."

We were frightened, oh yes, we were frightened alright, hearing her calm resolute voice and her decision. Our minds were on one thing only — conviction for murder. Perhaps that isn't quite fair. We were also, most of us, genuinely alarmed for the safety of Max. We had in all our different ways drawn close to him, become fond of him. At least that was what I thought at the time.

Simone asked no advice, merely gave a decision to which we all acquiesced. She would drive down there and stay with him until the baby was removed. Removed was the word she used, not born. It was a fait accompli, or almost accompli by the time she told us, this course of action having been in her mind as a back-up plan all along. We might have guessed that Simone was not one to get into something like this without a back-up plan of some sort. She never took unnecessary risks, as I knew long ago when she went into exams with information that she knew well written on her hands, "just in case . . . "

So they set off soon after five one morning — Simone driving, Max lying covered in blankets in the back seat. Only Julia saw them leave, and she told us later that everything was under control, whatever that could possibly mean.

They drove directly down through Estevan, Bienfait, across the U.S. border and down to Fargo. The one phone call we got — that is Julia got — simply said that the journey had been more or less uneventful and that everyone was O.K. The operation, she said, would go forward as soon as Max had recovered from the journey and rested up a bit. After that, nothing. No calls, no messages, just a terrible suspense that lasted a week.

The next thing we knew, Simone was back. I looked out of the window and saw her car on the street. I called her and there was no answer. When I called Julia, she told me to come over immediately. I arrived just after Lena, who had apparently been summoned before I called. And so, once again, for the last time as it happened, we all converged upon Julia's house and assembled, this time in the kitchen.

Simone told us in a calm voice that it had been a bad, dangerous business, "touch and go for a while." But Max had survived and would be coming back to the city "in due course."

The baby had not survived.

So we were free, out of danger.

"Well that's one problem solved," Lena said.

I guessed she meant the problem of what to do about the baby. Julia burst into tears.

"No Desirée," said Monica. "All the pretty little children gone away." She sounded so bereft that we all looked at her in alarm.

Someone asked at last if it was a girl.

"No," said Simone, "a boy. It would have been a boy."

We all stood around in silence except for Simone who, as always, was foot-tappingly impatient to be off to unspecified urgent commitments elsewhere.

III

It had been a long week. We had walked round the lake, gone shopping, watched television. I wrote three book reviews. We'd watched tennis matches, picking players to support as one might pick teams in football or baseball. We argued their various merits. I was nostalgic for Billie Jean King. Her age made her attractive to me, especially when she was in competition with teenagers.

But all the time I was thinking of something else, pursuing the same toy-train of thoughts that had been going round in my head for months. You can't throw the switch on a dream at a moment's notice. I was dreaming of Simone coming back with a baby in swaddling clothes and of myself saying, "I will take the child."

I was dreaming of moving my study into the spare room and of making the big sunny room I now used into a nursery. Of making my house baby-proof, as I had made it dog-proof when I so easily absorbed Dog. I thought of everything going on much as it had all year — Simone as the resident physician, saying, "She's only cutting a tooth."

I dreamed even beyond the immediate arrangements to future years, with the continuity of the group ensured by the child, but with everyone growing in wisdom and charity as Monica had grown less deranged and more stable. I thought of them all as benign aunts and myself as the matriarch. I pondered details — should I be Mother or Lucy, and thought that, in such cases, the child's own attempt at pronunciation would provide the name.

And always my dream would be rounded off with a twinge of anxiety. My possession of the child was by no means certain. Suppose Max had a change of heart and claimed the baby? Suppose it were a boy? Would I want a boy? Would Max's desire for a son prevail if he were faced with a healthy boy? And what of the others? Who knows what Julia would do, or whose claim Simone would support. And suppose the child were not perfect, not quite normal? Would I want a handicapped infant that was not my own? Of course I couldn't at my age be expected to take on that kind of responsibility.

There are days that are time out from the ordinary business of life, times of convalescence from shock that just have to be waited out. The day of Simone's return was such a day.

It was Friday. Simone had had time to become accustomed to the loss in the past few days — perhaps even before she embarked on the fatal journey. Who knows? But for the rest of us the shock was sudden and devastating. For eight months our entire daily routines had focussed on caring for Max and preparing for the arrival of Virginia-Desirée, and now we were suffering from a collective post-partum depression. Lena and I, following a well-established habit, carried out the physical routine — caring for Dog, walking around the lake, making endless cups of tea and coffee, watching the evening news, and shopping for groceries.

After we'd done most of those things and she was sprawled on the couch in my living room, I asked if she wanted to cook or go out somewhere for dinner.

"Where I come from we call it supper," she said.

I hated these moods of Lena's — sullen, hostile, ready to take offense and pick a fight at the slightest thing, usually on class grounds.

"Whatever you call it, it amounts to the same thing," I said. "What do we do about the evening meal?"

We ended up sending out for Chinese food, which we only picked at. It promised to be a long uncomfortable evening, and Lena showed no signs of going off to spend it alone. I gathered that she wanted someone around on whom she could vent her anger and so, to avoid a fight, I set up a table in front of the fireplace and got out the chess set. At least we could look at the board and figure out the moves as we brooded. When we finished one game, I got us each a Scotch and soda and set out a bowl of nuts. I should have left it at that and gone on to the next game. Instead, I made the mistake of saying casually how much I had wanted the baby.

"What difference would it have made to you?" Lena said.

Again, I should have dropped the subject, but I wanted to talk and thought that Lena might come out of her black cloud and be again what I thought of as her real self.

"I thought that, since no one seemed prepared to take on the child, I could take it on myself, adopt her perhaps."

"*You* adopt a baby? What could you do with a baby?'

"Raise it like anyone else. Like any other grandmother, since I'm beyond the age of normal mothering. There are advantages — I could afford help, give her a good home, holidays, education."

"Oh, sure. A nanny, a private school. Just the thing to make up for a normal home."

"Don't tell me you've got some objection to single parenthood," I said lightly.

"*Single parenthood?*"

"Well?"

"You actually have the nerve to try to identify with pregnant teenagers, deserted wives, mothers on welfare?"

"Oh, Lena, for Christ's sake."

"You know something? I've had it up to here with you middle-class feminists who make a career out of trendy feminist ideas."

"Lena, I had a job before I had what you call trendy feminist ideas. As a matter of fact, I made it in a male-dominated profession and survived in a misogynist institution. I've paid my dues and you know why I survived?" My voice was rising because, yes, she had done exactly what she set out to do — goaded me into rage. "I survived because I was tough and because I worked bloody hard and had more self-control and discipline than self-pity."

"Unlike me, I suppose."

"Well, you said it, Lena. I didn't."

"Do you realize what you said? 'If I can do it through sheer ability and grind and toughness, why can't you?'" She was mimicking my English accent at this point. "How often have I heard you say that merit alone isn't enough for women to succeed? That, you said, was the easiest argument in the world to shoot down. 'Just look at the few women and minorities in the professions, in music, in art.' But you don't fucking believe in affirmative action and equal opportunity, do you, Lucy? It's just another plank in your platform. You're so fucking comfortable because you have the world by the strings. If you want a baby, you can just adopt a native kid like all your fucking middle-class friends. It'll give you the authority of experience, or provide a good subject for a paper or a short story, or a focus for your deep incurable boredom."

"Lena, it's true a lot of my friends did adopt children. And we know now that those interracial adoptions and other adoptions didn't work out well for the children. But the people who took them in weren't motivated by malice. They didn't want power or control, they simply wanted to help. It was an act of generosity. *Is* an act of generosity, taking in a child when you fully understand what bringing up a child means. They got nothing out of it."

"You're so full of it, Lucy. They got all kinds of things. They got ... well, it was a fucking feel-good thing, like giving conspicuously to charity, like being a public saint. Oh they got something alright. Not to mention the arrogance of doing it — like fucking missionaries converting the heathens to a more enlightened religion, to the worship of the true God. I heard you admit it yourself. You said the men gained stature and the women raised the kids."

"Lena, this has nothing to do with my wanting to take in that child."

"Oh no? It has fucking everything to do with it. Why didn't you have your own child? Yeah, why didn't you? Are you barren or did you ever conceive a child? And if you did, if you aren't barren, what did you do with it? Did you have an abortion because it would have stood in the way of your career and ability to do good works?"

"It's odd that you suddenly have scorn for my work. It seemed very interesting to you at one time. I seem to remember you once saying that the Virginia Woolf seminar was the only course you ever took which had any bearing on your own life."

"That was back then, when I knew fuck-all and drank in everything you preached. Virginia Woolf, another middle-class hypocrite and snob."

"That is so stupid. Yes, she was middle-class and she was at times a snob ... "

"And a racist, don't forget that . . ."

"Even a racist. But she also suffered extreme deprivation. She was sexually abused, she was deprived of education, she was forbidden to have a child, and she was hounded to madness and death by doctors. But she left a legacy for the women who followed. She left something to build on, she didn't just whine."

"Here we go again with all our high-born heroines. Lady Victoria Sackville-West Nicholson of the beautiful gardens. Baroness Blixen of the coffee plantations. The exclusive feminist club."

"Lena, you're parroting the words of all those who hate women. Naturally middle-class women began the struggle. The average factory worker or peasant bearing children and toiling in the field couldn't take up a banner and change things . . ."

"Some did . . ."

"And they didn't get very far. It had to be your Harriet Beecher Stowes. And what about your revered male reformers — Gandhi, Tolstoy? Did their class stamp out their worth?"

"Crap crap crap."

"If it is crap, you hung around a long time eating it up."

"Profitting from your largesse — from the wisdom, from the exposure to the finer things, from the extensive library and the cultivated atmosphere. How grateful I am to have had the privilege of your friendship, Lucy."

"You have a habit, Lena, of getting in on the benefits of everything you dislike before you turn on it — on me, on the university, on Julia, who you didn't mind asking for a job one time while claiming to hate everything she stands for. Why don't you simply go and seek out other like-minded people — work in the inner cities, help people in a way that doesn't provide a living for you."

"Go back where I came from?"

"A lot of people wondered why I spent time with such a mediocrity, if you really want to know."

"Odd that they should have wondered that. It's always been clear to everyone that you regarded your work in this town as a kind of sacred mission to the unenlightened. Didn't you say yourself that you were in internal exile? Just a sophisticated joke, of course, not meant to be taken seriously. I was one more disciple, ready to do your bidding, run errands, act as an unpaid chauffeur and cabdriver, and keep you company. And be a surrogate daughter."

"Which you did gladly for quite a long time."

"And now I'm revealed as disloyal and ungrateful. You know why I was loyal and grateful for so long? Because I felt sorry for you!"

"*You* felt sorry for *me*?"

"Don't you realize how much they laugh at you? At the way you talk and the way you look and act? You should hear Bernie Woniger's take-off of you."

"Lena, am I supposed to be devastated by that? I'm sorry to disappoint you. You have the advantage of knowing what's said about me as I know what's said about you. And let me tell you, it comes as no surprise to me. I've heard it all before, said of any woman who gets a bit of power. And the more vitriolic, the more pathetic the source usually. Bernie Woniger. For chrissakes, Lena. He's so bloody pathetic and transparent. One-beer-Bernie, who can't take a drink without undergoing a radical personality change. Lovely company you keep, Lena."

"If it's all so obvious, why are you shouting? What happened to rational discourse?"

"Fuck off, Lena."

"Tut tut, Professor, don't you know that's a sadistic word that betrays male contempt and aggression towards women? Your language has really deteriorated."

It was an ugly evening with an ugly ending. If Lena didn't stomp off into the night, it was only because at the end of it we had both drunk the rest of the Scotch and got on to the good brandy, and neither of us was in any state to do more than flop on the nearest couch.

I wish I could say that the next day we laughed at ourselves, that we suffered from alcoholic amnesia, that we made up our quarrel. We didn't, of course, and the rift was deep because it wasn't a question of Lena's saying things she didn't mean. Max had been right when he tried to warn me and I wouldn't listen. They'd been there all along, deep-rooted resentments and grudges, fuelled by envy, anger, hatred, whatever. What was amazing was that it had all been kept in check for so long.

There was one other singular thing that I remember about that night. In the early hours of the morning, around two or three o'clock, the phone rang. That's a disturbing experience for me because a phone call after midnight has always heralded disaster, brought news of some fearful accident. I woke with a start to hear the phone ringing and then Lena talking to someone. When she came back to bed, she mumbled that it was some drunk who dialled a wrong number. She may have been telling the truth.

But the next day we learned that Monica had killed herself in the night. She had left Julia's house and Julia, being preoccupied, I presumed, with reestablishing a relationship with one of her boyfriends, had not paid any attention when she left. The next day when Monica didn't drift over, Julia went to look for her and found her in the attic of her house. At first Julia thought she had gone up there with a bottle to look for something, or to sit among the family paraphernalia she kept there.

Then she realized that she was dead.

I don't believe in ghosts, but I do believe in some kind of extrasensory perception or communication, and I'll never forget that phone call. I remember that I'd asked Lena the next morning as we glared at each other across the coffee and toast, both with fearful hangovers, sharing a bottle of aspirins, "That wrong number in the night, was it a woman?"

"No," she said, "it was a man. Or a kid, some teenager who'd had too much to drink or was on something."

Her answer sparked a vague memory of another lost message, but at the time I couldn't quite put my finger on what it was.

X

I HAD THOUGHT a great deal about the christening. I like tracing the patterns in people's lives, finding equations, parallels, and culminations, the figures in the carpet. On shopping expeditions I had gravitated to the baby departments and looked at cribs, lined with silk and satin. I thought that as we stood around that crib, everything would come full circle and close with healing. There would be the four of us, as we were the night of Jinny's death. How fitting that it would be the same time of year, with the warmth of summer but a slight tinge of fall in the air. Monica would enter my house for the first time. She would come eagerly as a welcome guest, all the old bitterness sweetened by our affection for the new child in our midst. What an age-old sentiment, to pin all hopes on the birth of a child:

> *You are the one*
> *Solid the spaces lean on*
> *You are the baby in the barn*

We would not have a religious ceremony but a celebration — a white cake in the middle of the table, light glinting in the rows of glasses, champagne cooling in the fridge. Instead of prayers, there would be toasts and wishes for her future. And, of course, the naming. Virginia-Desirée. If I thought at all about a last name and the necessary documents, I assumed that, as always, Simone would take care of that, as she took care of everything. But death intervened and instead of a christening we had a funeral.

It was Julia who did most of the planning for the funeral. Monica had a lawyer who oversaw her affairs, and he and Julia arranged it, assisted by a funeral director from one of the funeral homes that used to be grand houses overlooking the park. These funerals were always awful creepy affairs, with some Uriah Heep of a funeral director presiding, and organ music intended to produce an atmosphere of reverence and sounding like music piped into a department store elevator.

We held a short vigil there the night before because it seemed the normal thing to do, and no one had offered to take the responsibility for organizing any other kind of reception. We were a small group, sitting with bowed heads, all locked in our own separate worlds. I noticed that Lena had an absolutely ravaged look, and I wondered if she was mourning the end of our friendship more than Monica's death. Mrs. Pike, who had cleaned for Monica and looked after her, was there with both her daughters, and all three of them were sniffling and scrubbing at their eyes with tissues.

The disintegration of Monica's family had been pretty complete, and her daughters had been out of contact and unreachable for so long that no one expected them to show up for the funeral. It came as something of a shock, therefore, when Monica's lawyer told us that Renny had been notified of her mother's death and would be arriving from England. She sat among us, a little jet-lagged and dazed. All of us were engrossed in our own thoughts, mourning not only for Monica and Virginia-Desirée but for the accumulated losses of a lifetime, as people do on such occasions. Every funeral is a day of the dead.

The one surprising thing about that vigil was that we were all sitting there, morosely, listening to the awful music, when Max walked in. I was dumbfounded, seeing him neat and well-dressed and slim. It was as if the past eight months had never happened. He looked subdued, perhaps sad, but that may have been my imagination. For several months I had scanned his face, like an anxious mother, looking for signs of tension or trouble, and it was hard to break the habit.

He walked down the aisle briskly, entered the pew, bowed his head in prayer, and then sat beside us quite easily in the tacky funeral home. Before he left, he shook hands with each of us solemnly but warmly and said how much he had liked Monica and how grieved he was by her loss.

Julia asked if he wanted to come back to the house for a drink or go somewhere for one. I thought at the time that it was an amazing invitation, offered as if he were an ordinary friend she was in the habit of seeing on normal occasions. It was all random and vague, but he thanked her courteously and said (without any indication of irony) that he had a lot of work to be catching up on. He promised to be with us for the funeral the next day. And, you know, he was.

We concocted what we thought was an appropriate service, each of us going up to the lectern to read some poetry or prose. Simone read a passage from the Bible, Julia a passage from one of Donne's sermons, and Renny a fine paragraph from George Eliot's *Daniel Deronda*. I winced when Lena started to read Anne Sexton's signature poem, "Her Kind." It seemed in execrable taste with its reference to witches and madness, but as the refrains at the end of each stanza hung in the air, the selection seemed fitting, as if she were expressing her own kinship with Monica.

A woman like that is not a woman, quite
I have been her kind.

A woman like that is misunderstood
I have been her kind.

A woman like that is not ashamed to die.
I have been her kind.

I chose a passage on the immortality of the soul from the end of the *Phaedo* — the bit where Socrates gives his disciples instructions for the disposal of the body and tells them, "don't think it's Socrates you're burying." I've found his words the only consolation for that awful moment of seeing a parent or friend sealed in a coffin. Max liked it and nodded at me appreciatively. He sat beside me in the car when we rode out to the cemetery on the prairie where Monica was to be buried.

Would anyone have noticed anything unusual in our association with Max? Was there a certain emphasis when we asked how he was, or an innuendo in perfunctory remarks such as "How well you look" and "I'm glad you were able to come." We were a little restrained because there were strangers in our midst, and I wondered if, had we been alone, we would have asked about the journey to Fargo, about his recovery, about how he travelled back to the city. Did he rent a car and drive himself? Or did he fly?

After the service at the graveside, most of the people who had been at the funeral drifted away. Besides the group from the night before, a handful of neighbours had turned out who, as far as I knew, had little to do with Monica when she was alive. They may have been drawn by morbid curiosity, or hoping for an elegant reception afterwards. That, too, is a feature of funerals. I felt no obligation to cater to them and so the four of us and Renny returned to my house for drinks and sandwiches. It was mid-afternoon and we sipped sherry or gin and tonic and picked at the sandwiches. I don't know what the conversation would have been like without Renny (Lena and I were barely speaking and Lena and Julia always had daggers drawn), but she provided a focus for the occasion. Since Simone had known her in childhood, the two had a fairly cordial relationship based on childhood memories. Simone offered to take Renny on a guided tour of the new hospital. Renny also knew Julia's children as classmates, and Julia vaguely promised an excursion to her cottage at the lake.

If any of us had expected Renny to be grief-stricken, it was clear that either we were very much mistaken or that Renny was a master at disguising powerful feeling. Her dominant emotion seemed to be surprise that the mother she knew as a dysfunctional social outcast should have been part of such a closely knit group of friends. It was clear that Monica had met us regularly on social occasions and that we genuinely mourned her death. Renny couldn't figure it out and we found ourselves in the awkward position of having to account for it, yet not wanting to give anything away.

"It wasn't that I was estranged from my mother exactly," Renny said, "it was just that I found her totally inaccessible. The mother I remembered disappeared long ago. When I talked to her on the telephone she was usually incoherent. And yet you apparently didn't find her so."

"Oh, but we did," I said. "She was there and we hardly noticed her. I don't think I exchanged more than a few words with her in six months and yet she was always around."

"Julia talked to her though," said Lena, with a nasty edge of scorn in her voice. "She collects waifs. Has a whole menagerie of them."

"Don't be so stupid, Lena," said Julia. "She was an old friend and she was in trouble. She made a remarkable improvement in the last few months," she added unguardedly.

Renny leaped on the remark. "Was there any special reason that you know of?"

We all looked at one another, wondering what to say next, hedging, reluctant to give much away. Renny waited for an answer.

"In a way there was," Julia said.

"We had a kind of project," I said. "We were looking after a person who was going to have a baby..."

So there it was. Out in the open. And so far it didn't sound extraordinary or sensational. But Renny was not going to let the matter drop. She was like a dog with a bone. "You'd taken in this person?"

"Yes, we had. At Julia's house." I thought Renny must be trying to remember which one of us had a daughter or granddaughter of an age to need such help. I thought she might imagine it was a student of mine.

"And my mother?"

"She began to take an enormous interest in the baby," Julia said. "At first she appeared not to know what was going on. She'd always come in and out of the house as she wished, you know.

She'd wander about, sometimes sitting with the schoolchildren. Then suddenly she was aware of the baby and started knitting things for it. And she gave it a name — Desirée. I don't know if it was the baby that she wanted or if she just felt part of something, like being part of a family. I don't think any of us realized how much it meant to her until . . . you see it died. It was stillborn."

"But the disappointment would have been inevitable. The letdown. I mean, she couldn't have kept the baby," Renny said.

I don't know what made me jump in at that point but I said, quite unnecessarily, "No, it wasn't inevitable. Someone had to take responsibility for the child. I'd thought that I . . . Monica could have helped out. As a babysitter."

"And did you think that would have kept my mother on an even keel?"

"Maybe it would."

"But what about the child's mother?" said Renny.

"The parent hadn't the slightest interest in the child," said Lena.

"And yet she had not wanted an abortion?"

"It was too complicated," I said, and Lena and Julia chimed in one after the other.

"It was too late."

"It's not possible in this city,"

"In this province."

The three of us were almost too eager to provide answers to the question.

"It was an unwanted pregnancy and the parent was totally unfitted for child-rearing," said Simone coolly. There was a warning note in her voice. "Shut up, you fools," she was really saying.

"And where did Max Hoffman come into this?" said Renny.

"Come into it?" someone said.

"He was involved, wasn't he?" Renny persisted.

"In a way," said Simone. "Lawyers run into these cases as a matter of course."

"Why do you ask about him?"

"My mother thought the baby was his."

There was, I recall, a movement to the refreshment table, a refilling of glasses.

"Did she tell someone that?"

"She kept a diary, you know. Well, she wrote constantly, mostly during the night, an odd incoherent account of everything that happened to her. Most of it is pretty garbled and incomprehensible, but she had a good ear for conversations and recorded them in incredible detail."

Of course. I remembered Monica, sitting at Julia's kitchen table with her pile of newspaper clippings and scribbling on bits of paper.

"Have you read these . . . diaries?"

"Not all of them. Not by any means. There's such an enormous amount it would take days to go through it. And her handwriting can be pretty hard to decipher. But the later ones get clearer and I did look into them."

"And she thought the baby was Max's?"

"Not in the way that sounds, as if he were liable for a paternity suit. It wasn't that."

I remembered my first reaction when I saw Monica lying on the couch in Julia's den. How I'd been angry and alarmed, but Julia had reassured me that Monica was so out of it, she wouldn't know what was going on. But it had come out through her. "You damn fool," I thought now as I had then. Who knew where it would lead from here.

And so we ended up telling Renny everything. Again that overwhelming sense of déjà vu. As we explained what happened, it was like the other time, when we told Max. But this time we were all standing around holding glasses, and all dressed in black. And there was less incredulity because the diaries had prepared Renny for something bizarre. If we'd wanted to try out the story of what we'd done on someone else to see how it sounded, the result could not have been more gratifying. Renny, after her initial amazement, was full of admiration.

"Who hasn't thought of such a thing," she said, "without ever thinking it could happen. What an experiment. How clever of you. And how brave of you all to take such an enormous risk."

We started to look slightly pleased with ourselves for having done something clever. All except Simone, who was looking thunderous.

"Did you keep a day-by-day record?" Renny asked eagerly.

We said no, we hadn't.

"Why?"

"Well, really, we had our hands full with one thing and another."

"But wasn't that the whole point of the experiment?" she asked. It was hard to explain, and I for one balked at the word "experiment" that she kept using. It seemed too cold and calculating for what had happened to Max.

"But you must have kept medical records?" she asked Simone.

"Of course," said Simone evenly, "but I destroyed them when I got back from Fargo. It was over and there seemed to be no point in keeping around incriminating documents. Suppose that Max at some late date decided to sue us?"

"And so my mother's diary is the only written record. You have no photographs, no proof, nothing?"

"I think we want to put it behind us now," said Simone. She looked at her watch with her characteristic brisk gesture and began to gather her things together. Lena left at the same time and, to my relief, so did Julia. Renny and I were left to clear away the mess, wash the glasses and the silver.

"You still seem confused," I said.

"Well some things don't fit. I gather, for instance, that my mother acted as errand-goer for Max?"

"Oh, I don't think so. She couldn't have."

"She did. She was sworn or urged or whatever to absolute secrecy. She was always being sent to the mailbox to post letters. He told her they were birthday cards for Julia or you or one of the others."

"And she trustingly mailed them?"

"She mailed them. How trustingly or what she believed I don't know. She seems to have had lucid moments, you know. She noted the discrepancies in the stories. That the stamps were for postage to the U.S.A., for example."

"But who on earth would he have been writing to in the U.S.? Does the diary say?"

"I haven't read everything, but it doesn't seem to give the name and address."

"And you wonder why Monica left that out?"

"That's only one thing, but there are some more puzzling aspects of the whole affair."

"Such as?"

"How did Simone get this colleague to help?" Renny put vocal quotation marks around the word "colleague." "Did you ever talk to him?"

"*He* was a *she* Simone told us," I said, "and she participated on the condition of strict anonymity."

"Well, the ovum. Where did it come from?"

"Simone got it from the lab at the hospital."

"But it must have come from somewhere. I mean, it must have belonged to someone. You can't just have unspecified, unlabelled, unclaimed genetic material lying around."

I don't know why I hadn't thought of this and why it took an outsider to raise all these matters.

"You took a lot for granted."

"I see that now. We rushed into the middle of things when we should have begun with the egg."

Renny's last remarks were unsettling. She looked thoughtful as she set her purse on the radiator by the door and took her jacket out of the hall closet. Then she said two things that kept me awake long into the night thinking about them.

"Simone hasn't changed all that much, has she?"

And as she opened the door and stood in my little porch, she turned around and asked one last question. "Do you really believe that baby didn't survive?"

XI

RENNY. HOW CAN I speak of Renny?

She stepped so neatly into the space left by Lena that she seemed like a gift from above.

Lena was gone from my life after the evening of Monica's funeral. After that, it was as if she was transformed into someone else. Not someone different, but someone who had been there all the time, disguised as Lena, whom I hadn't noticed or hadn't chosen to notice. There'd been hints that this other person existed, but I had refused to face up to what was there. And then Renny's arrival erased all the memories and the regrets.

I wasn't in a particularly cheerful frame of mind when I went out to the airport to meet Renny. Even though I had fond memories of her, I was put out that it fell to me, who had no car, to go and meet her all by myself, but everyone else claimed to be busy.

The scene: The carousel at the airport, with throngs of people watching mesmerized as the conveyer belt carried tattered and tacky luggage round and round, some of it spewing out entrails like an old couch. There was the carnival atmosphere that characterizes these places during the summer months, when the celebrations of civic pride take place that recall the province's historic past — Klondike Days, Buffalo Days, Stampede Days, etc. A hillbilly band was making a racket, and the sheriff's men in ten-gallon hats and kerchiefs were grabbing arriving travellers, putting stamps on their hands to let them know they were welcome to the city or that they could go to the Exhibition for free or something. It was all very rowdy and good-humoured, and you could tell the strangers by their look of culture shock and their facial expressions that said, "Is it like this all the time?" and "Where have I landed?" or "What kind of *shtetl* is this?"

I searched the crowd for a dishevelled, grief-stricken person in mourning. No one matched the picture in my mind. I was trying to remember the last time I saw Renny as a youngster, in a striped overall with a snub nose, freckles, glasses, and a missing front tooth; my last image had been a photograph, enclosed inside a Christmas card, of a teenager in a long dress.

My eyes lit upon a smallish person, with dark hair swirled up into a kind of bun. She was wearing a beige jacket and pants and a jaunty emerald-green blouse and scarf. There was the glint of a gold earring. I forgot the person I had come to meet. Instead I found myself staring at this other self-possessed person.

She was happy, pleasant, alert, interested, an acute observer, taking stock of the scene. There was a kind of visible intelligence in the gaze she trained on everything. It circled like a searchlight from the luggage to the people and back to the luggage and inevitably fell on me and stopped because I was staring so. The gaze held me, caught staring. Then she smiled, as if to say "Isn't this too absurd?" and we both smiled. Then her grin faded. Well, how long can a grin last? She wasn't a blithering idiot.

Why did I not make the connection with my traveller? Because there was no trace of mourning? Then I realized with a shock that an unclaimed solitary traveller, a young woman with dark hair must be ... The men in baseball caps advertising farm implements, the women in square-dancing dresses, the cowboy boots, the jackets and shirts in bright red fabrics to warn hunters, all these blurred and receded. We stepped forward to shake hands and then hugged each other. It was Renny.

Later I tried to make something out of this meeting. What did she think? Why did she suddenly break into a smile? "You fishing for compliments?" she said. "I expected the lawyer and then I saw a familiar face. And you were staring so hard."

We collected the baggage, which was amazingly heavy. "Books," she explained. "I thought I might be here for some time. Very good of you to meet me like this."

"We'll have to look for a cab," I said, "because I don't drive."

"Me neither," she said.

I was surprised that she wanted to go directly to the house after her long journey, not pause at my place for a drink or a rest. She said she wanted to go "home" directly, and she wanted to go in there alone. So I was dismissed. But she relented, remembered her manners, and agreed to come over later, have something to eat with me, and let me know what immediate supplies she needed. It was between three and four when I walked back across the street from Monica's doorstep alone. I thought that I had three hours to kill before she would come over. Three hours to think what to offer, what to say, how to make her feel comfortable.

Later Renny told me it was her fate to close up houses and dispose of the contents, only she had trouble in finally letting the houses go. It had fallen to her to go to England when her grandmother died and sell the family home. Unfortunately, a deep recession had caused a total stagnation in the real estate market. Nothing was selling and renting was out of the question. So she had decided to move in and wait out the slump. She had gone to the University of Sussex and been offered a part-time job. It eventually grew into a full-time position and she had simply stayed on, commuting two or three times a week by train to the university.

Soon I was hoping that the same thing would happen again. There was no economic recession and houses were selling briskly in our neighbourhood, but Monica's place was so full of the debris of a lifetime that it would take months to sift through everything. Renny had a sabbatical leave from her job anyway and seemed in no hurry to get rid of the contents of her family home. She told me that it was her final connection with her past and that once she got rid of everything, that past would be gone forever.

She took the job seriously, had been shaken somewhat by finding out the extent of her mother's papers, and wanted to go through everything carefully. She accepted my offer to help and had no objection to my reading her mother's diary. She wanted to discover her mother in those pages, but my motivation was slightly different. I wanted to find out what had gone on during the past months that I hadn't known about.

There were pages and pages of semi-legible scrawl, rather like automatic writing. It's odd because I hadn't remembered seeing Monica write so much. She was often just sitting staring into space. But then, as she says over and over in her account, "nobody sees Monica." I remember Julia saying to me that Monica was writing again. There was so much of it and so many pages that it seemed to me that Monica must have been scribbling most of the time and squirrelling away the pages in her house. You wouldn't want to read the entire thing, though I've read it many times and it yields new secrets at every reading. But if you dip in here and there, into the sections I've placed at the beginning, you'll get the general idea.

Today Max said come in Monica do come in Monica How are you? Would you like to do something for me. Don't tell anyone. Don't tell Julia or Lena. You wouldn't tell would you? It's a birthday card for Julia. You like Julia a lot don't you? SO DONT TELL MONICA CAN YOU UNDERSTAND? the mail box is on the corner have a chocolate Monica and come back and tell me after it is in the mailbox see in your pocket right away while no one sees our secret card for Julia and spoil the surprise.

It was clear that Monica had bad days and good days. But even on the worst days she knew more than anyone had suspected, except perhaps Julia. How could we not have known that in spite of that pathetic, collapsed exterior, there was a human being inside? This was our shared guilt — Renny's and mine — hers that she had abandoned her mother, and mine that, during all the past months of concentrating on the needs of Max and the baby, I had ignored the one person who needed help, who cried out for help and could have responded to it. The word "inaccessible" came back to haunt us.

At first we assumed that the incoherence in parts of the diary was a kind of simple-mindedness, the result of regressive or drunken behaviour. We were making again the mistake we had made in judging Monica. For it wasn't simple-minded or confused, it was automatic writing that often tapped into an underlayer of her consciousness. It was vivid, spontaneous, alive. Why were we so ready to assume that she had passed out when we found her sleeping on Julia's couch? She had probably been writing most of the night and was catching up on her sleep. When Julia said once, "She doesn't drink as much as you think, she doesn't actually drink that much," I read that to mean that she had a low tolerance for alcohol and became hopelessly drunk after one glass of something.

I like to hear Max and Julia talking to each other even though I know eavesdropping is despicable. But can it really matter very much since I speak to no one, tell no one except my diary. Don't be shocked diary. If I lie down on the couch or curl up in a chair they pay me no attention. I become invisible. I know so much that the others don't know, that Max and Julia are very happy together. My darling, they say sometimes. Don't call me that it might slip out when the others are around. That is very interesting but not as interesting as when they talk about the others. How did you get on with her today? I'm terrified of her, really terrified. She's very strong and muscular for a woman you know. Are you afraid that she'll do you any real harm? I don't know what I'm afraid of exactly but I'm afraid alright she's so weird. Creepy. Do you know what Lucy thinks about her? Oh Lucy. Lucy thinks she's a victim of child abuse. Of sexual abuse. And doesn't know it. Only Lucy knows it. Lucy thinks she knows everything. She thinks she understands everyone. Well, she is pretty astute, you have to admit. I don't have to admit. And I don't agree. She thinks she is alright. She may be right about Lena you know. Oh she may be. There's got to be something back of all that rage. Why does Lucy put up with her? Who knows? Is there anything between them? How do you mean anything? Well, you know, sexually. Who knows? I don't think Lucy's that way somehow but I could be wrong. She never came on to me. I think Simone is though. No really? Did she ever come on to you? Not to me no.

So later I think about all this going on. I think of Lena who frightens everyone. Why are we all afraid of Lena? Is she a victim of child abuse? Who abused her? She had brothers and brothers often abuse their sisters. Tonight I read the diary of Alice James. Dear Inconnu, she writes. I write dear diary but I am writing really to myself. Who are we talking to when we write diaries? Dear Monica. Dear Monique. Dear Inconnue I like that dear inconnu it reminds me if I could talk to Lucy, if Lucy would listen to me I would tell some things she could write about Alice James. She would say oh I know that it's been done, Monica. Lucy always knows what's been done. This is a habit of hers when someone says something she says, ah yes, Matthew Arnold and the person who hasn't been quoting or echoing anyone else at least not consciously looks embarrassed. Looks caught out. I've seen this lots of times with Julia. They are all a little intimidated by Lucy. They don't like her much but they don't hate her because they laugh at her. Lucy has lots of books and she has read most of them. She reads all the time and there are books all over her house, face down on the chairs by her chair in the kitchen. People ask Lucy things. I don't though but I watch Lucy and listen to her. Do I like Lucy? I'm not sure. There's something cold about Lucy. Is she like that? I know something about Lucy that no one else knows. Dear Inconnu, shall I tell you what I know about Lucy?

How strange it feels to be undressing in a little cubicle, a tiny box with a stool, or a seat like a shelf along the side opposite the door, hooks on the wall on which to hang clothes. This may not be sinister, it may not be the prelude to anything dangerous at all. It could be the cubicle in a department store which one enters to try on clothes to see if they fit. To see simply if they are the right shape, colour and size. Or it might be the cubicle in the doctor's office which one uses to change into a robe before an examination, an x-ray, a mammogram. And even then that might not be sinister. One might well be told "no problem, everything fine." One might return to the cubicle, dress again and walk out into the sunshine. One might be told we'll be in touch with you and then be told later that there's something very wrong. A lump, malignant, cancer. I seem to remember these cubicles sometimes at swimming pools somewhere and there were pools of water on the floor. These dark moods come upon one so that every single thing or act contains all the fears. As if all the cubicles contain all the fears or not the cubicle but the head in the memory and then one needs to blot it all out. Thinking of cubicles I could go mad. There is one final cubicle that one never comes out of. A carrel in the library is another kind of cubicle.

Monica is writing in her book which Julia says is good Monica writing in her book Julia smiles at Monica the birds come to the bird feeder Julia put birdseed Monica eats bread and birdseed Julia does not say fuck off Monica but is no bird stop coming in here go home get stuffed

Julia is kissing Max says what about her Julia says she's O.K. Monica hurts no one Lena hurts Suzy went off Max sees Monica sometimes Lucy sees Monica simone sees monica is afraid of simone too

julia says don't be stupid monica is not stupid lena is stupid so julia says don't be so stupid lena stupid lena stupid lena fucking off but not near the children julias children in the school room reading rimplestultskin

mrs pike cleans monicas house every week sometimes mrs pike says honest to god what a mess what do you do in here monica what a mess talks all the time monica likes mrs pike cleaning saying what a mess and time for our coffee and see you in a few days and don't make a mess well its what im paid for so not to worry mrs pike doesn't know babies smile and sees how are we today fast asleep when I left last week poor old thing mrs pike says poor old thing i brought you a pie now eat it birds eat mrs pikes pies and mrs pike never says fuck off mrs pike throws the pie and says well i tried and it was a good pie too mrs pike says saskatoonberry pie and cranberry jelly now you eat it

if monica can't rock the baby mrs pike can rock it with the money from the mantelpiece under the blue jar if monica is asleep on the couch mrs pike can clean the baby max and julia will have a baby lucy is very grown up and too grown up for the baby is inside max

today i worked on the jacket for the baby i have finished about half of it i had forgotten how to cast off and mrs pike showed me she said how much better I looked

She asked me if it was a present and I said yes it is a present for a friend who is going to have a baby. Has she had one of those tests, she said. What tests I said. Well you seem so sure that its going to be girl. I shall have to stop now I said because it is giving me a headache. Knitting always does me like that said Mrs Pike anyway it's about time for our coffee and cookies. I brought some cinnamon cookies. Has the baby got a name yet? Yes I said but it's a secret. I remember when our first was born said Mrs Pike. Mrs Pike is so nice. I was getting sleepy and I said I think I shall have a little something with the coffee. Mrs Pike said now you don't need that do you. I said oh reason not the need and Mrs Pike said what? She said please don't so I didn't. Mrs Pike always calls Julia that friend of yours. Mrs Pike doesn't like Julia at all and wouldn't clean for her no matter how much she paid. She doesn't hold with a lot of the things that go on over there though she has to admit that Julia is one of the few people who is kind to Monica and gives her the time of day. You would think in a neighbourhood like this but that's the city for you. She calls Simone the lady doctor or your doctor neighbour. Tell that friend of yours it's time for your hair appointment you are starting to look very untidy. If she's too caught up with her boyfriends or whatever you want to call them I could get you there in a taxi. Mrs Pike is a grandmother. Rosalie has two children and Arla has three. She calls everyone by long names. Arla-that's-out-on-the-acreage Rose-in-the-north-end Monica the-poor-old-thing Mrs Pike that-comes-in-to-clean. The secret name is Desirée.

Julia said you handled Ruth Lawson's divorce didn't you? As a matter of fact yes said Max. Tell me, what possible satisfaction can you get from helping someone like Don Lawson take someone like Ruth to the cleaners? You're beginning to sound like Lena. Does Lena go on about Ruth? Not about Ruth no but she always goes on about something. Well I'm not bullying or haranguing or being shrill I'm just asking out of curiosity. I mean, what does it feel like afterwards? Are you asking about yourself, Julia? Well. You're hardly in the same category as Ruth Lawson. What difference does it make? That stupid bitch she's like a great spider preying on poor old Don all these years. She got her claws into him when he was too young to know any better he was a student when they got married. She put him through school. And stuck him with four kids. Or looking at it another way he stuck her with four kids and she raised them. What else was she fit for? Is that what you thought of me? You were so attractive I knew you'd be alright. Land on your feet. Meaning you thought I'd latch onto another lawyer, doctor or cabinet minister — in spite of my advancing years. I wished it might have been me, Julia. I still do. Monica wants to open her eyes to see what happens next but she sighs, stirs and settles into a deeper sleep.

I am the invisible one that no one sees. I glide in and out of rooms as I wish and no one notices. I lie down and close my eyes and hear everything. Once Lucy sat down at the table and looked at me, looked right into my eyes and said Oh Monica what are we going to do? I thought she was seeing me but I was still invisible and she was talking to herself. When did I become invisible? It was long before Suzy went away, long before I married Sam. Perhaps when I was a child but I think it was later when I was to stop being a child certainly it was when I lived with my mother and father and needed to fade away out of their lives out of their scrutiny. Girls do that they stop eating but I started to become *invisible but was many many years before I faded completely it was after Suzy went away.*

Renny would not have gone away if I had not been invisible Mrs Pike has two daughters and they are grown up and gone and I am her only daughter now. She comes in every day and keeps the house as neat as a pin. A person can live very well and privately under this cloak of invisibility. The milkman drops things on the step and Mrs Pike brings in food and all through the day I float about like a dream person and at night I start to write.

Max said today Monica I've run out of stamps I shall need stamps do you understand can you get me some stamps the stamps to put on letters on birthday cards it is easier and I have to send cards I smiled because he explains it as though I am four years old I say nothing and he shakes his head Monica do you know where Julia keeps stamps isn't there a desk or something please try and understand.

It is funny to see Max trying so hard to make me understand about the stamps wheedling I can easily get the stamps I have trained myself not to laugh and I never laugh but it would be so easy I bring old stamps to Max and he sighs and explains so laboriously that these won't do though they are very pretty stamps but he needs new stamps. O.K. this has gone on long enough and I don't want to torment him any longer I don't want to get like Lena so I bring him a book of stamps. He puts two on the letter because it is going to the United States and one isn't enough.

Smiles and laughs would betray me and I don't let them but tears come sometimes I like to hear Lucy talk she talks like an English teacher and says things sometimes they are from poems and plays a lot of Shakespeare and sometimes perhaps her own words it is soothing to hear Lucy speak Lena's words cut like knives. They laugh everyone laughs at Lucy. She isn't a real person she's so soaked in all those books she's become a character in one of them. But which one? She has no voice of her own, merely a rag-bag of hand-me-down words from the poets. Words are her medium, learning them, uttering them so that they float into the air and stir even the most leaden souls in the classroom. I've seen her do it, walking down a hallway looking for Sam. All her life she has been in thrall to words drunk on them like a mid-summer bee on pollen. Her words are her powerful aphrodisiac.

Aphrodisiac he said. Come on help me out even now she says especially now he says I need to remind myself I'm still a man and not some I close my eyes tight very tight until she says I'm getting a towel that's all it's like another time in their big double bed in the bedroom upstairs where I fell asleep they are getting undressed and my eyes are closed tight but I am not asleep carry her back to her cot she says the cot is in an alcove in their bedroom it is hard to keep my eyes closed but I do and when I open them it is dark but I hear sounds it is not dark now and I must fall asleep are you ready love he says I like it better this way don't you.

Max and Julia were talking today. Max said whose idea was it this pregnancy? Was it Lucy's idea? Julia said no it wasn't it just happened we sort of all thought of it together it evolved it's hard to explain really we were at Lucy's house though yes. Max said I somehow thought Lucy must have been behind it. No she wasn't said Julia she was out of it at the time actually you won't convince me said Max. We all started airing our grievances and saying if men could have babies and Simone said they could and that's how it got started. But why me said Max or perhaps I don't really have to ask I suppose Lucy thought of me immediately. It took us a long time to decide who to choose said Julia I don't remember who thought of you.

They all have secrets from each other they are all doing things they don't want the others to know about. Lena takes photographs with a little hidden camera that she carries in her purse or in her pocket it is so small. Sometimes Max knows and sometimes he doesn't but he won't tell he is very frightened of Lena it is a kind of blackmail taunting him not so well endowed but that's quite aesthetic like the Greek statues.

Simone is the strangest of them all. It's only you who keeps me from going crazy he says to Julia do you think you could love me after all this? What about the others he asks her Julia is very bad Mrs Pike thinks so but she is nice and she strokes so gently I AM JEALOUS OF MAX. Taking pictures never hurt anybody oh yes it did a very small camera they all have their secret equipment Simone's things in the black box, Lucy's little recorder to play things and to record what they say. They had a big discussion about television.

"Why didn't you stick him in front of the telly?" asked Renny. "Isn't that the great baby-sitter of our time?"

"As she says, we had a big discussion and decided against it for various reasons. We needed to be alert, vigilant, not lulled into inattention. Also it was noisy. We took a vote at last and the T.V. lost."

"Did Max want television?"

"I don't remember asking him. I don't think he minded not having it. It was Lena who mostly wanted it."

"A sinister character that."

"Yes, I see that now."

"All those photographs."

"Terrifying isn't it?"

"For him?"

"And for her. If she tries anything. He's powerful again and capable of being ruthless."

XII

ONE DAY RENNY came in briskly as she always did. She had a key and so she rapped on the door, rang the bell, and let herself in. I came downstairs, happy to have a reason to stop working and make coffee. Happy always to see Renny.

"You'll never guess what I've done."

"I wouldn't even try."

"I've sold the house. The FOR SALE sign comes down this afternoon. Don't look so horrified," she said.

I was horrified. I never thought she'd do it. And I hadn't imagined how I should feel her loss. Nor had she.

"Look," she said, "this is silly. You'll just simply come over and see me."

"And you'll never come back."

"I won't really have any reason to."

"And your mother's papers?"

"I thought I'd leave them with you, if that's O.K. You have loads of room, a few more boxes in your attic won't make the slightest difference. And they really belong to you. They are the only record of what you did. We daren't give them to the archives. And besides, we haven't really ever completely understood them, have we?"

I kept thinking how disaster always strikes when we least expect it. I looked out of the window at the blue sky and the weak sun, a day with no threats in it. And how I'd let the weeks slip by, taking Renny's presence for granted, believing that she would be here always. She had told me about going over to England to close up her grandmother's house and how she had simply stayed on, unable to leave. I'd assumed, since a mother has a greater claim on us than a grandmother, that she wouldn't be able to leave here. I had paid no attention to the FOR SALE sign, thinking that it would eventually be taken away, offer after offer, if they were made, being refused.

"When I went over to deal with my grandmother's house," she told me, "I hadn't been over there for years. I walked into the house and it was terrifying. It was a mausoleum, like the tomb of Tutankhamen. It was full of photographs, mementos, letters, the accumulation of a lifetime. Can you imagine living in a house surrounded by pictures on all the walls of *your* mother as a baby, as a child, as a young girl, as a bride, and pictures of Suzy and me? And every drawer full of letters — all the letters home my mother had ever written.

"My mother had written to her parents religiously every week of her life from the day she left home. There were letters she'd written on the boat the first time she came to Canada, postcards from holidays, all the birthday cards and Christmas cards she sent them. And you know what was the weirdest thing? After my father left and everything fell apart, she never said a word to her parents about what happened but kept on writing and recording life as it would have been. She described our birthdays, celebrations, our progress through school, holidays, all a fantastic piece of make-believe. Every letter began with 'Dear Mummy and Daddy,' you know the way English women do right to the end of their lives?"

"Yes, but how could she write coherently? My understanding was that she was crazy."

"It *was* crazy. She never veered from the theme of the happy family. And if she did lapse into incoherence, it just sounded as if she'd had too much to drink. They knew she drank, of course. So there was all that and I had to dispose of everything.

"And did you?"

"Of course not. I couldn't do it. I thought, if I wait a while, if I settle in, eventually I shall be able to get rid of all this debris."

"And you did?"

"No. It hasn't happened yet. Perhaps it will now."

"So you live in the house exactly as it was?"

"No, no. It's not Miss Havisham's place by any means. I've actually made it very pleasant. I got rid of the old rugs, curtains, furniture. I put in bookshelves and so on. I moved the photographs into the bedrooms, but they are still on the walls. I haven't been able to take them down. All the photograph albums, letters, and diaries I've put in chests. There's an attic, not a big one like yours, but one of those spaces under the roof. You pull down a ladder from the ceiling in the hall. It isn't morbid, really. Well, perhaps the photographs on the walls are a bit much. I do have to explain them to visitors, that they aren't my choice and so on.

"I actually enjoyed settling into the house. It's a cottage really. I think of it as my ancestral bungalow. From time to time I think I might move to a bigger house on the cliff road overlooking the sea, but somehow I never do. Or down nearer to the university, to Lewes or Brighton. But I'm used to going back and forth by train, and as long as British Railway functions, it's convenient. If I moved to Lewes, it would be rather less convenient for going up to town, which I do in the summer and in the university holidays."

"Renny," I said, "tell me. You couldn't bring yourself to close up your grandmother's house and get rid of her stuff, and yet you've managed so quickly to close up your mother's. Can you just let it go so easily?"

"There's one thing I haven't told you," she said. "It's that I think Suzy is in England."

"She is?"

We had been reading Monica's diaries, not the recent ones, but earlier ones when she was younger and less confused.

I lie awake when the wind howls around the house like wolves thinking of Suzy, wondering if she has a bed and a pillow and if she is spending the night inside peacefully somewhere. Each blow and cry of the wind pains me because I think that Suzy gone from the safety of the house must be buffeted and exposed — her thin shoulders shuddering, her decaying teeth chattering so that in the morning I wake from fitful sleep weary and exhausted as if I had endured the storm.

I wish I could talk to Suzy now. What a useless, impossible wish. If only time were not so irrevocable. If I now could talk to Suzy then. If only she had survived the rapids and lived, she could have spoken to me. I imagine sometimes longingly being able to dial a number and hear her voice.

I wonder does she have a warm coat, for she was never good at looking after herself but perhaps someone somewhere will care enough to see that she has a coat to put around her shoulders. And gloves. I remember how she hated to wear gloves and pulled down her sleeves to cover her hands. I said "you look like little orphant Annie." She would always lose her gloves and I bought pair after pair.

I can never leave this house for as long as I live. Suppose Suzy wakes one day from the nightmare of her life and thinks of home, of going home. Or perhaps on some journey of her transient life, finds herself by chance in this city and thinks I lived there once. And walks to the house with a growing sense of being home again, of having fallen into the orbit of the family. And she walks to the house with a growing sense of excitement which mounts as she gets nearer to the familiar street, the same path, the same trees, and knows that she can ring the bell, the door will open and she will say "Mother!" And all the lost years will melt like snow and Suzy will be home again.

The Christmas Suzy got a small cassette player she took it to her room and spoke into it all winter long. She didn't record music as we thought she might but read into it all her favourite poems and played them back endlessly to herself. Secretly when I am in the house alone and during the night, I play those tapes and listen to them before I fall asleep. I play them again and again hoping that if the disembodied voice speaks often enough Suzy will materialize in the room. And sometimes she does. I fall asleep and float into a dream where I meet Suzy and we walk together along the promenade under the cliffs and beside the sea where the equinoxial storms cast up great waves of pebbles. "*Ah love let us be true to one another*" *says the voice on the tape.*

And reading these, Renny told me how she'd been rushing down the street in Toronto and a voice had said, "What a pretty sweater." You got inured to street people when you lived in a big city. Beggars and bag ladies were everywhere, though not as many in Toronto as in the university town where she'd lived in the U.S. But she'd turned and stopped because the tone was so conversational, bright, social. And she'd been shocked because this was a young woman about her own age. She was a good-looking woman or, at least, might have been and might be again if her teeth were fixed and her hair cut and if she were fed properly and got enough sleep. She didn't have the mad wild look of many of them and she hadn't asked for anything, just admired the sweater, which was a very nice one, and she'd smiled. Renny had been so overwhelmed she hadn't been able to go to class afterwards. Then she went to class less and less often and then not at all. She was hanging around the streets and then around the shelter that the young woman went to. She was weary of academic work anyway.

"What's someone like you doing here?" one of the workers asked her. "You don't look like the kind for this place."

"You doing research for a paper?"

"You in sociology? We get a lot of sociologists here."

Renny changed her clothes so that she looked like the rest of them, but something still gave her away. Perhaps it was the way she spoke or moved. When she knew him better she thought she would ask Paul, whom she liked.

She had the impulse to give the sweater to the young woman everyone called Amy. Only it would have looked absurdly out of place with its bright flowers, even if they became muted and dulled by the dust of the street. But later, during the bleak winter days when the wind whipped round the corner of Bloor and Yonge and Amy came into the shelter in a thin sweater, Renny gave her her navy blue Eddie Bauer jacket. It was a good jacket, quite new and downfilled against the cold. About a week later Amy had shown up, with the weather still cold and the wind still biting, and she was shivering without a coat or even a sweater but just a cotton dress. Paul, giving Renny one of his withering looks, said Amy probably sold it for the price of a packet of cigarettes. Or perhaps, thought Renny, it was stolen. But maybe it kept her warm for one day or one night, in which case it was worth it.

There was something wrong with everyone at the shelter, and Renny found that comforting because their weaknesses were openly acknowledged, not hidden and festering. Amy was an extreme case, but the helpers were like that too. Paul and Reba disappeared and went on benders but, apart from that, seemed to function quite normally.

"Amy was looking for you," Reba said.

"Yeah, that's right," Paul said, "she was asking where Renny was."

Renny was extraordinarily pleased. When Amy came in she went to hug her, knowing that Reba and Paul were thinking "not a good idea." Amy, who was only looking for something to eat, said, "Get away, I don't want to catch anything off of you."

"You're getting quite a fan club here," Paul said.

Maggot-face wanted to take her out and gave her a number where she could reach him at a detox centre. He had been hanging around waiting for her.

"Got yourself an admirer," said Reba, and they all laughed. Renny was struck by how much laughter and joking there was at the centre.

Then Amy collapsed on the street and was rushed to hospital, and Renny rejoiced, thinking that now Amy would be cared for, would come back, be brought back to the normal world, and they could talk. And Renny went hurrying to the hospital carrying things — flowers, juices to drink, a basket of fruit. But Amy merely turned her face to the wall, staring at it. She paid no attention to Renny, who left the things on the table by the bed.

"Are you her sister?" one of the nurses asked.

When Renny went back, Amy was gone.

"Flew the coop," they told her. She had simply left in the middle of the night. No one saw her leave but, in any case, they had no means of keeping her there. It wasn't unusual, the nurse said, happened all the time. And Renny had despaired of ever seeing Amy again, but a few days later she walked into the shelter, coughing her hacking cough, her fingers blue with cold, dark circles around her eyes, wiping her nose on her sleeve, looking for something to eat.

"So where've you been?" Reba asked.

"Took a vacation," Amy said, "needed to get out of this bloody climate. What do you think of my tan?"

So many people at the shelter had colds, and Renny carried Fisherman's Friends in her pockets to hand out. The men shook their heads but Amy took them. Renny gave her the whole sack, and Amy sat reading the instructions with a slight smile on her face. "My daddy was a fisherman," she said. That could mean anything, a cod fisherman, a salmon fisherman, a sports fisherman going by helicopter into the northern lakes.

"Oh yes, where?" said Renny, but Amy had retreated into her own hermetic bubble. She ate all the Fisherman's Friends, though the instructions said one every six hours.

"Can you O.D. on these things?" she asked.

"Then I got a call that my grandmother was dying and I had to take off for England," Renny told me.

"I don't understand," I said. "Was Amy one of Suzy's names?"

"One of many," Renny said, "Alicia, Felicity, Penelope, Desirée. She liked names."

"She wasn't Suzy was she?"

"She was very much like her," Renny said. "I used to pretend she was. When you've failed one person, you try to make up for it by finding someone else and looking out for her."

"I know."

Then Renny told me that her grandmother's neighbours said

they remembered a young woman coming and going, "a hippie" they called her. She had stayed for a few days, sometimes as long as two weeks. They had seen her going in and out, taking walks alone at night, which was dangerous, going to the pub. Then she had disappeared. But someone had taken a picture of the grandmother and the granddaughter. Renny carried it with her — an enlarged picture of a young woman with hollow cheeks and hollow eyes, hooded eyelids, bad teeth, and a ghostly kind of smile.

"She's probably in England somewhere," Renny said. "I can't stay away. I have to be there."

"Have you tried to find her?"

"Oh yes. I try all the time."

"Renny," I said, "do you ever blame me for what happened to your mother?" I guess I was asking for absolution.

"It would have happened anyway," she said. "There would have been someone else, and back then I wasn't putting two and two together very well. She was such a mess. I knew we didn't have the kind of home that other kids had. She was always drinking and they were always arguing. I didn't even blame him, I blamed her. And then I thought of you as a normal mother, the mother we should have had by rights. I loved your house, all the books. I loved that summer we had with you. It was an oasis of happiness, a kind of Eden in that troubled childhood. You burned like a bonfire, Lucy, in that naughty world. A fairy godmother.

"That time you took us to Banff. I still have the little glass paperweight with the picture of the hotel by my bed. We had our own room at the hotel. I remember how we went to Lake Louise and it was full of tourists, a choir belting out hymns in the lobby, and it snowed in the middle of August. I can remember everything about that summer in incredible detail.

"It was a perfectly happy time. Except for Simone. Whom I hated. She was always going on about God and how we'd go to hell unless we went to her church and accepted Jesus into our lives. Suzy believed her and went to the church and even went through some kind of conversion ceremony. Got born again or something. Can you be born again if you haven't been born in the first place? Simone was a mean kid, you know. Suzy was worried about everything, and Simone preyed on her. I used to think Simone ruined my childhood, because I thought of that summer as my entire childhood. I didn't have any other.

"And then it was all smashed up. He came back from England and we heard him say, 'Lucy we have to talk.' We stood waiting anxiously and then he more or less told us to get lost. I knew it was over. We were up in our rooms, listening to your voices downstairs. You were crying and pleading with him. I should have protected Suzy. She was older but so vulnerable. I was a survivor even then. But when you're a kid you don't think of that. So there we are.

"He wasn't a bad person really. He tried to look after us and he looked after Mother in his own way. He always sent far more money than he could afford. So he looked after her and I looked after myself, but no one looked after Suzy, and she was the one who needed help. She was like my mother in temperament, too fragile for what happened to her, but I couldn't see it . . . "

"You were just a child, Renny."

It was painful when Renny talked about these things. She was perceptive and she had all kinds of theories about Simone then and later. She was a natural skeptic and there was no ridding her of the conviction that Simone had duped us, carried out some kind of trick or joke. It was the kind of thing she would do, Renny said. For the life of me, I couldn't think why.

"What were her clothes like, during that time with Max?" she asked.

"She wore a lab coat a lot of the time."

"Loose? Was it a loose coat?"

"Fairly loose. Not very. I don't think it would have concealed an eight-month pregnancy, if that's what you mean."

"Did she gain weight? Was she fuller in the face? Did her face change?"

I couldn't see how an elaborate charade would have solved the problems of Simone's own baby. If she had one.

"And Julia and Max. Didn't it seem strange the way they fell into each other's arms?"

"No, not really. Julia had a way of falling into people's arms. That was the way she was. It didn't seem odd at all."

"But you said she suggested Max in the first place . . . "

"I think she did, yes. Perhaps she did, but many names were mentioned, and when Max's name was brought up there was a general consensus."

Renny, the solver of everyone else's puzzles, couldn't solve her own, and so she went back to keep her vigil in the house of photographs. In the beginning I thought that I would go over and visit. I imagined arriving in the little seaside town and entering Renny's house. Of being taken on excursions, daily outings, having dinner, reading quietly, enjoying each other's company, as we always had.

But the realist in me knew that I could be only a temporary guest, a summer visitor, and not a part of her life. I'd be taken to the university, shown her office. And a colleague would come rushing up to greet her, then fall back seeing that she was with someone, was not alone. Not free at the moment. I would be introduced. "An old friend from Canada." And I'd sense or suspect the unspoken words passing between them. I'd make phone calls and wonder what I was interrupting. Lucy, the cold one. Lucy who knows everything. Lucy who speaks other people's words.

There was a final parting at the airport, the business of checking in her luggage, going with her as far as the security gate, hugging her for the last time.

"Hey, don't forget to write."

And then there was empty space where Renny had been.

XIII

AND SO, AFTER all these days, all these tapes, our memories at last converge. You have your own recollection of Simone and I have mine. It is a question of bringing them together, like matching the negative and positive versions of a photograph, comparing the skeleton of something with the fleshly version, the caricature drawn in a few rough strokes with the portrait in many dimensions. There are so many different manifestations of Simone and we have only two of them.

Let me tell you about the last time she appeared to me. It was summer, the first summer in a long time that I'd spent in the city instead of travelling to the house I'd acquired on an island off the West Coast. I'd had a double mastectomy and I was recovering from surgery, lying in my hospital bed, looking out over the prairie, drowsing. It was only natural that, being in hospital, I should have been thinking about her and thinking about the past. I turned my head and there she was, framed in the doorway, smiling.

"Am I dreaming," I said, "or is it Simone?"

Odd that you tell me she appeared to you in just the same way — a ring at the doorbell, running steps, exclamations, and you drawn slowly towards the door by hearing the cry "Why, it's Simone!" And you saw her, framed in the doorway, that magical aunt you never tired of hearing about.

I have to admit I was feeling sorry for myself. I was no longer a woman but a mere shell, a husk. They'd taken the uterus too, saying the prognosis would be better without it. The prognosis for what, I wondered.

Then there's something irrationally sad about being in hospital and having no one to see you in and out, bring you what you need daily. Oh, I wasn't alone, far from it. Friends, students, and colleagues dropped in constantly. Flowers arrived in loads, cards ... but they all seemed like painful reminders that there was no one in charge on a regular basis. They brought home to me the stark fact that there was no one in whose affections I stood first. I had the feeling that I'd outlived everyone. I was indulging, I can tell you, in some very melancholy thoughts. And, in particular, I was dreading the moment of departure — leaving for home alone, the nurses all gathering and asking, "Is there someone to take you home?" And I saying briskly, "I only live across the park, why bother anyone?" and leaving in a taxi.

And then Simone arrived as if in answer to a prayer. She was in and out of the hospital all week, coming early in the day and staying by my side for hours, and I must say her presence gave me some clout with the nurses.

"Isn't that ... ?"

"Do you know her well?"

"I read in the papers about that hospital they named after her in ... Africa, wasn't it?"

"Is she coming back to Canada to live?"

I couldn't answer all their questions because she was pretty vague herself.

"Why is she in town?"

"Oh partly business, partly to see people," she said. "Actually, to see you, Lucy."

Surely not, I told myself. But she insisted that this was so.

She was lighter-hearted than I'd remembered her. She went all over the cards and things that people had sent. I said we'd leave the flowers for the nurses.

"Don't be silly," she said, "most of them are plants. Just leave mine behind."

Hers was an exotic flower arrangement, one of those showy pieces designed to impress — birds of paradise, orchids, arum lilies, and so on. But we left it at the nursing station for the nurses' aides to wonder at, and she packed up all the dull chrysanthemums and begonias and took them over to the house. When I got home there were pots massed in the hearth and everywhere.

"How popular you are, Lucy," she said. "It looks like a flower shop."

"Or a funeral," I said. "I find myself looking around for the coffin."

And after I got home from the hospital, she came in every day, looking after me, doing the shopping, and preparing my meals.

"Like having a daughter," I said.

"Neither of us knows what that's like," she said.

During those days of my convalescence we often sat in the garden. It was one of those wonderful Saskatchewan summers full of blossom and sunshine, but never oppressively hot. Usually my garden was a scene of wild disorder, but the year before I'd had one of my periodic binges of landscape gardening. It was no Sissinghurst, but one of the local firms had done a fairly good job with cedar decks, pebbles, driftwood, flowering shrubs, and small trees here and there. It was as if I'd known I'd be spending the whole summer in the garden instead of travelling out to the island.

I'd be sitting there, a book in my lap, half asleep, and I'd wake with a start to see Simone standing over me or sitting beside me, looking at me with a smile on her face. You say that's how you remember her too — waking up to find her looking at you. Perhaps she was, after all, already dead and what we were seeing was a ghost.

She must have spent her entire leave between the two of us. I don't know if she planned to stay with me as long as she did or if it was finding me ill that detained her and gave me more than my allotted share of her time. It was the honorary degree, I discovered, that brought her here, though she may have had other reasons, other business to tidy up. Perhaps she knew then it would be her last visit to both of us. But she loved getting the degree and minded my not being there. She made it quite clear that it was me she wanted as her family in the audience rather than her real family. So we talked about that.

"Did Max ever get his degree?" she asked.

"Oh yes," I said, "I saw to that. I thought it was the least I could do."

"The least?" (Incredulously.)

"I wanted to make some kind of reparation. You know, compensate for what we put him through."

"But he got so much mileage out of it. More than any of us."

She was referring to the Tyler case — a notorious trial involving a woman who had killed her children. Max had made a brilliant defence. It was a tough case because Tyler was an unsympathetic character, the kind of woman who has everything — looks, money, an easy life. The kind that every loser who has a grudge against society can focus his anger on. The misogynist's dream of a pampered over-indulged woman. She'd been a model and her husband was a stockbroker. She went berserk one day from cabin fever or something and drove a carload of little kids into the lake, jumping out and saving herself at the last minute.

It was a hard sell, and everyone expected the defence to plead insanity and bring in childhood trauma and sexual abuse, the whole lot. And what did Max do? None of that. He turned every stereotype on its head. He portrayed her as your average harried housewife and — this was the real stroke of genius — he managed to make her an object of sympathy so she got a light sentence and the papers were full of editorials about young mothers needing support systems. It was an incredible performance. And Max was the hero of the hour. He amazed everyone with his understanding and sympathy for women. There were headlines in all the papers:

FORMER ABORTION FOE
BECOMES FEMINIST ADVOCATE

YOUNG MOTHER CAUSES
LAWYER'S CHANGE OF HEART

LAWYER TURNS OUT TO BE EXPERT ON GYNECOLOGY

His elevation to the bench and the senate was, more than anything else, the result of this one case. No one in the country could escape it. Every time you switched on the radio or television, clips of it were being played and replayed, sometimes the whole peroration. And you know what was so eerie? I was hearing all that stuff Lena bombarded him with, being played back to us as if he were mocking us. Which he may have been, but he appeared deadly sincere.

"For the hard of hearing you shout, for the half-blind you write big," he told the jurors (I'd had him reading Flannery O' Connor), promising to level with them, no exaggeration, no playing with their emotions. He talked about pregnancy and childbearing and post-partum depression, as if, in the words of one reporter, "he'd had first-hand experience." A walking example of empathy.

Then he topped it off with a fantastic flight of fancy. He had them imagining that Samantha Tyler had to take care of first one of her elderly bedridden parents and then the other, then her husband's. Would anyone blame her for going mad? No. And what's the difference between being a caregiver for four semi-ambulant, demanding, querulous, elderly people and four youngsters? Nothing. There isn't the slightest difference. Only the mystique surrounding motherhood decrees that Samantha Tyler should not only do it, but should get boundless satisfaction from it. And if she doesn't, she's a monster, an unnatural woman.

Well, he had the jurors not only shedding tears for Tyler ("she is your daughter, she is your granddaughter"), but champing at the bit to get the case wrapped up. They couldn't wait to get the hell out of there and go home to rescue their daughters and granddaughters before they did something drastic. It would have been funny if it hadn't been so damned annoying. It was one of the most fantastic episodes in legal history in this country.

"The degree came before the Tyler case," I told Simone. "I

pushed it before I had any idea he'd turn the whole episode to his own advantage without any help from me."

"Surely you could imagine something like that happening?" she said.

"Well I didn't, did you?"

"Not in the form it took," she said, "that we'd provide him with a crash course that fuelled his career. No one could have imagined that. But it's inevitable that whenever men do something it gets elevated into a profession with all kinds of rewards, prestige, status . . . So it was entirely predictable that in some way the whole experience would redound to his credit because it's happened so often before. It happened when midwives were replaced by gynecologists, when women cooks gave way to chefs, seamstresses to couturiers, and hairdressers to . . . "

"Of course, it's programmed into the language, plain English giving way to Latin and French," I agreed.

"And look who benefited from the so-called sexual revolution, and the women's movement. Women are magnanimously allowed to enter the work force and what happens? Half the time they're supplementing the family income, raising the kids, doing the household chores, and either feeling guilty for working or being grateful for permission to do it.

"So all along I had doubts. I thought that if men could carry babies it wouldn't change a thing. They'd be elevated to deities and saviours of the world. Women would be ministering to their care while they sat there enthroned like Buddhas."

"Buddhas. There's a thought. The role-model already exists."

"And so Max, the wily bastard . . . "

She didn't specify what area of his activities qualified him for that epithet, and I didn't ask. I surmised that it was everything — his career, his success, his popularity, and, most of all, Julia. They weren't married, but his wife's condition had deteriorated and she'd been moved to the long-term care facility. Julia had moved in with him as *maîtresse en titre*. It seemed a reasonable thing to do and nobody criticized either of them, especially as he was so good to Francine. He sent flowers every week, visited, nothing was too good for her.

"It wasn't you who proposed me for my degree was it?" she asked.

"No, it wasn't."

"I didn't think so," she said.

"Would it have made any difference?"

"It would have made a whole lot, Lucy. A whole lot."

"I hadn't the faintest idea that you craved such a thing," I said. "I thought you would have despised it. Besides, haven't you had enough recognition for your work?"

She took out the silver cigarette case she carried and tapped a cigarette against it. She was smoking now, not chain-smoking like Julia, but from time to time she'd light up one of those little foreign cigarettes — Gauloises. I liked the smell.

"I used to wish you were my mother," she said, "but you took in everyone else except me."

"Took in?" I said, and she seemed unable to explain, though I knew what she meant. I'd never totally responded to Simone as I had to the others, never confided in her, never really, until that past week, rejoiced in her company, looked forward to her walking in the door.

She went on, emboldened, to list her grievances as if I really were her mother and had been negligent in my obligations and had preferred all my other children to her.

"You made allowances for everyone but me," she said.

"Everyone?" I said.

"Well, for Renny," she said.

I smiled because in Renny there was nothing to overlook or forgive. But Simone was terribly jealous of Renny. I'd noted the furrowing of her brow when she perused the cards in the hospital and saw and read the one from Renny, examining it closely, as if decoding a secret message. She was conditioned from childhood for jealousy and rivalry was Simone.

Once upon a time I would have defended myself vigorously, but now I merely nodded. I admitted my weakness. "Oh that the gods a gift would gie us / to see ourselves as others see us." They had given me that dubious gift in the form of Monica's diary. I'd read it and never felt the same about myself again.

How many of us ever have the luck or the misfortune to come into possession of an account of ourselves, detailed, written over the years, day by day, by a perceptive observer? This is what it must be like to read a biography of yourself. In the beginning you resist, you say, "This is not I." You feel like the old woman in the song who falls asleep on the king's highway and wakes to find her petticoats cut off. But gradually you begin to acquiesce, you grant the truth of the observations, and eventually you accept the portrait totally. You become that person, you grow into her. When friends looked at Picasso's portrait of Gertrude Stein, they said she didn't look like that. "She will," he said. And so I grew into Monica's portrait of me, seeing myself as she saw me.

One day, Simone said to me, "Do you know what the most devastating thing about my childhood was? That it was lived absolutely under the cloud of your derision. Everything I or any member of my family did was a source of amusement and mockery. This scorn — call it what you like — this superiority was a steady drizzle. It was the one constant. And it achieved a definite purpose. It kept me loyal to them. No matter how much I resented them, your scorn made them seem vulnerable and I felt protective of them."

"Was she right?" you ask.

You must have many questions, but you seem reluctant to ask them, except when you flip a tape or take up a new one.

"Yes, I suppose she was. I was snobbish. It goes with the territory, bred in the bones, like racism, like alcoholism. It's inscribed in the language, and the vocabulary's already there and waiting.

There are all these words for every shade of bad taste and so-called vulgarity and lack of proper decorum, the way the Inuit have dozens of words for snow, or wine-tasters for every slight variation of flavour and bouquet. Even when you leave the country, it takes a long time for the tares to work themselves out."

"Then why did her saying so bother you so much?"

"Partly because I'd never for a moment imagined that my amusement (I prefer even now to call it by a softer word) was so transparent. I'd thought that I concealed it, that in any case they were too self-centred, too self-righteous themselves to notice it."

"They were . . . "

"Yes."

"But she wasn't . . . "

"No, she wasn't . . . "

∼

Simone told me she remembered asking once when she was twelve or thirteen why I never wore the make-up I bought from her mother. Without thinking I'd said, "Because I don't want to look like a tart." Then I'd caught myself, adding hastily that my hands were unsteady and I'd look as if I had jam all over my mouth.

"I knew what a tart was," she said, "and I knew exactly what you meant."

"My mother," she went on that summer day in the garden, "was not an educated person. She wanted more than anything to go to college, but there was no money. There wasn't a great deal later for us, especially after my dad lost his job, but she managed to find it. She gave us all the advantages that she'd been denied, and that was admirable, Lucy. Since when has it been alright to laugh at ignorance and poverty?" I felt ashamed, hearing her ask the same question Julia long ago had asked more gently.

It wasn't just the fact that I had caused her pain that mortified me. It was that it replicated exactly the pain of my own childhood.

It was unthinkable that I, who suffered that same lofty disdain from my classmates and teachers, should have visited it on her and assumed that she wouldn't notice and suffer. But, of course, that's how it happens. "Man hands on misery to man / It deepens like a coastal shelf."

"Did you ever have an abortion?" she asked me one day that summer. She popped the question at me without warning, just as she used to ask questions when she was a child and I never had the nerve to answer them directly and truthfully.

"I did something else," I said, "something so terrible I can't think about it. Why do you ask?"

"I always wondered why you never had any children. Were you not able to or didn't you want any?"

So this was how I came to confide in her, telling her the secret of my life, as I'm telling it now to you. It was a peace offering, to excuse my coldness of heart and make up for the confidences I'd withheld over the years. Even then I couldn't speak directly about my younger self. I had to invent a character and talk about her in bits and pieces, forcing it out. I said I wanted to tell her about someone who was close to me a long time ago, someone who no longer existed.

Sometimes she had to leave on one of her engagements and I hoped that the story would end there and I wouldn't need to go on, but inevitably she made me continue. After we'd exchanged greetings, talked about what she'd been doing, settled down, she'd say, "Go on with the story about that person you knew in your other life." And not looking at her, but looking instead at the sharp edges of the monkey-puzzle tree against the blue sky, I'd pick up where I left off the day before.

And when it was over, she left. I'd begun to dread the moment of her departure, and she knew it. She told me that she wanted to drive across the prairie to see Andrea and Ken. And the kids. She added "the kids" as if it were an afterthought, not returning confidence with confidence. Of course it was you she was coming to see.

She asked me one last thing about my story. "Can I ask you something?" she said. I thought for a moment she was going to say "Is it true?" as she used to. Instead she asked, "Did the others know?"

"The others?" I said.

"Renny."

"No," I said, and she looked pleased.

And so she was gone and I never saw her again.

But a few days later you say she appeared in your life, the same apparition, the golden girl, *jeunesse dorée*.

I can well imagine everything you tell me, especially the disapproval that she stayed in a hotel. Tell it to me again, beginning when Andy asked her, "Where are your things?"

"'Where are your things?' my mother asked. I mean, the one I called mother.

"'Things?' said Simone.

"'Your suitcases.'

"'Oh, I left them at the hotel when I checked in.'

"'*Hotel?*'

"'The Holiday Inn. I didn't want to cause any inconvenience ... you have so little room, someone would have to sleep in the living room ... and besides, Andy, there's a very good pool at the hotel. I need to swim every day, twice a day if I can manage it. The twins will love the pool. They have swimsuits, don't they? It'll be a holiday for them.'

"And it was. We'd never been in a hotel before. Not one like that. And we'd never been with anyone like Simone before."

"I didn't imagine she'd be particularly good with children."

"Not in the usual way she wasn't. She didn't play games much, but she talked to us a lot, and listened. To me in particular. She wanted to know everything about me. About my life and my friends and my interests and schoolwork. That's very flattering to a kid, as you know.

"There was never enough food at home, and we always left the table hungry. If there was a pie it was cut in half and we got a quarter each, an eighth of the whole pie. The other half was for the next day. There were never any second helpings. What was left over was for the next meal, the next day. Oh yes, Simone sent plenty of money, but we didn't use it all. We tithed strictly, and a tenth of anything that came in went to the church, more than a tenth, I suspect. How else would my dad have become a deacon? So I remember all the food on the table in the hotel coffee shop and Simone urging us to have more. As much as we wanted to eat.

"'They look hungry,' Simone said, 'and they're both so thin. Are they getting enough to eat? I could send more.'

"'We use as much as we need, no more,' my mother said, 'the rest goes to the church, to the poor. There are others need it more than us.'

"'Their clothes are shabby, Andy. They need new clothes.'

"'Their clothes are clean and sufficient. We wear our clothes as long as we can, patching them when we need to. That's what we believe in. Waste not. Want not.'

"'You all seem to be wanting a lot.'"

"It was clever of her to devise that way of getting you to herself, to have you stay in the hotel, the pool, the dining room. But creepy and a little sad what you say — all those times in the night you woke up to find her watching you with that intent look, a kind of hungry, yearning look that you didn't understand; which a few years later you interpreted as her wishing that she too had had a child. Your memory of that time is uncannily exact — five short days and you say you remember every single minute, but especially her standing beside your bed when you woke, covering and uncovering you, splashing you when you took your bath, giving you soft drinks from the bar in the room that fascinated you. And your anguish when your parents joined you for a meal and you couldn't have your wonderful aunt to yourself. And your constant fear that you wouldn't be allowed to go back to the hotel. Your delight when your brother didn't go but chose instead to go somewhere else, to play with other friends. The picture of you writing on the thick hotel paper and her saying to you fiercely: 'You must write to me. Promise. Promise . . . ' And you kept your promise faithfully and wrote to her every week afterwards, and made drawings."

"Yes, and years later I found all the letters, stamped but never mailed, in the bedside table drawer of my mother, of the one I called my mother.

"One thing I could never understand was why Simone and my mother — those two sisters — hated each other so much. Little as I was, I could sense it from the way they talked to each other. I couldn't bear Simone to be out of my sight. I followed her around like a dog, and when she was talking to my mom in the living room I was usually behind the couch listening. I heard a lot that I didn't understand then, but I remembered all of it. It's just now beginning to make sense.

"One day, my mother and my aunt were drinking tea and talking while I played with one of the new toys.

"'The kids have been raised in a Christian home,' my mom said.

"'Then no harm can be done in five days. To the pure all things are pure,' my aunt said.

"'Then there's the smoking,' my mom said. 'When did you take up that filthy habit? And the drinking. You drink a lot now, don't you? And not just wine.'

"'For god's sake,' my aunt said. 'Don't forget who pays for a lot of this, all this.'

"My dad was unemployed and my mother found work when she could get it as a nurses' aide in a home for old people. I heard one thing that astonished and sort of frightened and excited me.

"'I could take the kids away legally, you know.'

"'You wouldn't and you couldn't the way you live, they don't allow it. And I don't even think you could do it legally after all this time.'

"'But you wouldn't want to risk finding out for sure would you?'

"I remember our birthday. It was mostly little kids from the neighbourhood, the grown-ups in the background. But she gave me a watch, which I loved. My mother disapproved.

"'It's too expensive for a kid. What if it gets lost?'

"'If it gets lost,' Aunt Simone said, 'I'll send a new one.' Was that such a surprising thing for her to say?"

"No, it wasn't. I'm not astonished at the gift or at your mother's disapproval. But something suddenly occurs to me when you mention your birthday. She couldn't have driven directly to see you. She must have gone somewhere else for at least a week. I wonder where she was and with whom and if we shall ever piece together her life."

"It's possible that she wanted to be alone."

"Possible. Anything's possible. But not likely."

XIV

EVERY TIME SHE RETURNED from one of her errands that summer, Simone came hurrying out into the garden to find me.

"Go on with the story about that person you knew in your other life," she urged me, and I tried to, proceeding haltingly, circuitously, trying to extricate it from Monica's words. There's always one story you can't tell. And usually it's the one you have to tell before you can go on to the other stories. There it is like a roadblock, your story. And you think of reasons to avoid telling it. You start it often, but you don't finish it. Or you trick it out with a forced resolution, an ending, or one of those non-endings over which a listener frowns, looks out the window, remembers, and is moved. But really there is no ending to this story and no beginning. It goes on wherever you are. And all the other stories are weaker because of this untold story. It makes them into evasions, digressions, wanderings off the beaten track.

The first scene is Elmsville, Indiana, in the mellow fall. Season of early morning mists and mellow fruitfulness, the frost on the piles of pumpkins stacked on the roadside stands. It seemed to me exotic as I breathed the clear air along the banks of the Wabash. I'll never forget the beauty of that place in the late summer and early fall — the golden corn, the lush leafiness, the maples in their autumn colours. You have to remember that I'd never even seen corncobs, pumpkins, and maples before I left England. I wrote rapturously to all my friends back home, evoking scenes with rustics like the first act of *Giselle*.

"Go on with the story . . . " she said.

I was married.

If I talk to you now with the same hesitation it's because it's still difficult. It comes back to me shot through not only with echoes of Monica's diary, but with the changing expressions that flitted across Simone's face, the smell of her Gauloises.

When I first saw him I thought there was something freakish about him. Foreign students were not a rarity in English universities, but the Americans stood out among them. They came on a larger scale than other nationalities, sprouting taller and bigger than the Italians and Germans from whom they were descended. Was it dietary — all the milk they drank? Or was it the sun and space and over-indulgence in sports? There's something about tall men from big countries.

Then there were the clothes. He wore army jackets, khaki pants, sweaters, windbreakers, sneakers. All these garments for sweating, sneaking, breaking wind, loafing. It was impossible not to think of the Americans as slightly degenerate and déclassé even before the ubiquitous blue jeans.

Yet for all their shoddy clothes, they possessed a miraculous freedom. They weren't cramped by protocol and penny-pinching. They went rushing off to London on a whim to see a show, stay the weekend. In the Turk's Head they stood round after round of drinks, unworried about making their scholarship funds last. I was enchanted. I thought that the freedom might rub off on me. After I crossed the Atlantic, it was I who was the freak. I had good clothes with BY APPOINTMENT labels sewn into the linings, but they were so ugly and tweedy, and so few. I was an object of curiosity, amused tolerance, and sometimes awe.

This neighbourhood is an extension of the university and there is no getting away from any of them. The department head lives a few houses up and we walk to his house every Friday night. I hate these get-togethers — the smoky room, the crowd, the cheap wine, being a faculty wife, a wife. People see me standing by myself, feel sorry for me, and come up trying to be friendly.

"You're Monica aren't you? I read one of your stories in a magazine."

"Don't you want to join faculty wives? We do lots of interesting things. We have a potluck supper once a month at the President's house. It's so much fun because there's a lively group of young wives."

"Come on, Shelley, there's a lively group of wives who aren't young."

"Oh I know. I shouldn't have said that. Anyway, Monica, you'd really like this group. All the wives join."

"Hello, Monica, why have we never gotten together for coffee?"

"Have you met any of our creative writing people?"

So they detach the creative writing people from the animated conversations they're having, lead them over to me, and they talk to me dutifully, their eyes roving about the room. Then they excuse themselves, saying they need to fill up their glasses, and on the way back to me, get waylaid and drawn into more interesting discussions.

It wasn't altogether unpleasant being a curiosity, having a different accent, different clothes, different manners. And the glorious freedom my American husband had all his life was now mine. I felt like someone above and beyond all the rules. How else could I have been running around the countryside with Kit? At first it was innocent — going to antique shops and nurseries, picnicking on the way. Then Kit was lending me books, reading whatever I wrote, bolstering my confidence, fanning my ambition. I began to have dreams for my future and it was a future without my husband. He was an obstacle to my growth. Only as Kit's protégée could I fulfill my potential.

It was Kit who arranged the rabbit test.

"Poor rabbit," Kit said, "with all the liquor you've been drinking lately, its head must be spinning on top of everything else."

"It's not funny," I said.

"Go on, it is," Kit said. "Lose your sense of humour and you're really done for."

"I'm in pig," I told Kit when I got the result. "We have to decide what to do about it." So Kit decided.

"If he finds out, you two will be bound together for life and you'll lose all the lovely freedom you keep talking about."

I hate living in this place. I will never get used to it, this arid, flat land, I'm used to gardens and country lanes, the smell of fields, the mists rising in the morning from the meadows. He hates it too, it makes him sullen and restless. If we lived somewhere else he wouldn't always be staring at young girls, and ones that are not so young. He stands at the window watching the women who live on the street — our glamorous neighbour with her boyfriends going in and out, the ugly professor with her briefcase and armful of books. They are both divorced women, they couldn't keep their own men, but because they live alone, they are temptresses, who draw all the bored husbands like magnets.

Leaving my husband was easier than I thought possible. Afterwards I told myself that he had yearned to be free as much as I had. The marriage was burdensome and caused friction with his parents, who found much to criticize. "Why doesn't she clean the house?" "Why is she always running off with that new friend of hers?" "What's this idea of suddenly wanting a job?" "Why doesn't she do volunteer work — raise money, like we do, to send terminally ill kids to Disneyland? There are oodles and scads of good causes."

We shared none of the same interests and if we had not met each other as foreigners, nothing would have drawn us together. Yet if he had known about the baby, things would have fallen out otherwise. He knew nothing of the daughter he had fathered.

It is a frozen day in mid-December, by noon the skies have darkened, the snow is falling fast and there are blizzard warnings. The children don't go back to school in the afternoon. The snow falls steadily, heavily, sealing us into the house, piling up around the doors and windows, obliterating the paths and sidewalks. On the roads around the city there is a white-out, we are enclosed, isolated like a small island in the middle of the ocean, only the occasional car creeps slowly up the road, its lights catching the snowflakes, he calls home to say that he is working in his office, will get home when he can, not to wait for him, not to hold up our dinner. I know someone is with him there, a student perhaps, they are together in that enchanted tower room above the library, their eyes shining at each other, the curtains drawn.

A strange thing happened. The foetus that I carried inside me took on a character of its own. From the first moment, while Kit was saying "it," I was calling the child by her name. I knew exactly what she would look like and how she would be. She would be my own child with a face that had come down through the ages, though I had known it only for two generations through photographs. I have photographs of myself and my father at the same age, looking exactly alike, so it was easy to imagine my daughter. She would be curly-haired, sturdy, her two legs slightly apart, resentful at being made to stand still for the photographer, absolutely refusing to smile. My daughter. None of this could I explain to Kit, for whom she did not exist.

He has made his office at the university into a second home, he has most of his books there, a white bear rug on the floor, a divan along one wall, an armchair with cushions. It is austere and yet comfortable, the divan he says is for catnaps in the afternoon or if he works late into the evening, that's what he says. It is a bright airy room, high up like an aerie with a view over the prairies, sometimes he draws the curtains so as not to be distracted when he works at his desk, he likes a flowering plant on his desk, for inspiration he says, he is as fussy as a woman about arranging his room, the pictures on the wall, the little table by the armchair. But it is not only for working, and for escaping from crowded disorderly conditions at home, it is so that he can invite women inside, entertain them with drinks and conversation, I imagine them sitting in his office, discussing books, ideas, I imagine him offering something to drink in one of the cups or glasses on the tray that sits on the table by the chair. I imagine all kinds of things.

With complete clarity the child whom I now called Lucia grew like a sturdy tree in the barren landscape of my mind. Every day I thought of her, knew how she looked, how she would look. My family photographs filled the gaps in my imagination, for the family resemblance ran down through the generations — the Henrys, the Samuels, the Joannas, and the Lucys, and on into the future with variations on the same face, like variations on a theme. But I would not see the faces of the future if I lost my child. I would break the chain, abdicate, step aside, let the face pass into the hands of strangers. Where my child should be, there would be an empty space.

The three of us have cornflakes for dinner. I have a glass of whiskey and then wine with the meal and more whiskey afterwards, the girls watching my glass anxiously all the time. "What's the matter with you two? Eat your cornflakes." So they eat their cornflakes. They in their tower room are drinking too, raising their glasses to toast each other. In the early hours of the morning, the snow stops, the moon shines through my bedroom window for I have not drawn the curtains. They have opened the curtains and are lying, their heads together on the white rug, looking at the moon. She is saying lines of poetry "On such a night as this . . . " He picks up the refrain "On such a night . . . " They are in a state of ecstasy. I do not know how I know this. It is now all over between him and me and after this night nothing will be the same. Not for him, not for her, not for me, and not for the children. Our family has come to an end, it is finished.

I said, "I'm not sure what I want anymore." Kit said, "You're not kidding. You don't plan to keep this kid do you? You? A kid?" I pressed my hand to my temples, feeling trapped. "Do I have to decide now?" I asked. "Decide now?" said Kit. "You're almost into the third trimester."

I was beginning to realize that Kit liked challenges, enjoyed making complicated arrangements, especially when they revolved around me, cutting off my ties to other people, allowing me to escape from my husband. Kit had worked out an elaborate plan that involved referrals, clinics, journeys, convalescence — all resulting in my freedom from everyone and everything except Kit. When I said I wanted to keep the baby, Kit sighed long-sufferingly and said, "Well, this is a whole new problem, isn't it?"

She is a divorcée and everyone wonders about her husband. Rumours get passed around as if she is a mystery woman like Rebecca de Winter. Someone said she was married to an Englishman, very rich, very aristocratic, that he kept her locked up in his castle but she didn't want to be a chatelaine, a lady of the manor, she wanted her own life, she wanted to be educated, and so she fled to the New World. When I asked Sam, he said, No, no, don't believe everything you hear. It was a short marriage, a mistake. She was very young and a Fulbright student came to her university in England, swept her off her feet and brought her out to some boondocks in the Midwest. It is hard to imagine her of all people being swept off her feet, the very idea is laughable, risible she would say in that eccentric way she has of talking, she is a shrewd, calculating, dangerous woman. People always imagine that a woman alone is vulnerable, they feel protective. In her case, it is a delusion, she knows exactly what she wants. I am obsessed with her. I watch her through the window, look at her house when I walk down the street. I hear her voice even when she's nowhere in sight. She's ruining poem after poem for me because even if she hasn't quoted it in her well-modulated voice, I hear it in my head spoken by her. She is there, always the centre of attention, always with a circle of men around her, leaning to catch her every word. If he is not among them, he is looking at her from across the room. She isn't even beautiful — she is ugly — with her lantern jaw, her prominent teeth and owlish glasses. But she talks all the time, her voice is the powerful aphrodisiac. Did Sam say that? I watch and watch. When the party is over, they offer to drive her, escort her to her door. She laughs and strides off alone, her voice floating on the night air as she marches through the fall leaves or the snow. If she walks with us, he goes ahead holding her elbow. She talks and talks. "Monica, are you grieving over goldengrove unleaving? It's like a stage set from Swan Lake." "And who am I?" he says, "Siegfried? Am I effeminate enough?" He pirouettes in the snow because he has had too much to drink and she says, "'Effeminate' now there's a sexist term. Monica and I disapprove of that entirely." The way she talks to me shows she thinks me negligible. When she looks at me a kind of polite glaze covers her entire face and I am invisible to her. Then she looks back at him, alert, her eyes dancing, flirtatious, saying something rude. He can't take his eyes off her.

I put my own picture beside my father's to show Kit, who said, "You look pretty browned off." "Well, wouldn't you?" I said. "In those clothes?" I pointed to my father's elaborate lace collar, to my own dress, painstakingly and lovingly made by my grandmother, that same father's mother. She made both our clothes, a skilled needlewoman. "That's what she'll look like," I said. "Now you stop that," Kit said angrily. "That's the way to drive yourself crazy. You and me both."

The Western Humanities convention in Winnipeg. She's invited to come along with us but accepts instead a ride with another woman in the department, not wanting to be squeezed into our crowded car. She wouldn't be crowded, being offered the front seat beside him. Is it her refusal or our presence that fills him with rage? He is silent and angry, ready to explode at the slightest thing. The chil-

dren in the back seat sense his fury and keep as quiet as little mice, frightened. Perhaps he is thinking how it might have been if just the two of them had driven together, she prefers it this way, not wanting to encourage gossip. It is a long day's drive for the children, they grow restless, begin to squirm, whisper to each other, and finally fall asleep, he says nothing to me the whole journey, watching the road, brooding. When we check in at the Holiday Inn there is the usual poisonous-looking chlorinated pool surrounded with plastic rubber plants, but to children at the end of the long drive it looks magical. They run to it, brightening up, reviving after the gloomy trip. But no, he forbids it, they might catch cold, and swimming in the depths of winter is too risky for children with weak chests, asthma, susceptible to every germ that comes along. Their faces fall, hers back into the mask of sullenness that is becoming permanent. She is a disturbed child, they stand watching the others having fun, her stare remote, unseeing, turned inward. When we are having our supper in the coffee shop, the bitch waves across the room from her noisy table to our silent one, eat up eat up he says. There is a paper in the evening and he goes to it, stays out very late. I drink and drink falling into a stupor from which I stir when he creeps into bed, carrying her smells. Bitch, bitch, I think. I wish she would die, drown in that green pool.

Kit was beginning to find me more trouble than I was worth. No sooner was I extricated from one mess than I got into another. But the sequence was wrong. The second mess happened before the first one, and it wasn't a mess. "You said you wanted your own space," Kit said accusingly. I was too timid to say that Kit had invaded that space so completely that I was unable to breathe, let alone think and much less write. I might as well have stayed married. I thought lovingly of space, with just myself in it and Lucia. Lucia would be in a little wicker cot and I would rock the cot gently with my foot, the two of us, Lucy and Lucia in harmony. There are common rhythms in the bodies of mothers and daughters.

I want so badly to protect the children from everything, the little one is buoyant and cheerful as she goes about her business, the older one is different, withdrawn, she knows something is going on, and why shouldn't she, I'm tense, irritable, I cry a lot he says I'm hysterical, she sees me crying and doesn't say anything but she's upset. He took them over to her house this morning when he went to borrow a book. Everyone borrows Lucy's books, they are what she offers the way other people offer something to eat, something to drink. She is even seducing my children, my little girls, they came back excited, carrying gifts she'd given them. Books, of course, everyone leaves that house carrying books, they are only loans, she doesn't give books, even to children. She wants them back. She has a library of children's books that she uses to lure children into her house. She also gave them coloured stones, the kind you pick up in cheap souvenir shops at resorts, she had them on her desk, they thought they were something special, that she was something special.

At the hospital they knew nothing of me or my husband. It was not the Good Samaritan or any other hospital in Indiana. It was in another state. They expected me to be happy. "A lovely little girl," the nurse said. Perhaps it would have been different if I hadn't seen the baby. Babies don't look like anyone. It was just my imagination. That it looked like my father was nonsense. But if I hadn't seen the baby I wouldn't have imagined the likeness. It was all Kit's fault because it was Kit who made all the arrangements. It would have been different if I hadn't been conscious during the delivery. I should have been anaesthetized, woken up after the baby was taken out. It should have been like having a tooth out, but it was more like having a limb amputated. The phantom limb. Only the child was not a phantom. She existed in the world, growing older each year, becoming a teenager, being exposed to all the dangers of the world, to illness, abuse, to the most terrible accidents, and deprived of the protection of a mother.

Perhaps if we were in a different place he wouldn't be so drawn to her. Perhaps it is partly through the boredom and frustration of living here. But maybe if we lived elsewhere, it would be someone else. The universities are full of women like her. When I was a secretary I watched them as they hung about my desk, bringing me their messy pages to type up and arrange. They were clever and confident but it was me he wanted, he chose me. They don't want to marry and have children, they want their independence. They are whores. There are all these restless men on the prowl so they never lack for companionship, for sex. They have everything they want.

Kit became an albatross around my neck just as my husband had been, as the child would have been. "I love you, Lucy," Kit said. "You'll get over all this and we can make a life together as we planned." But I escaped from Kit's clutches as from a trap. It was a long ungodly struggle to throw off all these ties, but I took comfort in the knowledge that all the efforts would be justified by what I would produce — my work, my teaching, and my writing, which would benefit so many people. Every writer knows her book will change the world.

How can a family be over, like one of those prairie gardens that people plant in the spring and take up in the fall? How can we go off with a nod and a handshake like strangers who have met in a seaside hotel, promising to write and send cards at Christmas? None of it makes sense. How will we tie up the ends? What shall I tell my mother and father? What about his, who are no longer my parents in law or out of law, but still the children's grandparents? Monica you are like the daughter we never had, his mother said. My head spins with confusion. What I fear most is that they will regroup with her in my place because I am the one who caused the disaster — not her, not him, not the blizzard or the snow, but me. I am unable to hold a job or take care of my children because I am a sloven and a drunkard. But he will survive and she will survive and the little girl will survive too, they are survivors all, the older girl and I will drown.

These terrible accidents happen at the crossroads. Oedipus, an irascible man, flew into a temper and killed a stranger. It was a misjudgment and someone should have restrained him. If he had the time to think he would perhaps have acted otherwise and the tragedy would have been averted. Yet already the oracles had spoken, so perhaps nothing was to be done. But I had nine months in which to weigh my decision. Well, not nine because at first the rabbit had not spoken, the annunciation had not been made that I should bear a child and call her name Lucia. But I had six months to think about what I should do. And still when I came to the crossroads, I acted wrongly. Twice in my life I did terrible things. That was the first. I let the child go. The nurse walked away, her heels clicking on the linoleum of the spotless corridor. Then she turned the corner and disappeared and I packed up my things and left.

At first, there was no danger that what I dreaded most might happen, that he might move across the street, that was not part of her plans. It would have caused a scandal, an inconvenience, a threat to her free, independent existence, I know something about her that he let slip out, a man can tell when his lover has borne a child, and he saw she had a baby once. What did she do with it? I asked him, but she hadn't told him that. Perhaps it died, he said, and he looked angry. That was one thing they shared, she didn't want to be caught up in a family and neither did he. His early glee faded and he became sullen again, if it weren't for us, he thought, they might be together, just the two of them, no ties, no obligations, just their books. They might combine libraries, live together, tossing lines of poetry and ideas back and forth, like performing seals tossing coloured balls in a circus.

"It won't be half as bad as you think it's going to be," Kit had said. But Kit was lying. Not lying exactly, but not understanding, not imagining. What does anyone know about giving away a child? It's always a mistake to trust your life to someone else. Anyway, I shed Kit soon afterwards. I thought that by shedding the only witness, I could erase what I had done.

A cab drops me at a house in a rundown neighbourhood near the hospital, it isn't the usual doctor's office in a highrise building with an elevator, it is a white frame, ordinary house and a woman is busy in the kitchen, the place gives us a cloak of secrecy and it makes mad people feel normal, a lot of people crack up in the middle of winter in this climate. I know I am in the right place because the woman directs me into a room with a sign that says waiting room. The doctor's voice is soft and low and he urges me to talk in a way that suggests the visit is casual, he relaxes, takes no notes, but looks at me, watching, noticing. The arm of the chair is threadbare because so many people have plucked at it and pulled on the threads. I have a mug of coffee in one hand and with the other I pluck the arm of the chair. It is frightening alone with him in the room, a cat springs on to my lap and my coffee spills hot on my lap and I start to cry. The things I want to say disappear and other unexpected ideas pop into my head.

I went on moving north and then west and into another country until I reached the prairies where I finally ran out of steam. All the past had now fallen away. But there was one person in the world who knew my secret. This was Kit. When I learned that Kit had died, I rejoiced because the secret died also. Now it belonged only to me. Yet still I was sterile. Even with all the space and time and freedom, the great magnificent work I'd planned for so long refused to come into being.

Now i have yellow pills and when i mix them with wine and whiskey they bring instant happiness nothing matters then not Sam going away not being alone not even the children i see the moon a white shiny circle through the branches of the trees and lie in bed with the curtains drawn back and wait for the trees to be lit up by the passing cars everything is so beautiful i think i will write a poem but when i wake again it is the middle of the day and not so beautiful the poem has disappeared and so the days and nights pass perhaps they will take me to hospital and put me in a white bed and look after me again

There are shameful things in every life. If you put two of them together they seem worse, as if the first happened one day, the second the next. It wasn't like that. They were done by different women in different countries, one young, one not so young. There were extenuating circumstances. I tried not to dwell on these disasters but to go on. I developed powers of self-preservation I had not believed myself capable of. Some would call it ruthlessness. It was painful telling all these intimate things to Simone during those summer afternoons, while she nodded and nodded. I could only guess what she was thinking. When someone promises to make a clean breast of it, something is always left unsaid. So perhaps she was wondering what I was keeping back. Perhaps she was simply thinking, now I know all about Lucy. I know more than the others do. Lucy is now bound to me by this confidence.

XV

"I AM NOT HERE," I thought, "and this is not really me." Either the medication or the barometrical pressure at the end of a hot day made everything surreal. Or maybe Julia had mixed a drink too strong for my weakened condition. She'd said it was mostly tonic water with a whisper of gin, but Julia was careless and might not have thought about the combination of drugs and alcohol. Then there was the sweet, warm smell of the room itself, full of abundant growth — plants everywhere ripening and decaying with the rich fecundity of nature. I closed my eyes, shutting it all out.

It was the last time we came together, the five of us who remained. We met by accident during the summer of my illness. Perhaps I should qualify that. Knowing, as I do now, that many things we assumed to be random were orchestrated by one person, I wonder if this last meeting was contrived. Naturally I've gone over every detail of that evening to see if it contained any clues to what happened afterwards. But at the time, I was not on high alert.

In any case, it seemed fortuitous. Simone said she ran into Julia who said, "Bring Lucy over to see my garden. It'll be good for her to get out. How about tomorrow?" And so we planned to drop by for a drink. Julia had been the chatelaine of Max's house for many years, growing into the role that suited her perfectly. Max was in Ottawa as he usually was during the week.

Just as we were about to set out, who should turn up but Lena. She'd heard about my operation and arrived on my doorstep as if there'd been no rift and she'd been dropping in regularly. Of course she resisted being taken along, but Simone talked her into joining us, saying she'd be interested in the house and that we wouldn't stay long. So she drove down the road and around the corner, parked in front of the house, and waited for us, the same old Lena, sullen and ungracious, in spite of her success.

It was a late summer evening, layered with memories and full of strange vibrations. There was the faint acrid smell of smoke from forest fires in the north. The park was full of people, and merry voices and laughter floated on the air. There were plenty of mosquitoes so we sat on the glass porch. Julia had fixed it up as a conservatory with large potted plants and lush greenery and her trademark white wicker furniture. The same white furniture as before.

At first they focussed on me and the fact that I was refusing the follow-up course of chemotherapy. Simone had mounted a campaign all week to get me to change my mind. She'd explained the benefits and had me read numerous articles, so she was none too pleased when Julia weighed in on my side. She needn't have been annoyed because I'd never for a moment wavered in my decision.

I was a shell of a woman now, a scarecrow in a field of ripe grain. My female organs were gone, and there were two long scars like the sound holes on a cello where my breasts used to be. (Was it Flaubert who spoke of playing a woman like a violin?) My body had delivered me into the hands of the tyrants. But I wasn't ready for complete surrender. I intended to keep my hair and my mind and I refused to let them fry my brains. My last vestiges of power lay in refusal and renunciation — no chemo, no radiation, no tamoxifen, no prosthetic devices. It wasn't vanity that fired my resistance but fear of further indignities — a uniformed official making a pattern of dots on my flesh, swinging a machine over me, setting a timer, and leaving the room while the deadly rays did their work.

I had little fear of death, but I was mortally afraid of what might precede it — of being at the mercy of some authority figure who could decide when I might or might not have my next shot of morphine. I had already decided, when the time came, to take matters into my own hands by following the Hemlock Society's instructions for a quick exit. I'd confided in Julia and she'd promised help if I needed it.

"If Lucy doesn't want to be nuked," Lena said, "that's her own business."

It brought me close to tears that I, so used to directing conversations, was now the subject under discussion, and I wished fervently that I'd stayed home. Finally I put a stop to the debate by saying that I wasn't going to play Camille and I'd be back on my feet in a few weeks. So the focus shifted to their lives and successes.

We were in two different worlds, they and I, for "everyone who is born holds dual citizenship, in the kingdom of the well and the kingdom of the sick." I was a resident alien, a second-class citizen, stripped of my right to vote. From across the frontier, I listened and spied on them.

For the first time, I compared their breasts. Simone from adolescence had the full bosom of a nursing mother; Lena was as flat-chested as a young boy; Julia had delicate breasts that would fit into champagne glasses. That was what we said back when shallow, wide-rimmed glasses were preferred to tulips and it was still acceptable to compare the female body to food and drink.

What were breasts anyway but troublesome appendages, treated as public property or a national resource, to be brought under governmental control? If you don't follow certain guidelines, you deserve what you get. Eating high-fat foods and refusing to breast-feed could lead to cancer — no matter that toxins in the air are concentrated in breast milk and can slow a baby's mental growth.

In school they horrified us with rumours. A member of the lacrosse team from St. Agnes said the nuns told them about a girl whose boyfriend got so excited by petting that he bit her nipple right off. We knew it wasn't true. It was apocryphal, like the myth of bra-burning, but it served its purpose — making us repressed and fearful. Best to be a nun and avoid petting and cervical cancer. But then you'd avoid breastfeeding too, and increase your chances of coming down with breast cancer, so it was hard to know what to do. You could become a wet-nurse and wear a gas mask, but you'd scare the baby to death. The Amazons cauterized their daughters' breasts to prevent them from getting in the way of their bowstrings. There are no cancer statistics available so far on them.

My reverie was ended abruptly by a commotion in the front hall. Suddenly a lock turned, a door slammed, and bags were dumped on the tiled floor. It was Max, who had returned early. We looked at each other in alarm, feeling caught like schoolgirls at a midnight feast, surprised by the housemother's flashlight. Julia looked especially put out, a raw expression of dismay flashing across her face.

Then the three of them sprang back to life and she controlled herself, explaining how it had come about so that he wouldn't think we'd planned a meeting in his absence. What went through his mind I can only guess. He didn't explain his own arrival, and I wondered if he liked to keep his comings and goings unaccounted for, even to Julia. It seemed to me that the normal thing to do would be to pick up a phone before leaving Ottawa, or at least from the airport.

Anyway, we all recovered and he rubbed his hands and started to play the genial host. This gathering calls for champagne! Had we been offered any? And Julia rose to the occasion, matching his performance in a perfect duet. She updated him on our various activities, as the wife of an absent-minded politician might prompt her husband when he meets his constituents.

"Isn't Lucy looking well?" she said, and he seemed momentarily confused. I couldn't believe he needed reminding that I'd recently had major surgery, and wondered if he was shocked, seeing my deflated chest, flat as the prairie landscape. I didn't want my health discussed again, and I was relieved when the conversation turned to Lena and Simone, those beings who had come down among us from Mount Olympus.

He wanted to know first about Simone's life. He was curious, he said, not just as a friend, but as a government official seeking precise information. She told him in great detail and promised to let him have complete documentation of the project she was involved in. This was the first time I realized that her present work might be a mere stepping stone to something more important. If she had political ambitions, she'd know that no one could be more helpful to her than Max. When her work was finally exhausted as a topic, he turned to Lena.

We all knew about Lena's life. You couldn't pass a bookstore or take a flight without seeing stacks of her novel in the shop windows. I'd never quite got used to its strange cover. From a distance it looked like a pickle jar on a kitchen window-sill, its contents catching the sunbeams. When you looked closer, it was less cozily domestic — a specimen jar in which a snail-nosed human embryo, preserved in formaldehyde, mooned and glowed.

His remarks to Lena struck me as offensive and condescending. How does it feel? You've come a long way since, etc. He said he'd noticed her car outside the house, a lot different from the old broken-down Volkswagen she used to drive.

"I live in the country so I need a good car," she said.

"I'm very much looking forward to reading the book," he said. "I've heard a great deal about it from Julia, but my time hasn't been my own lately."

"Naturally," said Lena in a dangerously sarcastic tone.

In spite of his evident weariness after a long flight, he dominated the conversation like a principal at a class reunion. And when he ran out of questions, he allowed us to inquire politely about his life.

"Not much new," he said. "As you see, business as usual."

Like Lena's, his life was so well covered by the media that anyone who was half-awake and able to read the newspapers would know all about him. He hadn't had to go to Africa to get a reputation. And he wasn't famous for a mere work of fiction on a subject that coincided with a trendy interest in recovered memory. His work was much more important, coming as it did under the rubric Public Service. It was crucial to the national interest and involved tight security, all-night sittings in the Senate sometimes, knowing about all the current legislation, and so on. With his air of complete confidence and invulnerability, he seemed to have reverted to his younger self.

Once, long before I'd cooked his dinner, long before his captivity, I'd had a professional consultation with Max. I was under siege at the university. Besides the graffiti and the jokes in the student newspaper about a certain female prof giving an A for a lay, I'd been receiving anonymous letters. These materialized in my office mailbox, and it was clear they were written by someone who was watching me constantly and who knew every detail of my daily routine. Neither my department head nor the dean were inclined to take these letters seriously. (I have to admit I balked at showing them the actual letters and only described them.) But they knew about Sam and me, and they probably thought that anyone who led such an irregular life should expect unpleasant consequences. It was Julia who suggested I see Max Hoffman.

"He's the last person to be sympathetic," I said.

"He's a lawyer," she said. "He's into clients and fees, not sympathy and causes."

"I couldn't afford the fees," I said.

"If he takes on a case," she said, "it's because he knows he can win and neither of you would be out of pocket."

She convinced me that I had nothing to lose, and I guess I was desperate enough to make an appointment. It was a totally humiliating experience, going to his office. He was ensconced behind a large executive desk, with his diplomas and a glamorous studio portrait of his wife prominently on display — visible proof of his personal and professional success. The whole *mise en scène* was calculated to reduce the client to the status of supplicant.

"What should I call you?" he asked, with a tinge of mockery in his voice. "Professor? Doctor? Ms.?"

"Whatever you wish," I said. "What should I call you? Doctor? Sir? Mr.?"

He didn't just look over the letters, but he read bits of them aloud. Naturally they sounded ridiculous.

Dearest Lucy,

    I have been watching you for some time now. I sometimes go up to the fourth floor of the Humanities Building and watch you below drinking coffee and conversing with others. It distresses me greatly that it is not me sitting across from you but some Shakespeare wimp. Due to an overwhelming urge I have to tie you to my bed and smother you in chocolate, I remain permanently frustrated.

At night I stand under a tree on the street and look up at your lighted window. Yes, I know that you have a lover but what is that these days. It's been reduced to promiscuity and dissatisfaction, come on, admit it, what you need is a change. One round with my whips and leathers will make you feel like a new woman.

On and on he went, reading out more and more sordid details of someone's crazy erotic fantasy. Finally he broke off, laughing. And then, leaning across his desk, he said, "Come along, dear lady, this is a student prank. It's a joke."

"I'm not your dear lady," I said, feverish with embarrassment.

"No indeed," he said, "and I can assure you, you won't be anyone else's if you don't develop a sense of humour."

"But I'm frightened," I said, "it sounds sick, and whoever wrote it could be some dangerous psychopath."

"I remember that kind of thing from my student days. Letters being sent to uppity girls. Jokes cooked up over beer in the fraternity house. My advice to you, Professor, is to ignore it. If more letters arrive, leave them unopened in your mailbox, go about your work as usual. I guarantee that will be the end of it." Somewhere during our exchange he managed to hit me with the word "hysterical," that ugly knot in the cave man's club. I was to try not to be hysterical about being stalked.

Perhaps he wanted to make amends and keep on friendly terms, because he sobered up quickly from his little bout of merriment, saw me to the elevator, and patted me paternally on the arm. He never sent me a bill for the consultation. I couldn't decide whether to be offended or grateful for that.

And, in fact, nothing happened, so perhaps he was right in assuming it was a joke. The letters stopped, the writer probably grew tired of the fun, and the exercise in intimidation was over. I wasn't attacked, but it was harassment all the same. We didn't name it back then, and there was no committee to appeal to. I no longer worked in my office in the evenings and on the weekends. I was too scared. Every footfall in the corridor outside my door gave me a fright.

Eventually I got to know Max better and stopped hating him. He became a different Max, no longer arrogant. But that summer evening at his house, seeing him restored to his smug and successful self, I began to hate him all over again.

They say that the angry ones are the ones who survive. Maybe that's true, for I was consumed with rage. I thought, you're all so alive and brilliant, but I could survive the lot of you. I might have the last word yet. Three of them were famous, they'd made their mark on the world, done something heroic, and here was I fading mutely into oblivion, being treated with benign condescension, like a quaint grandmother cherished for what she once was.

It wasn't just the illness. That was merely the outer manifestation of my inner obsolescence. My time had passed, my ideas were outdated, and I'd now become a dinosaur, like those gentlemen-scholars of the old school. The three of them had ridden the tide, but I'd been drowned by the cresting wave. I belonged to another era, all the theories and beliefs that fuelled my work had been superceded by new ones. And I saw now that all our efforts had failed. We'd tried to change the institution in which we worked, but it was still the same old oppressive feudal system, and we'd succeeded only in replacing one power structure with another.

Perhaps something similar had been stirred up in Lena by Max's smugness because she abruptly changed the congratulatory tenor of the conversation by throwing down a gauntlet of her own.

"That was very convenient for you, Max," she said, "the Tyler case coming along when it did."

"Convenient?" he said urbanely. "Tyler cases had been coming across my desk for years. There was no bolt-out-of-the-blue about that coming along when it did. I didn't plan the case and I certainly didn't plan the fall-out."

"Come on, Max," she said, "that's not true. How many cases of women killing their own kids have you had in your life?"

"Well, no two cases are exactly the same. But I've had numerous cases of women in trouble, abused women, farm wives deprived of a livelihood when the marriage ends, and so on. I championed those women for years before the Tyler case came up."

"And turned a nice little profit along the way."

"Not always. In certain cases I waived or reduced the fee."

"And you championed a few men too along the way."

"They were entitled to a defence too, Lena."

"And none brought you the glory of the Tyler case, did it?"

"The result there was not of my making. I took the case in good conscience. Perhaps my younger self wouldn't have handled it quite the way I did. We all learn from our experiences."

"You didn't calculate on being hailed as a hero? A saviour of womankind? A defender of beleaguered women? Come on, Max, I saw one of your news conferences. 'It wasn't easy to overturn the convictions of a lifetime, to say I was wrong about everything I grew up believing.'"

"It wasn't, you know."

"How is that you managed to turn everything to your own advantage? There are women who've been working behind the scenes or on the barricades for years, and you come along, take a stand, and suddenly you're the champion of the oppressed, the authority on the subject, the high-profile, well-paid consultant."

"A convert is always more interesting than a lifelong believer, Lena. Tyler was a flamboyantly beautiful woman and that got a lot of media attention. These cases do, inevitably."

"That peroration you made . . ."

He began to look flustered by this time. If, for one second when he'd walked in on us, he'd seen his worst nightmare materialize, that premonition had been fulfilled. Lena turned to the rest of us.

"You won't believe this. The other day in a bookstore I picked up a book of great speeches. And guess what was in it? Mark Antony's funeral oration, Oscar Wilde's 'The Love that dare not speak its name,' Martin Luther King's 'I have a dream,' John Kennedy's Inaugural address, and, as a nod to Canadian content, Max Hoffman's defence of Samantha Tyler."

"It was a good speech," Julia said.

"I've always thought Sorensen made Kennedy's speech too contrived, too eighteenth century," I said in a weak attempt to change the subject. I was ignored.

"I puked when I saw that," Lena said. "This from someone who once said it would be more accurate to speak of 'unwanting' or 'rejecting' mothers than unwanted children. 'Women are requesting therapeutic abortions because their child represents an inconvenience or a nuisance.' You can't get more 'unwanting' than Samantha Tyler."

"I would think you might take a modicum of credit for that particular speech," Max said, addressing Lena very reasonably.

"How so?"

"You were the one who was always reversing sex roles and situations and coming up with clever little anecdotes about violinists and so forth. I took it all to heart, Lena, and when the time came, I used it."

"And when that reporter pressed you on the subject, you made a clever little joke. 'Maybe in a previous incarnation I bore a child,' you said."

"It was an injudicious remark I came to regret."

"You know what I'd like. I'd like to pick up a magazine and see a picture of you on the cover and a spread of pictures of you inside — all in your maternal guise — under the caption 'In A Previous

Incarnation I Bore A Child.' They'd have a field day with you, Max. They'd crucify you."

All this was said so vehemently that it shocked us into silence. Except Max, who had blanched a little but made a quick recovery. He had tremendous self-control. I suppose bombshells in the courtroom were nothing new to him and he was trained to look undaunted in the face of new evidence.

"Faked and contrived photographs appear in the tabloids by the dozen these days," he said lightly. "No one takes them seriously. And if that's a veiled threat of blackmail you're making, it's a criminal offence," he added.

It sounded eerily familiar. We'd fallen right back into our former roles. Lena hostile and aggressive, Julia vaguely alarmed, and Max on the defensive. I expected Simone to step forward, take charge, and tell Lena to shut up. Then Lena had a sudden change of heart. Either she bethought herself that attacking Max could rebound, or she lost interest.

"Lucy's totally exhausted," she said. "I'll take her home." Everyone got up, relieved to have the confrontation over. We said hasty good-byes and left. It was true that I was too tired to walk back to my house. Even going out to the car I leaned heavily on Lena's arm. She parked at the curb in front of my house and helped me up the path and inside.

"Can I come in, Lucy? There's something I want to ask you."

I thought for a moment she was going to ask if she could stay overnight, but she simply settled me on the couch and sat down beside me.

"If you survive me, Lucy, will you take charge of my books and papers?"

"If I survive you!" I said incredulously. "Just look at us." It was patently absurd because Lena, with her figure of a stripling, looked even younger than she was, and I . . . "I have one foot in the grave."

"Simone says you're going to be O.K.," she said.

"It would make more sense for me to be asking you," I said.

"Well, let's make a pact then. Whoever survives. It'll make me feel better to know you'll take care of everything if something happens. I've got these forms. All you have to do is put your name here."

She fished out a pen, and being too tired to protest or even read what I was signing, I wrote my name and she wrote hers and that was it. It seemed so ridiculous and I just wanted to put my head down and fall asleep. I guess fortunes have been lost in exactly the same way. She put the papers in her bag, looking relieved and pleased.

"Now can I get you anything or help you to bed?" she said.

"I'm going to rest here for a while," I said. I stretched out as I often did on the sofa. She pulled my plaid rug over me, tucking me in as if I were a child.

"Lucy," she said, "you will have the treatment, won't you?"

Those were her last words to me, that evening and ever.

When I woke up it was morning, the sun was pouring in the window, I was alone, and I felt nauseous and hung over. Then an alarming thought occurred to me. I might have made Lena heir to everything I possessed. The first thing I had to do, when Simone came in, was get her to help me make another will.

XVI

THEN THERE WERE just the two of us, Julia and I, neither of us in very good shape. Julia had lost one lung, but she was still smoking as heavily as ever. She was beautiful now in a different way — her long hair streaked grey and white, and the lines and wrinkles giving her face more character.

I had to do some preliminary sorting of Lena's papers, for I'd become her literary executor, having committed myself to the job that evening when I was too tired and ill to know what I was doing.

It seemed to follow naturally that I would write the story of her life. Someone would do it — her murder ensured that, as much as her novel — and I couldn't bear the thought of anyone else going through her papers. Also, the prospect of another biographer producing a big florid tome aroused my professional jealousy. I was no longer capable of a definitive scholarly work, but I could manage something between a memoir and a biography. An editor from a small press had approached me with a suggestion for a short book with plenty of photographs. I would have *carte blanche* to do exactly as I liked. There would be no hard and fast deadline, my reputation was not at stake, and I felt no compulsion to write an exhaustive account.

So the project suited me perfectly. It gave me the illusion of being employed instead of sidelined, as I'd been for too long. The university librarian offered to set aside a small office for me and I was delighted to be returning to work.

But before I began I had to go through the papers, separating what I needed immediately from the material destined for the archives. Nothing had been removed from the studio where Lena had lived in seclusion during the years she worked on her book. After the shooting, the police had sealed off the whole place, but now the investigation was concluded we had permission to go in and retrieve what we wanted. When I was finished my sorting, the archivist would go out with a van, box the rest of the stuff, bring it back, and catalogue it. She was more of a professional associate than a friend, and I'd turned down her offer to drive me out there. I knew that going into Lena's place would be disturbing. I certainly didn't want to go alone, and Julia, weak as she was, was the only person I trusted to go along with me.

She agreed, on condition we didn't set a specific day. She had bad days and good days and wanted to be able to decide the same morning when we would go. I was quite willing to be flexible and we left it at that. It would be a long drive to the southwest corner of the province, but I thought I could find what I wanted in a few hours. I said we should take a lunch, stay at the house all afternoon, drive to the nearest town for dinner, and spend the night in one of the motels along the highway.

All this was decided, and then for a long time nothing happened. I began to suspect we would never make the trip, that Julia would never have another good day, and that I'd end up making another arrangement. I was just wondering about getting a student to drive me out when early one morning Julia called. "I'm O.K. today," she said. "Can you be ready in an hour?"

I hadn't realized that she had so many bad days, but she seemed fine when she arrived at my door. Not only that, but it was a lovely spring morning with a slight wind blowing over the prairies, an uncertain wavery sun in the sky, and the smell of streams running again.

"Dressed for a day in the country, are we?" she said, in that amused way she had of appraising my outfits. She opened the trunk and I stowed the two large canvas bags I was bringing. "That's some lunch you have there," she said. Since I was at the point of giving up on our excursion altogether, I hadn't anything in my fridge for lunch and we had to stop along the way and buy provisions. The bags, I told her, were for carrying stuff back.

"So this is an illegal operation," she said. "You scared of what you might find?"

"You bet I am," I said.

"Must have been hell for you waiting this long to get out there."

"I kept having dreams about a fire."

"Nightmares?"

"No, just the opposite," I said, for I remembered the shock of reading Monica's diary. I had no reason to think that Lena's would be any less devastating, because she knew me better.

We stopped for coffee mid-morning, parking under the trees of a small town off the highway to share a thermos. We were both thinking about Lena's death.

"Any word about the investigation?" Julia asked.

"Not that I know of. I thought you'd hear more about it than I." I assumed that through Max she had contact with some of the bigwigs on the police force.

"What about your own theories?"

"Well, there's no shortage of suspects. Or motives," I said.

"Right," said Julia. "I was often tempted to wring her neck myself. And then the book's full of clues — all those lovers she dumped. Who would have thought our Lena was a *femme fatale*?"

"It was a novel, Julia. That part was pure fiction."

"Some of it surely was. Like the physical attractiveness of her heroine. Or maybe that's how she saw herself."

"A mere convention of fiction, the beautiful heroine," I said.

"So you think that part's fiction, and yet you accept the terrible childhood and the sexual abuse as something that really happened to her?"

"That's not unusual, Julia. That's what fiction is — imaginary gardens with real toads in them."

"And you have absolute confidence in your ability to separate the real toads from all the other creatures in the imaginary gardens?"

"Max couldn't have had anything to do with it could he?" I asked, changing the subject. I couldn't really imagine Max, even before his recent decline, getting involved in murder.

"In the shape he's in?" she said.

"He has lucid moments, doesn't he?"

"Not that lucid, and not that often."

"Anyway, I didn't mean actually do it himself. But arrange it."

"With what motivation exactly?"

"I should have thought that was obvious. You remember how she threatened him with photographs that night."

"Could it have been suicide, do you think?"

"It's not been ruled out, but it seems highly unlikely to me that someone dropped by afterwards and stole the gun. Besides, suicides usually leave notes, as Jinny did."

"I didn't know Jinny left a note. You never told me that."

"I didn't tell anyone. I don't think about it very often. I can't afford to."

"Poor Lucy. What did it say?"

"The kind of thing that children say to their parents, that they've ruined their lives and so on."

"Could have been some drug deal gone wrong."

"Lena wasn't into that," I said sharply.

"Oh no? You heard her — sniff, sniff, sniff all the time like a rabbit."

"Allergies, she suffered from allergies. That's why her skin was so sallow."

We'd gone over, through, and around this subject of whether Lena had a drug habit many times before, and on this day I didn't want to risk bringing on a coughing fit, so I let the matter drop. But all these ideas floated in the air like the clouds of Julia's cigarette smoke — who could have done it, what would we find when we walked in, and most of all, what would I find when I started to go through the papers?

It was early afternoon by the time we reached our destination. It was a wooden shack at the end of a gravel road that dwindled into a dirt road and finally into overgrown track, chosen, I suppose because it was the farthest Lena could get from civilization. It had belonged to what was originally a small farm, but the land had been incorporated into a larger one, and most of the buildings left to fall into decay. The old farmhouse was a ruin, but the stable or cattle-shed had been taken over by an artist and converted into a studio. Lena had found it and moved in, using the lower floor as a workroom and the small loft as her bedroom.

When you enter a room where violence has taken place, you expect to be shocked by something unspeakable. Not long ago there must have been blood everywhere, but when we walked in, there was nothing to suggest a crime scene. The police or someone else had cleaned up and there was only the musty smell of an enclosed space full of books.

We stood together in the doorway, looking around. The only morbid touches were the objects that decorated the walls — skulls of cows and sheep, curious hornets' or wasps' nests, and amputated limbs sculpted out of papier-mâché. I don't know whether they were Lena's ornaments or those of the previous tenant. Our eyes moved about the room, taking everything in. It could have been cozy if it had been fixed up properly.

"All that money she got from the book," Julia said, "what happened to it?"

"It was left to a sister," I said.

"She had a sister?"

"Not that kind of sister, a nun."

"She didn't get religion did she?"

"Not as far as I know. I believe this was a teaching sister who'd written something about the book."

At the far end, where there had been a feeding trough or

manger, there was a rudimentary kitchen with an iron stove. The floor was badly stained, but the stains might have been spilled coffee or soup rather than Lena's lifeblood. I opened two of the windows and we stood breathing the spring air and looking out across at the fields. Two dark figures carrying hunting rifles appeared over a rise on the horizon and disappeared again behind a stand of trees. I remembered reading somewhere that the land was part of a Hutterite colony.

"Well, not so bad," Julia said.

"No."

"So you may as well start."

It didn't take much of an inspection to find what I was looking for. They were on one of the bookshelves, their spiral spines neatly aligned, just fitting into the shelf space. On the cover of each was the date, and a quick check showed that she had filled two or three a year, going back for some years.

Seeing them all before me brought back a familiar sensation. There was a time in my life when I travelled long distances to work for a week or two in university libraries. Often they were in southern climates and the air would be heavy with the scent of blossoms. It was ceremonious — signing in, carrying the approved materials, pencils, five-by-eight cards. And the moment when the archivist or librarian set before me a great box of letters was a moment of almost erotic excitement. You never knew what secret you might find hidden in some letter, the key that might open up a whole life. On the other hand, you might find some detail that would reverse all the theories you'd developed so far and undermine the whole project. It was habit, the rush at seeing those rows of spiral notebooks, and it was mixed with fear this time.

Now I see myself as I was at that moment, in the stable, Julia lounging on a day bed, coughing and coughing as the dust from the books filled her lungs. From time to time the coughing stopped and I knew that she'd dozed off. And then it would start again and I'd turn and see her leaning forward to light another of those long brown cigarettes, and she'd lie back wreathed in smoke. Or, oddly in the circumstances, she'd pull out a long tube of lipstick and apply it.

There was plenty of reason for me to be nervous — what Lena might have written about the Max affair, and what she might have written about me. Also, any information about her enemies could put me in a dangerous position. So there were all these floating concerns and the problem of where to start in on the diaries — with the early ones, the middle ones, or with the last ones. It would be possible to remove and dispose of some of the pages and perhaps even some of the books, but not many, for the bookshelves would have been carefully photographed, along with everything else in the place. The pages of the notebooks were numbered, so tampering with them was likely to be noticed later.

Then there was her novel. I had assumed that the trauma of her main character was based on her own childhood experience, and I was confident in my ability to distinguish felt experience in fictional works. All the same, I couldn't completely suppress the few teasing doubts thrown up by Julia or by my own imagination. Suppose I found out that Lena had an idyllic childhood, in a big warm happy family, the brothers and sister gambolling happy as puppies among the haystacks and orchards of a prosperous dairy farm? That would torpedo the biography I had in mind.

What I remember best is the conversation I had with Julia when I took a break in the late afternoon. She'd poked around and unearthed a cache of blackberry wine. She was drinking a lot of red wine to soothe her throat. So we were drinking Lena's wine and eating the food from the deli. All the leftovers would go into the bag to be burnt later with the pages I'd ripped out of the notebooks.

Maybe I'd mentioned that the shock of reading Monica's diary made me nervous about Lena's, and that's how we got on to a subject we'd never broached before — what had gone on between Max and Julia in that upper room. Julia hadn't eaten much, but then she never did. She was stretched out on the day bed, her wine and her ashtray beside her. When I told her what Monica had overheard, she swung her legs around, sat up and looked at me incredulously, and said "Lucy! You didn't believe that?"

"Why wouldn't I believe it?" I said. "She was right in everything she said about Sam and me."

"Was she? Well, maybe that fit into what she expected. The eternal triangle sort of thing. Anyway, you can't be sure she got it right. You've always been crazed with guilt on that subject. But it certainly wasn't the usual sort of thing with Max and me."

"But the stuff she wrote down that she overheard?" I quoted from memory some of those phrases that had embedded themselves in my mind.

Julia laughed until she brought on a coughing fit, and when it passed she looked at me soberly. "Lucy, that's pure Harlequin romance. That just wasn't Max. I'm amazed you'd even think it was for a moment. Max is the most . . . well . . . he didn't talk like that, as you know. Monica was totally out of it, don't you remember?"

"But she was intelligent. Or had been before she lost it completely."

"Through no fault of yours, Lucy. The trouble is you've always been irrational about the Werners, all of them. You simply can't get it through your head that what happened was inevitable. Given Monica's mental state and that Casanova . . . "

"He was the love of my life, Julia."

"Oh, he was a charmer alright."

There was something about the way she said it that made me look at her sharply. "Why that sly smile? You didn't know him all that well, did you?"

"No, no, relax, Lucy," she said, "it was only a one-night thing."

I'd thought I wasn't beautiful enough to keep him, and now I saw I hadn't really ever had him. He was just Julia's cast-off. If she'd been interested in him, I wouldn't have stood a chance.

"Don't you remember Mrs. Pike?" she said.

"Of course. Mrs. Pike and her two daughters."

"You weren't in a position to know this, but Mrs. Pike was not overly conscientious about cleaning up the house. Oh, she brought things for Monica to eat and looked after her, and they really got along well, but what they were doing most of the time was watching the soaps. And I'd say that's where most of what she wrote about Max and me came from. As did her name for the baby."

"Desirée. I thought at the time it was . . . "

"There you are. What Monica always did was weave romantic stories around people. Don't you remember those piles of clippings from supermarket tabloids?"

"I didn't think they were *romantic* stories. Weren't they all about house fires and death and disaster? Hadn't she published a prize-winning collection of short stories at one time? I thought she was talented."

"At one time she may have been. Well, fairly. I've read that book of stories. They were over-written and they all had these melodramatic plots. Not quite bodice-rippers, but not far from it."

"So there was nothing between you and Max?"

"Oh there was something alright. But it wasn't that and it's a long, complicated story."

"There's something I've always wondered about," I said. "Did he have stretch marks?"

"Good old prurient Lucy," she said.

"Not prurient," I said, "just curious. It's a legitimate question. 'The indelible stigmata of motherhood.'"

It actually wasn't something I'd always wondered about, but something I had just thought about. The phrase came from a page I'd torn out of the last notebook I'd read. A repulsive description of myself with no clothes on.

"There was a scar alright," she said. "As for stretch marks, I don't think so."

And then for some reason, smoking and coughing in a musty old stable in the middle of fields being prepared for spring planting, Julia started telling me about Max. And inevitably about her own life, which she divided into two parts — a.m. and p.m., before Max and after Max. And in spite of the magnitude of the task at hand, I sat down and listened.

It's a family story that starts with the arrival of a cherished first-born, the son and heir. The event is greeted with huge delight and relief because it's his destiny to carry all the hopes for the first generation in the new land. He won't be an alien, speaking a foreign tongue, but a real native-born Canadian. He'll redeem or increase the family fortunes, perpetuate the family name, extend the dynasty. Since he's the bearer of the family hopes, everything is lavished upon him — attention, admiration, praise, love, the best that money can buy in the way of education. It's a situation that carries the seeds of disaster, likely to produce a spoiled and pampered brat who turns out badly. But actually he fulfills expectations and grows up brilliant and charming. I was thinking while Julia lit up again that, yes, I could see Max in all this, knew it all from the interview I'd done.

The seeds of disaster are elsewhere and otherwise. There's a second child, a girl. It was natural to want the second child to be a girl, a companion for the mother, someone to look after the parents in their old age. Naturally, she won't make a name for herself or even perpetuate the family name, but she'll be decorative, musical, play the piano or sing delightfully. She'll marry well and bring a fine son-in-law into the family, fine grandchildren to fill out the family portraits.

Even if she isn't sweet-tempered, gifted, and decorative, things can be arranged within the community. She can still make an advantageous marriage and provide a full quota of children. And even if the marriage isn't exactly advantageous, nor exactly happy, that too can be arranged. It can be propped up with money and influence, the errant husband brought back into the fold and set on his feet again.

As it happened, it turned out worse than anyone could have imagined. By some medical misstep or accident of genetic development she was born brain-damaged, a severe and irremediable case requiring one surgical procedure after another. Incontinent, arrested at the age of three, requiring perpetual care for life. In a more enlightened time her condition would have resulted in a malpractice suit, but it was interpreted as an act of God, considered a sign of bad blood, of the sins of the father being visited upon the children even unto the third and fourth generation.

Family life ended with that birth. Afterwards, the home was a garrison that nobody entered apart from close relatives or hired help. The parents moved into separate bedrooms, the father and Max sharing one, the mother and the daughter another. The mother withdrew from all social contact except for necessary shopping excursions and religious observances. And the burden for Max to succeed increased a hundredfold. His slight frame bore all the weight of the family's self-respect, all the responsibility for redeeming the father's shame.

"What was her name?"

"Whose?"

"The sister's?"

"Esther, why do you ask?"

Even after he went to college and out into the world, he couldn't shed the home. If he made friends, he couldn't invite them to meet his family. And it was understood that the sister would pass into his care when the parents, already middle-aged when she was born, could no longer care for her. So his choice of wife was limited for that and another reason. Julia paused and swallowed, as if weighing what to say next.

"Another reason?" I said.

"He wasn't the ideal sexual partner..."

"For a woman?" I said.

"No it wasn't that."

"He didn't dress up in women's clothes and paint his face did he?" I said, remembering Julia's speculations about Simone's father.

"No. He wasn't Wally," she said, laughing. "There were just physical problems."

I nodded, understanding that dysfunction was plausible under the circumstances, and thinking of the biblical connotations of the verb "to know." How accurate they are, because you never really know people or guess their vulnerabilities until you know them sexually.

"Francine was a cousin and came with enough baggage of her own to make marrying Max the best she could hope for. He'd be a good provider, even if being provided for came at a high price. And so, in a small family ceremony, the sad little wedding took place."

"A marriage of convenience!" I said.

"Most marriages are marriages of convenience," Julia said, quoting myself back at me. "And then, just as they'd worked out a *modus vivendi*, the impetus for the marriage was removed."

"She died?"

"No, she didn't die. The parents did though, and that freed Max from any need to provide a home for the sister. He placed her in an institution in California. She didn't know where she was anyway."

It was the stock excuse of everyone who puts away a child or an elderly parent. I was tempted to challenge it, but I kept my questions for later, reluctant to interrupt the flow of Julia's story.

"Francine offered to release him, but he wouldn't hear of it. He'd been brought up to disapprove of divorce, as well as drinking, smoking, gambling, fiction, and almost every other human activity except breathing. Most of those interdictions gradually slipped away."

"Except the ones that ruled female behaviour," I said.

I'd always thought it out of character for Julia to latch on to someone simply for the material benefits, and I wondered now if she'd felt sorry for him, or guilty. Then again, guilt wasn't prominent in Julia's repertoire of active responses.

"He was a good man," she said, "kind and generous."

"So we picked the wrong person," I said.

"We couldn't have picked anyone who'd had a more difficult or tormented life."

"Did you try to atone for getting him involved with us?" I said.

"It was you who got him involved."

"But you suggested him in the first place."

"No, Lucy," she said. "I brought up his name, but it was Simone who planted the idea in my head."

Yes, it would have been, I thought. I should have realized that.

Then Julia talked about Max and herself. How for most of us there's one thing loved above everything else — one dog, one city, one house, one human being. "When he got to the end of the road, so did I."

It wasn't Max's getting to the end of the road that started your decline, I thought, it was those damn cigarettes. It's a wonder they didn't catch up with you sooner. But I let Julia go on in this tranced way.

"You never believed in marriage, and perhaps you were right not to. Well, we never married, weren't able to. You said once that every marriage becomes a *folie à deux*. We didn't come together when we were young and full of dreams, and cling together when those dreams turned into nightmares. But it was a kind of marriage, all the same, of true minds. We'd been part of each other's nightmares.

"You thought, as everyone did, that I had a whole raft of lovers. It was a picture of me you all cherished because it fitted some idea of glamour you had. I remember you examining that old photograph of me ridiculously dressed up as a courtesan for a costume ball. You borrowed that picture, by the way, and never returned it. Why did you want it, Lucy? Because it fitted the image you had of me? You and all your talk about stereotypes!

"Well, I wasn't a latter-day courtesan. I had one lover for a very long time, an old high-school sweetheart. And when you and Simone commandeered my house and my life, I had to let him go. I didn't resent it at the time. I'd known that it had to end, because the other life he had elsewhere was making stronger claims and he couldn't extricate himself from it. And so I made the best of it and thought that at the end of those months I'd emerge healed and whole-hearted. I was grieving, and into the void came Max.

"We shared ideas. That was something you craved, wasn't it, Lucy? Sam and you, working together, reading what each other wrote, talking about it endlessly over drinks, over the dinner table, forging a partnership.

"We often worked together on his speeches, I lying on the couch by the fire, like the courtesan in the photograph. He wrote at his desk, reading paragraphs aloud, adding sentences that I tossed out to him, striding across the room with pages for me to read. Often when a speech was finished I'd feel it was more mine than his. And when he was very busy, I'd sit at the desk and rough out the whole thing. As a boy he'd dreamed of being a great orator and moving people to tears or to action. He kept that dream long after the scope or need for oratory was gone. And I helped him fulfill that dream."

"You wrote the Tyler speech, didn't you?" I said.

It was so obvious, the astonishing thing was that I'd never thought of it before. That was Max's secret, far more incriminating than any photos that might have been taken when he was pregnant. No wonder he was tense when he saw us all together. I'd said that speech sounded like something one of us might have written. Well, one of us had. Julia — who teased me by quoting my words back to me. Julia, who was so casual about her property, intellectual and otherwise. Julia, the only one who would expect nothing in return and have so little concern about honesty that he'd never feel like a fraud, never even think about it. Who even now didn't understand the enormity of what she'd just told me. Who was thinking that helping some man to achieve great things was my idea of personal satisfaction. Who was thinking "poor Lucy."

"I've been lucky," she said.

And not because I thought so, but because it was what she

wanted to hear, I agreed with her that she had been very lucky, that she'd had more out of life than most of us could ever hope for.

By the time she finished talking it was late, and I hadn't made any further progress with the sorting. We had food and wine, and Julia had enough cigarettes, and so we decided to stay where we were and settle in for the night.

Something seemed to be required in return for what she'd told me, and I might have spoken about my own life. Instead, I told her what Renny had found out about Simone. Worn out by coughing, she fell into a sound sleep on the day bed long before I'd finished. I brought a large Hudson's Bay blanket that I'd seen on Lena's bed, folded it into four pieces, and covered her with it, as Lena had often covered me up. It was a surprisingly tender gesture, coming from her. Then I climbed up the ladder into the loft and stretched out on the pallet.

I lay awake, looking at the stars through a skylight and dwelling on what Julia had told me. I thought that even though she'd scoffed at Monica's description and called it a Harlequin romance, Monica hadn't been far off the mark when she wrote about Julia and Max; nor had I been all that gullible in taking Monica's words at face value. In the morning I intended to ask Julia a lot of questions. Among them, how much of Max's true feelings and convictions, if any, went into the Tyler speech.

I suppose I was trying to keep myself from thinking about Lena, all those spiral notebooks, and — most of all — her terrible death in the room below where I was lying.

XVII

THE FIRST TIME I saw Lena she was a blurry presence in the back of the classroom. The class was The Art of Conversation. I know, I know, it sounds absurd. Although I offered it only once, people asked me for years afterwards, "Are you still teaching Conversation 101?" It was a joke, of course, but originally it was one of my own making.

I thought the whole Department of Extension — that supposed bridge between the university and the community — was a joke. Mickey Mouse courses, taught by unqualified people, under the aegis of an incompetent dean. I was drawn in against my will because whenever I proposed a course on women writers my department head, a gentleman of the old school, skilled in masking condescension with courtesy, had the same reaction. He went through the motions of considering the proposal judiciously and then advised me to offer it through Extension. That put me in a bind. Either I colluded in marginalizing my subject or I didn't offer it and denied it to those who might profit from it. So I capitulated. I was on the roster of Extension teachers so often that I qualified every year for the Dean's embossed Christmas card.

Unexpectedly, I grew to enjoy the non-credit courses. I liked the freedom from grading, the relaxed Sunday afternoon atmosphere, and above all the motley group of students they attracted. There were committed feminists, senior citizens, recent immigrants trying to improve their language skills and unconcerned about the subject matter, people wanting a taste of university, and lonely souls who treated it as a singles club. Soon I threw myself into the task of thinking up courses for the smorgasbord.

I was complaining in the hallway one day about a party where banalities were recycled like bad air in a jumbo jet. I remarked casually that a course in the art of conversation was sorely needed. The walls had ears in that place, and my remark was relayed to the Dean. The next thing I knew I opened the local paper and saw a huge advertisement for the course. Before I could object, the Dean was on the phone telling me that enrollment was high, the class was the most popular of the spring offerings, and he'd had to turn several people away.

The group — so enthusiastic that I felt ashamed at having dreamed up the course so frivolously — included members of the Toastmistress club, two Shriners and a Rotarian, three students from Hong Kong, one from Quebec, Tiam from the People's Republic of China, and Lena.

When she responded to the roll call, her gruff voice with the timbre of a non-English speaker was already familiar. She'd called to say she'd never taken a course before and asked to audit it. I reassured her that it would be a very relaxed class and she could participate only as much as she wanted to.

As I read out each name I looked up, trying to match face with name and fix both in my memory. But Lena, her face bent over the desk, didn't return my smile. The initial shyness didn't last long before her natural contentiousness took over.

For the first assignment, the class (with the exception of Lena) paired off, exchanged information, and then composed short introductions of each other. I gave a peroration about the difference between a dull passport profile of a person and an array of evocative details.

Mavis, a Toastmistress, introduced Tiam by describing his early reactions to Canada: all the people looked alike and he had to get used to potatoes with every meal. He couldn't stop laughing when he saw people out walking with pet dogs on the end of leashes, some of them actually wearing little coats and all of them with leather collars. This observation sparked a lively discussion about different cultural attitudes to dogs. Someone asked Tiam if dogs were regularly served up in restaurants in his country, and there was a lot of silly giggling and histrionic shudders of revulsion.

Suddenly a deep voice emanated from the back of the room. When people were starving, it said, they couldn't afford to be so picky about what they ate. They took whatever was necessary for survival — birds, rats, and, yes, dogs. It was not that, but the waste of food that was obscene. There was a moment of astonished silence in which everyone turned round, craning to see where the voice came from. I was prepared to deflect the attention and save her from embarrassment when someone else spoke up, offering televisual documentation. "It's true," she said, "there was a program about the war in . . . " This led through a series of non sequiturs and irrelevancies to cannibalism, vivisection, vegetarianism, and ended with someone offering a recipe for meatless lasagna.

The time passed quickly and no more introductions took place that day. I summed up, trying to validate the discussion by congratulating Mavis on her choice of provocative talking points. What we'd learned, I said (they copied my remarks into their notebooks), was that conversations, like rivers, should be allowed to find their own courses; the most interesting ones developed from unexpected detours and digressions.

We dispersed contentedly, they having reaped as much profit as they expected from the afternoon and I pleased that the class had coalesced and that a group dynamic had established itself. I saw that Tiam, now renamed Timmy, was well on his way to becoming the mascot of the Toastmistress club. Walking home across the park where the sap was rising in the trees towards a new leafing out, I felt a similar rise in adrenalin such as comes after a class that's gone spectacularly well. And I meditated upon the strange presence of Lena Stone.

When I had my appointment with the Dean to go over the class evaluation forms, he raised his eyebrows at the one insulting submission. "If thered been any pearls in this class theyd of been cast before swine." It was anonymous, but I thought I could guess its source.

Such were my first impressions. It was the last class I taught on that topic, but the first of many in which Lena enrolled. At the beginning of the next semester my phone rang and I immediately recognized the voice of the woman who had reacted so strongly to the subject of eating dogs. Because she hadn't finished high school, she needed special permission in order to be admitted to a credit course. This I granted, and eventually her good grades erased her probationary status and she entered the degree program.

Her performance in the conversation class was typical of future class participation. She generally remained silent until a sense of outrage caused her to cry out, as if a subterranean river of molten rage was ready to erupt under the slightest pressure. One spectacular outburst happened during a class on *Jude The Obscure*. We'd laughed at the episode in which the child, Old Father Time, hangs himself "because we are too meny." I'd made it worse by quoting Oscar Wilde on Dickens: "One must have a heart of stone to read the death of Little Nell without laughing."

From these incidents I formed the impression of Lena as someone who had known deprivation too well to bring fastidious judgments to its fictional representation, however clumsy. The terms "sentimental," "clichéd," and "melodramatic" offended her, and I was not inclined to defend their use. Her strong feelings for the dispossessed intimidated me, and perhaps that gave her a sense of power over me. Besides, her literary judgments were already being vindicated, as better critics than I were rehabilitating *Uncle Tom's Cabin* and other previously disparaged books.

It was through these flare-ups that I started half-consciously to assemble the jigsaw puzzle of Lena's life. I began by creating an exotic picture, with literary antecedents in *The Painted Bird*, *Darkness At Noon*, and *The Diary Of Anne Frank*. Its backdrop was an Eastern European ghetto or feudal village on the edge of a primeval forest, in occupied territory, her people persecuted for some accident of race, religion, or birthplace. Stone, Stein, the name could belong anywhere. I constructed her as a witness to horrors that most of us only see framed by the television screen. Later I wondered how much she colluded in my picture, for she did little to correct or deny it. If I asked, "Where did you come from originally?" which I did more than once, she was evasive. "It was so long ago," she said, "it's hard to remember." Once, mocking my own manner of speech, she said, "Lucy, it doesn't bear thinking about . . . " Of her ethnic background, she told me, "I'm a mongrel," and I thought of the *mischlinge* of Nazi Germany.

When we were alone together, there were no outbursts, at least not at first. She kept her scorn in check and plied me with questions. After driving me home from a class on *A Room Of One's Own*, she extracted every last detail about Woolf's life — her racism, her snobbishness, her animosity towards the suffragettes. Lena's curiosity went well beyond the literary to include manners, social conventions, the whole texture of a society that seemed more foreign to her than if she'd come from China. Opening a drawer one day when I asked her to set our two places at the table, she peered in surprise at the array of knives. "What's this for?" she asked, flourishing a butter knife with an ornate handle. "And this?" holding up some fish knives, bought on a whim at a garage sale. I explained they were relics of the pretentious *nouveaux riches* of nineteenth-century Britain. She wasn't much given to mirth, but these trappings of an overbred civilization brought her close to laughter. She shook her head in disbelief that grown-up people could concern themselves, then or now, with such trivia.

Thus, with no large picture on the box to guide me, I fitted together the pieces, following a pattern in my own head. It evolved very slowly until the months with Max, when the process accelerated. None of us appeared to advantage as we took our turns in that claustrophobic upper room, where too many bodies were jammed into too little space, and too many minds rubbed up against each other, all of us terrified of the outcome. With Lena, that undercurrent of poison I mentioned earlier was drawn to the surface. Later I understood that each day must have delivered jolts like electric shocks to the most sensitive places.

If she was surly during the day, at night she was frightening. She'd wake up in my bedroom after one of her nightmares, in the grip of an almost murderous rage. Day after day I lived in dread of her violence, fearing for Max, myself, and all of us. I felt sure then that she'd been not merely the witness of atrocities, but the one on whom they'd been perpetrated. Yet the more I found out about her, the more the picture wobbled. At times I doubted that her persecutors were human or had any existence outside her own disordered mind.

Sometimes, after she was quieted, lying soothed or drugged into a calm sleep, I looked down at her and thought it wasn't fury I was seeing but madness. If I imagined my future self in a prison cell, I imagined Lena in an institution, with cropped hair and vacant eyes, sitting at a table covered with glue and bits of coloured paper, trying to make something. Occupational therapy.

In optimistic moments — as we all do in the midst of great upheavals that are removing any possibility of future normalcy — I tried to believe that at the end of several months we would all get back to where we were before. My optimism was never put to the test because when the crisis ended, she receded into the shadows. My life resumed its uneventful routine, and the anxiety that she might reappear on my doorstep like an avenging fury gradually faded.

And then her book burst upon the world. At first, reading about it in the papers, a dread of what I might find about myself in its pages kept me from rushing out to buy it. Finally Julia turned up with two copies and we sat down together to read, our silence punctuated by the flick of Julia's lighter and her snorts of disgust or derision.

A Vast And Frozen Sea tells the story of a nameless woman who is an exile in her own country. She leads a restless, wandering life, searching for a place in which she can belong. Like a cuckoo, she settles in the homes of others, but always as an alien, forced at last to resume her wandering.

She touches the lives of many people, but as intimacy grows, now with a woman, now with a man, she panics and is driven away by a wild fear of entrapment, as if a monstrous demon is pursuing her. She takes on the colours of her surroundings, wearing them like a garment, establishing a life until the time comes for another casting off. She sloughs the old skin and surfaces elsewhere, born again, the old life apparently erased from her memory.

In an early incarnation she is a hired girl doing the work of a hired man on a subsistence farm. When the old farmer senses her yearning to leave, he tells her, "Only one way you'll git away from here and that's in a wooden box." From that time onwards, she makes her departures without warning. One minute she is stepping out on a small errand, and the next she has disappeared without a trace.

One night, driven off course by a blizzard, she arrives at a Mennonite farm. She is taken in and becomes a member of the community, comfortable with their austere customs. She wears a long black dress and headscarf, speaks their language, and becomes a favourite with the elderly widowed patriarch of the clan. Next she finds employment for a time as housekeeper in a house of ill-repute, observing all that goes on and befriending the girls. Later, in the darkroom behind a photographer's studio, she works such magic that she triples the studio's business.

She adapts to every situation, developing the necessary skills and making herself so indispensable that every disappearance adds to the crowd of discarded people in her wake. She becomes more and more fragmented, leaving a part of herself in every place, in every life she touches.

Most of the story is told in a spare unadorned prose, its starkness achieving a gem-like purity. It is Lena's unmistakable voice, that same voice I heard so many times raised against me in anger and disrupting the class discussion.

She manages the impossible feat of creating a central character who is believable and yet has the insubstantial quality of a somnambulist. The woman moves through territory that is at the same time everywhere and nowhere, each scene realized with amazing clarity — northern wilderness, western mountain range, windswept prairie, teeming city — each mirroring the ever-changing landscapes of her heart.

The climactic ending is almost unbearable in its impact. One afternoon in a grey city with the wind blowing off the lake, the woman enters a small art gallery in the wake of a group of schoolchildren. While they are escorted through the permanent collections, clustering around landscapes and portraits, she turns in to a side gallery. The exhibit here features the decaying corpses of rabbits. She stands before them in the warm enclosed space, the children's piping voices mingling with the steady trickling of a water fountain.

The light plays over the small iridescent bodies in such a way that they appear to stir and twitch. She picks up the corrupt smell of rotting vegetation, of rotting flesh, of blood. Moving closer she sees that the bloated belly of one rabbit is full of foetal young. She puts out her hand to touch the silky membrane and sees that her finger is smeared with coagulated blood.

As she draws back her finger, she is shaken by a chill of horror, for she no longer recognizes the white flesh as her own. The hand seems to belong to someone else, who has reached out to clutch her and draw her down into a bottomless pit. She whirls in a vortex of strange sights and sounds, and in the confusion a memory that has been long buried in her mind is dislodged from its burial place.

She finds herself looking at a small girl on the verge of puberty, but who has the swollen stomach of a famine victim or a pregnant woman. Scene follows scene rapidly — the stomach lifts and heaves, the pain tears at the girl's loins, she gives out the screams of a trapped animal, her waters break, gouts of blood spurt, and a mangled knot of flesh is delivered from her torn body. At last a profound and unearthly silence spreads over everything. It is her younger self and she has given birth to a baby.

Time stops for the woman in that deserted gallery. When she regains consciousness it is much later and the light outside is beginning to fade. She is like someone emerging from an anaesthetic after a surgical procedure. The children have gone, even the fountain is quiet. The ghastly vision has faded, but the unearthly silence remains. A uniformed official touches her elbow, saying it is time to close the gallery, asking if she needs help. It's not the first time this exhibition has made a lady sick. One lady vomited so much she had to be taken to the emergency room. If it was up to him, they'd throw out the whole mess and not call it art. "No," she tells him, "it's very wonderful and very moving." It overwhelmed her for a moment, but she is now recovered.

She feels that her heart has been long marooned, like a freighter arrested in a vast and frozen sea, but the ice has suddenly thawed, releasing the freighter so that it can speed on its way.

"Bullshit," said Julia, slamming the book shut.

It was late in the evening for us too, and we'd switched on the lamps by the time we finished reading. "Absolute bullshit. I can't stand that feverish ending. Her heart marooned like a freighter! Isn't that a mixed metaphor or something?"

Julia was capable of reading intelligently, but Lena's book never stood a chance with her because there was too much bad blood between them. I had several tries at explaining its merits, but she remained obdurately literal-minded. Our arguments always ended with Julia picking out an incident and saying, "Well, was she fucking him or was she not, that's what I want to know." Finally it became one of those subjects that, by mutual agreement, we no longer discussed.

"Absolute bullshit," she said when she finished the book that first time. But my hands were trembling.

They were trembling still when I wrote my letter of congratulation to Lena. For all the times she'd accused me of never feeling anything unless I'd read about it first in a book, I couldn't resist including a poem with the letter. It was Anne Sexton's "To A Friend Whose Work Has Come to Triumph," a poetic meditation on the flight of Icarus. Lena sent no reply of course, and I expected none.

Yet during our reunion at Max and Julia's house, she turned to me as if the lines of communication had never been broken and said, "Hey, I liked that poem."

"Good," I said. "I worried that you'd take it the wrong way."

"How was I supposed to take it?"

"As a compliment," I said. "I was thinking of your great work forming in your mind while none of us noticed. I was thinking of how marvels happen while the world goes about its business, not even noticing. People wait for a miraculous birth, unaware that one is taking place before their glazed eyes."

"Yes, yes, I get the point," she said. "I thought you were referring to his plunge into the sea, predicting my downfall." And then before I could protest, "It's just like old times, Lucy. I always enjoyed listening to you interpret stuff." I like to think she meant it affectionately.

Reviewers, baffled by the book's power, vied with explanations, often heavily dependent on Freud. They said the structure was patterned after his description of dream-work; the protagonist's flights were symptoms of neurotic behaviour and compulsive-repetition; the ending was a classic rendering of the return of the uncanny; the book was a clinically accurate account of recovered memory syndrome.

For myself, the book contained all I needed to know about Lena, for she'd finally delivered her life to me in the form I was best equipped to handle — between the covers of a book. My early struggles with a vague and changing set of symptoms had at last been superseded by the presentation of the corpse, dismembered to be sure, but with each individual cell intact and loaded with genetic information, which I could decode.

That final vision — with its grotesque components of menstruation and maternity, conception, birth, and death — was my key. I discerned behind the scene in the art gallery the contours of a second scene — that upper room in Julia's house in which another grotesque pregnancy had run its dangerous course. It was there she had relived her torture, not in a single afternoon in an art gallery, but day after day, month after month. When she reworked it into fiction, she'd condensed the time from nine months to a few hours and displaced the setting. But the motifs were the same — the house full of children, the belly swollen with new life, the bodily functions, the sounds and smells.

And did I believe the hideous memory that had been revived? Without a moment's doubt. I had no need to bring together the hints and echoes in Lena's conversations, for every word of the description in her novel was shot through with the flavour of pure and unadulterated truth. On its authenticity I was prepared to stake my reputation.

The wonder was that at some point during those months she hadn't taken flight. I recalled several times when, standing in the doorway, she'd announced that she was going on an errand in such a weighted tone of voice that I'd looked up in surprise, wondering what I was hearing.

"I'm just returning these books to the library, Lucy," or "Anything you need from the liquor store?"

Sometimes she was gone a long time. Perhaps she started out, travelling a few miles on a journey away from me. But she always turned back, stayed on, and endured right to the end, and in my hopeful, needy way I now took credit for those averted flights and for what she produced. Her ordeal with us had worked like an exorcism, preparing for one last repetition of the trauma as she wrote it out.

I saw Lena's life in three parts — first, the terrible childhood that had been erased by amnesia; next, the slow process of its retrieval; and finally, its reconfiguration into fiction. In that tripartite structure I had the field-marks for my book. Over her years of wandering in the wilderness, I intended to draw a curtain, for it was beyond my scope to trace all the incidents of her life before I knew her.

All the same, I had not totally abandoned the rigours of my old profession. I had to moor her childhood to a specific time and place, and I needed to travel to authenticate the facts. The diaries were my guide for that journey, not to some distant country, but due north from where I was.

Julia was dead, and there was no longer any student I trusted enough to make privy to what I might discover. But I thought it could be done, if I took it slowly and in gradual stages by bus and taxi. At the end of it I would need a driver, indifferent enough to be incurious, and a priest, doddering enough to be compliant; neither requirement was impossible in those remote northern regions. And so I set out on my way.

Physical evidence was sparse, as I knew it would be. I expected no marble or granite headstone, no house built solidly enough to have remained standing. If there had been wooden crosses, they'd decayed long ago, and all that remained of the shack was a heap of planks, barely enough to make a small fire. They stood in a clearing amid a scatter of rusty wheels and pots. And by a freakish chance, a mismatched pair of men's shoes was preserved intact, nailed high in the branches of a pine tree to serve as birdhouses.

Although the abandoned church was no longer under his jurisdiction, the old priest (encouraged by the presentation of a bottle of brandy) had no objection to opening the record books for a member of the family (I signed my name "Lucille Coté"), who had come so far to find them.

The facts were spare — a brief chronology, a few lines interwoven with their neigbours' lives — but they gave the outlines of a family history: the marriage date of Thérèse and Louis St. Pierre; the baptismal date of Madeleine Thérèse, the oldest of the children; the others in quick succession, serial pregnancies year after year — Jean-Luc, Hubert, François, Jeanne-Marie, Giles, Marcel, Maurice, Delphine, André, Charles. And thirteen years later the event that brought the family to an end: in the same month, the death of Thérèse and of her last child, Marionette.

Then nothing more of the St. Pierres. After the death of the mother, there was nothing more to record. The father, always absent for long periods, had disappeared completely. The youngsters were parcelled out to foster homes. Madeleine Thérèse, the only one old enough to fend for herself, was left to struggle along as best she could, gravitating to the nearest town, migrating southwards, undergoing her various transformations, and eventually, as Lena Stone, arriving in the city, two hundred miles to the south, where she drifted into an unlikely class in the art of conversation.

It was the blueprint of a life, preserved in the records of a deserted church. It had all happened, just as she had told it in her book. The enclosed space swarming with small children, the prolonged and painful vigil over the prone figure on the bed close to the stove in the main room, the pregnancy moving towards its terrible climax, the baby thrust out, caught, held, and buried.

Only one detail had been changed. It was not Madeleine who had borne the baby, but her mother. Though watching day by day, the oldest child, the little helper who moistened the cracked lips, brought wet rags to place upon the feverish forehead, sacks to cover the shivering body, had felt it so acutely she had claimed it as her own.

The phenomenon is not unheard of. The old mystics manifested the stigmata of the crucifixion in the palms of their own hands. Lena's story would have stood up, I believe, under hypnosis, under a lie detector test. And it was good enough for me.

Of course, skeptics would demur. Julia would have said it was a ploy to guarantee the book's commercial or artistic success. After all, the death of a woman from the complications of childbirth is no more remarkable than death in a car crash caused by a drunken driver. On the other hand, who would not feel the strongest revulsion at the violation of a child?

That was a doubt I didn't permit myself. The reason was not only my loyalty to Lena; nor was it my obligation to her loyal fans, who expected the biography to bolster her iconic stature. It was my conviction that even the most diligent investigators can never be more than half sure about what happens in another person's life. I kept her secret safe and preserved the image of her that would satisfy her readers' expectations and fulfill their requirements for her martyrdom.

The reviews were more or less predictable. The name "Stone" was irresistible: BIOGRAPHER LEAVES MANY STONES UNTURNED, BIOGRAPHER CASTS THE FIRST STONE, BIOGRAPHY OF LENA STONE A DEAD WEIGHT, HEATHCOTE KILLS SEVERAL BIRDS WITH ONE STONE.

Their contents ran the usual gamut: I'd colonized a life, replicated the original violation of the body by laying bare the woman and penetrating her text. I'd appropriated her voice, speaking as her, speaking for her. I'd been self-serving because I devoted so much space to the minutiae of our months together caring for "M," our pregnant friend. I'd been boring and pedantic because I included so much textual analysis of the novel. I'd engaged in a vengeful exercise because Lena's book was manifestly more successful than *The Uses Of Adversity*, my own generally overlooked memoir of surviving breast cancer.

One dear old soul, Sister Jocelyn, read *Lena Stone: A Life* as my own spiritual journey, a kind of pilgrim's progress. It was influenced by my early "religious experiences," as revealed in my breast cancer book. I'm supposed to be a witness ("aware of the shadings and valences, theological as well as legal, of that word") to Lena's days on earth. That's superseded by my role as interpreter of Stone's texts as if they were the teaching of Christ. Finally I become a pilgrim, finding the truth behind the figures that appear in Lena's writings, paying homage at the shrine.

It's a fanciful theory, a bit off the wall, but quite gratifying after all the malicious ones. We all need some saintly mother figure to put the best light on our endeavours.

I especially cherish her praise of my ending. I'd taken the liberty of dramatizing my visit to the church in a painterly and novelistic way. I gave the St. Pierre family the physical monuments that were rightfully theirs by transferring the record of their lives from the old record book to the inscriptions on a granite tombstone. I had myself standing before it in a shaft of sunlight. And — a harmless poetic touch — I filled the graveyard with imaginary characters — young Lena, dressed for her First Communion and surrounded by her siblings.

So everything's there for you to look at, if you're interested in the details. I'm incapable of throwing anything away, not even the stolen page from the church record book. Go over it all, if you care to. But, of course, it's not Lena's but another story that you have been waiting so patiently to hear.

XVIII

I WAS HURT that Simone confided in Renny rather than me, for who was more qualified than I to understand disappointment in love. But perhaps qualifications don't apply in such matters.

"When you run into someone unexpectedly in a strange place, there's a bond," Renny said. "And maybe Simone told me her story as a diversionary tactic. After all, it wasn't her blighted love life I was curious about."

They'd run into each other in London, of all places, and Renny called me soon afterwards, her voice excited over the long-distance line. She swore me to secrecy but apparently felt no obligation herself to a (implicit or explicit) pledge of secrecy. I kept the secret as long as Simone was alive, but I believe that death releases us all from our vows of silence. So it wasn't discretion but only time and forgetfulness that affected the story I told Julia. And she fell asleep before I was halfway through.

I'd often seen Simone in her lab coat, but I saw her again as she was when she first entered medical school. He was in the row in front and turned, mocking and playful, to say to the person behind him "Excuse my back" (it was his old-world manners she liked always). And, to his amazement, he saw *her*, all white and gold like an angel, smiling uncertainly, unsure whether or not he was kidding. If there was ever love at first sight, this was it. Afterwards, as they filed out, he lingered and, walking beside her, suggested coffee.

That was the beginning, simple as that. She felt like an outsider among the medical students, most of whom were affluent and sophisticated, coming from the rich families of doctors and dentists. She had the money neither for a car nor an apartment. She travelled up to the school by Greyhound bus or hitched a ride with a classmate or a neighbour. She preferred the bus because the meandering three-hour journey put some distance between herself and the family. She rented a room in the house of a good Christian family, recommended by church connections.

Although he was a foreigner, he fit in better than she did because he had a good car and lived in a fine new apartment building overlooking the river. He'd actually bought his apartment, intending to sell it again at the end of the course. He'd worked for several years and had plenty of money for movies and restaurants and trips.

She was enchanted by his apartment from the first time she saw it, coming in one evening after they'd worked in the library and he asked her out for a late supper. He'd stopped by, saying he'd left something, would she come up while he searched for whatever it was — his wallet or his driver's licence. She walked to the window and saw the city spread out under an early snowfall, all the lights twinkling.

The room she rented was totally depressing. It was cold, cramped, noisy, full of the smell of cooking, and dark because it was overshadowed by the brick wall of the office building next door. When she complained, he invited her to work at his place. He worked at a desk in his bedroom, while she made herself comfortable at the dining room table. She left her books there in piles, trusting him completely by this time, feeling at home. And all the time, falling more and more in love.

Without needing to mention the fact, they slipped into habits of secrecy. They rarely sat together in class, found other lab partners, and left the buildings separately. They met as if by accident in places where they wouldn't be observed — in the parking lot or on some side street. She set out for home, knowing that before she had walked many blocks a car would pull up to the pavement and stop. They used the staircase rather than the elevator to his apartment, and he checked that the coast was clear before they walked down the hall. When his brother came into town on his way to Vancouver, it went without saying that Simone would make herself scarce.

The weather helped, the snow and the cold imposing on everyone a universal disguise. Encased in their arctic parkas, hoods up, wolf-fur around their faces, they could walk along the path by the river, hands in each other's pockets, or both hands in the same huge fleece-lined mitten. "Hold my hand," he sang, "I'm a stranger in paradise." He liked Borodin.

And she was spending more and more time in the sealed warm world of his apartment, working there, eating there, watching television, and listening to his records when they were too tired to read any longer. They watched old movies — *Casablanca* and *Rose Marie*. They watched *A Touch Of Class*, and Simone wept along with Glenda Jackson and George Segal, all four of them watching Celia Johnson and Trevor Howard in *Brief Encounter*. Everything they saw became woven into the texture of their intimacy.

Claiming that her room was too noisy, she moved to another house, owned by an elderly widow. It was even more depressing than the first, but it afforded anonymity. She didn't have to go to church with the family, and she could slip in and out unobserved. She spent most of her free time at his apartment, but never stayed overnight. It would not have been scandalous to do so at the time, but it was too daring for her.

Going home for Thanksgiving and Christmas by bus or with Andrea, who sometimes insisted on coming to fetch her, she felt again that her allegiance was split between two warring countries, and that crossing the boundary between them was dangerous.

As she indulged in the subterfuges that had long been second nature to her, she was barely conscious of their familiarity, of their continuity with the habits of her childhood. Perhaps she regretted (I think she certainly must have done) that her friendships had to be conducted under a cloak of secrecy, shot through with an element of the forbidden. But she never understood that the secrecy and transgression was not an accidental but a necessary ingredient of her erotic needs. Eventually, forced to acknowledge that she gravitated to dark-skinned men of alien races and religions, she thought she was vainly seeking a substitute for her first love. But the force that drew her into these relationships had been in place from childhood, the conditioning behind it complex and convoluted.

Holidays became something to be endured until she could see him again. He spent his in Toronto or Montreal with friends of the family he spoke of vaguely. Only later did she learn that he was seeing a woman he was expected to marry, an arranged marriage.

"I'll write every day," he said.

"Oh no," she said, aghast.

"They don't read your mail, do they?"

"They'd notice."

"Can you write to me?"

"Yes, I can do that."

"Every day?"

"Perhaps not every day."

But she did manage to write fairly often, telling him what she was doing to pass the time — mostly physical activities such as skating, cross-country skiing, bowling, going to a neighbour's party on the Sunday before Christmas. Mischievously, he sent a postcard and signed it "Alice."

> I hope you are having a good time in the snow. Here it rains all the time and the pavements are full of "slush." My new boots with the Cuban heels now have a white tidemark around them. I am pretty bored most of the time and have been going to the movies. My friends have been trying to fix me up with an eligible bachelor! I got my hair done at Eatons Beauty Salon. See you in January. *Alice*

"You never mentioned anyone called Alice," Andrea said, turning the postcard over.

"There are a lot of people in my year I never mentioned," Simone said.

Dear Alice,

My sister brought in the mail and said who's Alice? I said I don't know anyone called Alice. Well she's sent you a postcard from Toronto she said. I said, There's a girl in my year called Ally, that's who it must be, but I think I turned red. It's funny what you said about the boots because they have got white line from the salt on the roads and I did get my hair cut at Eatons. It must be ESP. Please don't send another postcard as my sister is very nosy . . .

For some reason the postcard ended up on the mantelpiece among the Christmas cards. She got a fright every time she saw it.

She suspected he might ignore her plea and made an effort after that to get to the mailbox before anyone else. So when the second one came, she was able to carry it off to her room before Andrea saw it. After the initial shock of seeing his handwriting, she laughed and laughed. She'd never been playful, even as a child, and he was the first person with whom she'd shared private jokes.

Dear Simone,

It's good to know you're getting plenty of exercise but you don't mention curling. Perhaps you don't know any curlers there and are giving it a rest. There isn't much curling in Toronto, it doesn't seem to be as popular here as on the prairies. But we can make up for it when we get back to school. What time are you getting back on Sunday? My plane gets in at 4 in the afternoon. I'll give you a call so we can set up a schedule for curling.

Your skip, *Alice*

So they went on for almost two years, the knowledge that they had no future together making the time all the more precious to them. Finally it ended with Andrea's wedding. All year Simone had been dreading the summer, knowing there was no way to avoid spending it at home. For weeks the house was full of relatives, and Andrea oscillated between euphoria and despair. The euphoria was part triumph because she was getting married first, and the despair was over some trivial detail — the flowers for the bridesmaids' bouquets or decisions over the registry of presents at Eatons.

The bridal showers were the worst, with everyone telling Simone she would be next. It might have been easier if she'd had a boyfriend who was to be a groomsman, but having no one meant she was the object of speculation. Was there anyone on the horizon? Or did she intend to be one of those "career women"? The phrase was spoken contemptuously, her grandmother's mouth tightening. Usually the subject didn't end there.

"What I can't stand are these career women who decide to have children when they're in their forties and then act surprised when nothing happens."

"Or decide to have them on their own, without men. The arrogance is what gets me. No thought for the kids, bringing them into the world without fathers!"

She was under a cloud of suspicion. And if she couldn't bestir herself to agree when they discussed it over supper, Andrea would flare up and accuse her of things.

"People are beginning to wonder if you're a Christian."

And then Ken would chime in on Andrea's side. She couldn't stand Ken. Andrea had met him at the Bible College, which was better than university because it operated on trust, with no locks on anything. He didn't read fiction because it was immoral. He hadn't finished the course at the Bible College, not because he flunked out but because the course content or the professors failed to reach his high moral standards. Everything had to reflect on his piety, and Fern drank it all in and thought he was wonderful. There was going to be no liquor at the wedding, that went without saying, but no dancing either, because that wasn't suitable for such a solemn occasion.

And for a honeymoon, they were joining a group that was going to Tijuana, to a poverty-stricken Mexican shantytown, to donate labour and expertise and show support. They would sleep in an orphanage there and work on building homes during the day. It was the third such venture they had been a part of and they always returned with slides and made presentations all over town. As a concession to the honeymoon, Andrea and Ken were leaving the group at the end of the project and instead of returning with them, were spending a week in California. The contrast between the shantytown and the sights in California, captured on film, would be grist for the slide presentation.

When yet another crisis blew up over wedding presents or the reception in the church basement, Simone couldn't resist suggesting that it might be simpler to ask for donations, financial and otherwise, to the Mexican project. It was a mistake because she could never win an argument with Andrea.

Every so often, Andrea intercepted a postcard from Alice. She knew Simone well enough to sense her alarm, but she didn't say anything. She had a suspicion, but it was so awful she was afraid that if Ken got wind of it he might kick up a fuss that would torpedo all the wedding plans.

"He makes my faith look like milk and water," Andrea said, and her mother nodded in approval. He was just like a son already, she said. No one asked why he was alienated from his own family, or perhaps he had explained that he couldn't approve of their lax United Church morals. He'd joined his new family's church, become a deacon, and spent all his time on church work because he couldn't get a job anywhere else. In spite of being unemployed he offered expert opinions on everything, resented Simone and baited her constantly. "There's something very wrong," he said, "when doctors have a convention and all they talk about is fees."

He said he wouldn't allow Andrea to work after they had children. As a matter of fact, he blamed all the unemployment on the large numbers of women in the work force taking jobs away from men. He didn't believe in women working except in cases of dire necessity. Fern's going back to work was a case of dire necessity, caused by Wally's loss of his job and Simone's medical school fees (though it was understood she'd pay them back once she graduated).

Once he came into the kitchen and looked at a shopping list Simone had stuck behind a magnet on the fridge. "I don't think Simone's going to make a good doctor," he said (he had a way of referring to her in her presence in the third person). Naturally her mother asked why. "Because I can read her handwriting." It seemed the only time he made jokes was when he jeered at Simone. Andrea dimpled up to him and laughed, but if Simone didn't do the same thing she stood accused of having no sense of humour.

All their lives the terrible rivalry between them had been a ruinous destructive force that crippled her and, more than anything else, determined her destiny. It was a triangular relationship really, with Fern at the apex. She'd fulfilled Fern's ambitions, and Fern was proud of her, but she didn't like her. The education she'd promoted and fostered so single-mindedly became a wedge between them. The more Simone learned, the more she was able to stand up to Fern and argue, and win, and so there was always tension.

And from the moment the second daughter was born, there was a war between the sisters, a war that Andrea always won. Simone was more intelligent, but Andrea had the kind of cunning necessary to get the better of her sister. She didn't do well in school and she couldn't compete in any subject, so her chief weapon was piety. Perhaps things might have been different if she'd had other talents, been better at sports or music or dancing, but in everything Simone was superior. The only area in which Andrea could excel was in self-righteousness. "I want to be a nurse," Andrea said, "because I'm a people person and I want to work with people and help them. That's more important to me than making money." By being the more dutiful daughter, she pushed Simone into the role of "difficult one." Andrea had no unsuitable friends, never resisted what Fern decreed, never argued or opposed her wishes. She always watched Simone, and while she knew enough not to tittle-tattle, she could challenge her at the supper table and draw her into saying things that the parents disapproved of. And so Andrea and Fern formed a tight unit against Simone.

By the end of the summer of the wedding, Simone knew she had two choices: she could give him up or she could run away with him and yield the field to Andrea. What she couldn't do was let things slide, because they were reaching the point of no return. They were becoming more and more entwined and devoted. It could only end in disaster, and the longer it went on the more calamitous the disaster would be. She couldn't face the disapproval, the ostracism, of becoming, in the eyes of others, a fallen woman. But most of all she couldn't face leaving the field to the triumphant Andrea.

Sometimes she imagined announcing at the supper table that she intended to marry him. In this *mise en scène* her father burst into tears, Ken quoted the Bible, Andrea said, "Those people don't believe in Jesus Christ our Lord," and Fern said, "But my grandchildren won't be white." She knew that if she did go through with it, she'd have to say good-bye and never see any of them again.

The ending was terrible for both of them. There were no arguments or recriminations because he understood her reasons only too well. He was feeling exactly the same kind of pressure himself from his own family. It was getting more and more difficult to put off the marriage they planned for him.

The saddest part was that they couldn't make a clean break, and so the agony was drawn out. First one and then the other would plead for one last meeting. The only good that came out of their misery was that they threw themselves wholeheartedly into studying as a means of keeping their sanity. They both did well, she far more brilliantly than anyone had expected.

Painful as it was, it wasn't in Simone's nature to romanticize her loss. She would have despised herself if she'd burst into tears when she heard Borodin, and scoffed at the idea of telling someone never to play that tune again. She had a resolute streak, fuelled by rage and a lifetime of being outmanoeuvred by Andrea.

She came up with the perfect idea for solving all her problems. There was a prestigious prize, the Balfour scholarship, which had been established years ago to send "young colonists" to Oxford. The purpose was to solidify ties between England and her colonies, to give young colonists instruction in life and manners, and to add breadth to their views.

What she needed at the time was less breadth to her views than distance from her family. And, more than anything, glory, because renunciation had fanned her ambition. As it happened, this scholarship, established by men for men, was for the first time open to female scholars, and it was just what she needed. With her brilliant academic record she felt she was a strong contender. It's interesting to think how differently her life (and ours) might have unfolded if she'd won that scholarship.

When she spoke to me about her plans I was unenthusiastic about such a colonial scholarship, but I agreed to write her a letter of recommendation. Someone else suggested that she talk to Max Hoffman, who was on the selection committee. He received her in his office very courteously, and talked to her kindly about her future career. She'd already been nudged from gynecology, which she'd really wanted to do, into the more suitable area of pediatrics. He approved of that change, said it was a wise move for someone who was sure to have children of her own soon.

He asked about her participation in sports, the arts, volunteer work, for these were included in the definition of manliness, which was a not-yet-updated requirement for the applicants. He mentioned in passing that he had been an accomplished musician in his younger days. She told him frankly that she hadn't had time for music lessons or volunteer work. But she took the hint and annexed to her application form an account of Andrea's work with disadvantaged Mexicans. She wondered if that backfired, because at the interview she was asked, somewhat pointedly, why she had been helping Mexicans when there were plenty of poor people at home.

Anyway, for whatever reason, the sole Canadian scholarship went to someone studying at the University of Toronto who was editor of the student newspaper, a hockey player, fundraiser for the United Way, and male. For all we know, Max may have supported her application, even fought for it. But she never believed that, and the loss of the Balfour scholarship was at the bottom of the grudge she held against him. Her escape route was cut off, she remained on her home turf, and her heartache wasn't eased.

He met her for what was supposed to be the final time two years later, when they were both interning, he in a city hundreds of miles away. He flew in to see her and tell her there was still time . . . his marriage was all arranged, but it was not too late to change all the plans, and he was prepared to do it.

For the first time she brought him home. Everyone was away, there were no lights on next door, so they slipped into the empty house furtively through the side door. She pointed out the mantelpiece where his first postcard had been on display all through the Christmas season, brought out the family photograph albums and showed him herself at four and six and ten. Finally she took him up to her childhood bedroom. He stayed most of the night and by morning was gone again.

I can see it all so clearly: the two of them, Renny and Simone, running into each other accidentally, perhaps on the street or in an art gallery.

"Surely it's Simone!"

"Renny! What are you doing here?"

"I live here, at least only an hour away by train. I come up all the time to wander about the streets. And you?"

"Well, I usually break my journey in Paris or Frankfurt, but I decided to stop over in London for a change. I'm staying at Brown's."

"Wow!"

"It's just for a night or two."

And so they go off for lunch together, perhaps to one of those pubs where there's something about the atmosphere — all the oak benches and red upholstery — that seems designed for illicit meetings.

Most of the lunch crowd has gone and they have a corner table in the snug. They order wine and the seafood platter. Actually, they're both famished and the wine and the food and the meeting all make them giggly. They reminisce about this and that, and naturally about Lucy.

They are like sisters, alienated for decades, who meet by accident after the parents have died and all the old rivalries have faded. They establish a temporary armistice or a permanent peace.

"Do you remember those lunches at The Bay? Those movies?"

"I remember the ice cream afterwards."

"I'll never forget that movie about the dead whales."

"Dead whales?"

"The valley of the dead whales, where the whales came to die in mountains full of caverns, peopled by Vikings with those horned helmets?"

"And how did we get from there to here? We should be housewives dragging a load of kids across the Albert Street bridge to the park by the lake."

"I never wanted to get married. Not for a moment. I've always been solo, the influence of family disintegration was too awful to risk a second time. I guess I never recovered from that first time. And you? Did you never want to get married?"

"I did, yes, once fall in love, but it was impossible."

"And there were no others?"

"No there weren't. If there had been, it would probably have been the same thing all over again."

"Sounds like one of Lucy's prognostications."

"Lucy knew nothing about it."

And so (I imagine) they sat until the evening crowd started to drift in, and they gathered up their things and walked out, temporarily blinded by the sunshine after the dark interior, and still enchanted with this talk of old times. Perhaps Simone suggested that Renny come back with her to Brown's and they prolong the conversation over dinner. Perhaps she said, "It'll be on me," knowing that they would never meet again. And Renny either did that, or she went off to Charing Cross to catch the train home, carrying Simone's story like a chalice.

Only there's more to it than she told Renny. She didn't confide it to me either, but it was among the things that came to me after her death. However much they all hated me, they all trusted me to take care of what they left behind. Not the bodies, the money, the jewelry, or anything of material value, but the written remains. "To dispose of as she sees fit" was the phrase they used, or "For whatever purpose she deems appropriate." It was a tribute to my reverence for the printed word, as safe as sealing up their precious scraps in a time capsule. So now you can have the bundle of letters.

Dear Simone,
 Your namesake is now ten years old and looks nothing like you. Everyone has their own version of her name — Simmy, Simca, Mona. Only I call her Simone. I think she came to fill the emptiness left by you, her birthday so close to yours, which I never forget. When I named her, my first-born, it was assumed I was disappointed because I'd wanted a boy. It was too soon after we separated for me to think what I was doing. I think now that I named her so that when I thought of that name or stumbled on it, it would lose its charge. Did I ever tell you about the time a patient came into the office, a mother with a little kid and I said automatically what's your name. And she said Simone. Not the way you say it S'mown but Sea-moan and the tears started running down my face. I never wanted that to happen again. It's unfair that you'll never run into anyone with my name. Does anyone else have it?
 Your old friend,
 Alice

Dear Simone,
 Thank you for the card. Hope you like this one. I hope you managed to get away as you planned to see the old woman before she had the operation. Aren't the survival rates for those jobs improving? It always seems funny writing to you on the prairies. I try to imagine you there and I always see you arriving at the bus station. I hope you have a happy birthday in your old stamping ground.
 Alice

Dear Simone,
 I'm going to be a shameless boastful parent. My Simone has turned out to be a very clever girl. Why shouldn't she be with you as her namesake? Her sisters will be content to be traditional brides but not Simone. I sometimes think the name must have had a special power. She is going away to school in England. My sister and

her husband live in London and she will spend the holidays with them. So my heart is broken once again. *Alice*

Dearest Simone,

    I hope you got back safely. I'm writing out of turn but I feel I must, I've so much I want to say because we said so little when we were together, seemed not to need to. Ever since then I've been overwhelmed with images of you — waking up to find you standing in the window, pulling the curtain aside to look at that scrubby jardin publique, your beautiful hair shining — going back to your room to rumple the bed and make it look slept in. I've been torn between misery at thinking that we might have had that always, and gratitude that we had it when we did. That one thing you said keeps coming back to me — "Why didn't we have more courage?" *A.*

Dear Simone,

    It's been so long since we exchanged letters but there's no one else I can write this to. You know my Simone was everything to me, so full of promise, so intelligent, so beautiful. She's thrown it all away, her family, her friends, her future, to live the most abject life that's bound to end badly. You asked once when it was too late why we didn't have more courage. This isn't courage it's recklessness and blindness because she's so young and so inexperienced. I could have countenanced any kind of marriage she wanted to make even at her age, but he's so unworthy of her, old enough to know better but completely irresponsible and unconcerned for her wellbeing. What can a parent do? It's already too late anyway. Simone, I don't even know if this will reach you or where you are. If it does, get back to me immediately. I feel I must talk to you, see you if possible. I'm at the same address, always have been, always will be, waiting desperately to hear from you. *A.*

XIX

IT'S FUNNY HOW a routine establishes itself even in the most unlikely circumstances. When you disappear for a day to forage for supplies, I'm restless and uneasy. I fear that you won't return, that you'll have an accident, feel a sudden urge to make a getaway while you can, break for freedom.

I wonder what it is that keeps you here beside me. I can't believe that it's affection for me or a sense of obligation or even that my story holds you. I'm trying so hard to remember everything, but you know the ending (you are the ending) and so it can't be the desire to know what happens.

When you are here and I have no pain, I feel perfectly happy, as contented as I ever have in my whole life. I cherish our quiet days and want them to last forever. I receive the sunrise as a gift, and your coming to sit here in this room. I know my story makes you angry sometimes, but on days when you sound pleased and understand how it all came about, I bask, washed with your pleasure and warmth like a seal on a rock in sunshine.

When we eat our meal, and you light the candles and bring up the good wine and reassure me that the store is still holding out, I feel — to use your word — blessed. I even like the food you manage to find — the acrid goat's cheese, the coarse bread, and the bitter fruits. You have very funny eating habits, you know that. If I don't eat much, it's not because I dislike the food. It's because I want to put off the time when you have to go out and forage for more.

Even when I'm unable to go on with the story, I like lying here, listening to you rustle through the boxes, reading clippings, studying photographs, placing cool cloths on my forehead.

~

All night I heard the rain pounding on the roof. I believe now that what I most dread has happened. I listen for sounds in the place below or outside, for the footfalls on the stairs, one light and one heavy, that will never come. I try not to panic, but to be reasonable and balanced. The last months couldn't have been happier, no care more solicitous and loving. It had to end. And if there was no warning, no good-bye, that's no cause for resentment. It's too painful always to say good-bye. How could it have helped? I might have lost control and pleaded, "Stay with me, please stay. I can't last much longer and . . . " Once I told you, "Go when you must, it is kind that you came at all and stayed so long."

Perhaps I'm uneasy for no reason. But what makes me think the worst is that I found, in the kitchen, three bottles of brandy brought up and set on the table. They seemed to say — You're alone and it will be hard, but here, take us for solace. And beside them was your recorder and a few tapes. Surely you wouldn't have left your recorder behind if you'd gone for good. And why would you leave the tapes?

Now I start to worry that there were parts of the story you rejected. I tried to tell it so as not to hurt you, to make it as palatable as possible, but often I forgot and veered into byways that must have been painful to you.

"Was I an accident?" you said.

"No," I said, firmly. "For one thing, Simone didn't have accidents."

"She had one," you said.

I don't think it was an accident. She was careful, she knew how to protect herself. It was a calculated risk she took, going to such dangerous territory. And it was a calculated risk going into that building after the explosion. She brought out three people before the second bomb went off. I think about those lives she saved. Were they worth saving? I'll never know because it all happened so far away.

∽

All these days I've sat listening to you, Lucy. Like they said, your voice washes over everything, embalms everything in words, Lucy's trained hypnotic voice interprets everything. You talk and talk because you're in love with your own voice, your own story. It's like solo sex for you.

I've sat at your feet like one of your disciples, catching the words as they come out of your mouth on my little machine so that I can play it over, my gospel, my life-story. You said to me one day, about your failing sight, that seeing wasn't everything, that hearing was good too. But you hardly ever heard me. If I did say anything, you never listened. It wasn't — what's the word — appropriate? significant? You never saw me. Perhaps you never saw anyone who wasn't shaped in your own image. All you were left with was listening, and you had a short attention span for that. By your own admission, you're a selfish half-blind old woman. If that's mean, why shouldn't I be mean?

I thought that when I walked in the first time, you might put your hands on my face and say, "Tell me about yourself, let me feel your hands." But no, you launched right away into the story, your story. Those women you spoke of — Lucia, Jinny, Monica, Lena, Julia, Simone. Anyway, they were not really people but characters you invented. You thought you heard me smiling, heard me laughing. It was disbelief you heard in my voice. Or yawning.

What's weird is you don't even care about me, don't know whether I'm man or woman, male or female. You know how I was raised, though. You heard about Andrea's twins when she got them, but you never guessed where she got them from. You were too busy catching up on your work and revelling in Renny's company. And a lot of religious people were adopting native kids. Simone never had accidents you said. Oh no? It must have been a lucky accident finding another dark-skinned baby so she could pass us off as a matched pair and throw you all off the scent.

You don't need to hear much, do you, Lucy, to put together a tale. A little bit goes a long way when you get hold of it, talking up a storm, molding characters, inventing motives. Half the time you forgot I was there altogether. The only time you listened was when I said what I remembered about Simone. You perked up pretty fast then. How sad, you thought, seeing Simone's face hovering over mine. Then you took off, like a preacher on a Sunday, preaching your own sermon based on those words I said. "Simone appeared at your bedside, you say ... She appeared at mine too ... lit up like on a stage ... " and on and on you go.

I'm not a talker, Lucy. Though if I hung around you for much longer I would be. Getting up in the morning, I'd look out the window and your words would come floating out of my mouth like bad breath. If you'd taken my hands, you might have understood something. You would have found them strong and muscular, gnarled, unusual for someone my age. I don't trust talkers myself, I trust hands. Yours are very soft, as if you've worn gloves all your life and never washed a dish or scrubbed a floor.

I've been asked plenty of times when I got off on what I do. It was Christmas at the church. We were always at the church. Old biddies set up a crèche. Mary, Joseph, a hut made out of pizza boxes, a crib with a kid in it, and some animals. Farm animals and zoo animals. It was the animals I wanted. When I got hold of some playdough, I made one of my own. "What is it?" they asked. "Is it a pig? Is it a sheep?"

It was a creature. This was the first time I put my foot down. Here's what a cow looks like. Make a cow. The more they pushed, the more stubborn I got about these creatures. Then someone said, "This child has talent." That surprised them. Some person in authority, a bit like you, made a declaration that came down over me like a sheet. Or like an antiseptic wash over the exposed nerve in a tooth. "A remarkable talent, quite unusual." So the stuff about "Is it a pig?" stopped.

Then some other person came up with another sheet, another antiseptic bath. It had to come from somewhere, this talent. Because of my dark skin it must have come from an ancestral gene. They encouraged it by giving me pictures of animals carved in wood and bone and soapstone. Books about totem poles and canoes full of animals dressed up like people.

My dumb brother looked at them all and tried to make things — pigs and dogs. By that time they'd caught on that creatures were O.K., they didn't have to look like something. Suddenly the pigs and cows got no praise, however much they looked like real pigs and cows. The poor thing was beaten out by me once again. Sun and moon we were. I might look funny, but I was smart, they said, I was talented. God balanced it all out — the bad things and the good things. I had this lame foot, but I had a gift with my hands.

She brought me one day to a place, I thought it was another hotel. "Where are we going, Auntie?" It was a long drive and it looked like a hotel to me, with its big windows overlooking a park, and statues all along the drive and in the trees. I was a bit shocked because I hadn't seen too many statues of people with no clothes on. But it wasn't a hotel and there was no swimming pool. It was a house where rich people lived. There was a man who looked at me the way my aunt did. He took us upstairs to where there were a lot of little statues and pictures on the walls like the ones in the books. I'd never seen such a big house, with a long driveway that ended in a circle round a flowerbed. My aunt and the man kissed each other. He was short, and when they kissed he had to reach up because she was taller than he was. They watched me at first and then they stood by the window, talking and whispering. I was left alone and I could just look, walking around the room. Some of the things were on islands by themselves, and I looked up and walked around them. I'd seen ones like them in shops and in books — seals and birds — but never ones so big.

"Which ones do you like best?" he asked.

"The funny ones." There was one great yawning mouth like a shark's jaws on little legs.

"Funny ones?"

"That don't look like people or animals. What are they? Demons?"

"Not demons but spirits." And he told me what they were and something about them, but I wasn't listening. I wanted to hold them.

"Would you like one to take home?"

"Oh, that's impossible," she said. "You know that."

"Impossible, why?"

"They're valuable, for one thing. And where would they keep it, and where on earth would I say it came from?"

I wanted one. Not one of the great big ones — one of the little ones I could keep hidden in my pocket and stroke secretly.

"You keep it until such a time . . . "

"That's what I've been trying to tell you," she said, "there won't be a time . . . "

Perhaps she called him "Max," or perhaps I've added the name after listening to you.

"Let me give you one," he said.

"I'd like that one," I said, pointing.

"You shall have it."

I sat down and held it on my lap. It was a person but with two heads, joined at the waist, very peculiar. They were talking again, standing by the fireplace. " . . . to have everything. I have no one else to leave it to . . . where I'm going is . . . you can't tell what will happen."

"Then why go?"

"I have to."

"Then you'll surrender everything, all control."

"This is where you come in."

"Me? Why me?

"You know what we agreed that time in the car going across

the border? You'd be free from responsibility, but you'd help later if I needed it. I need it now."

"I'll do what I can, but you have to make some arrangement. I can't just burst in on them."

"I want that foot fixed." (I always perked up and listened when people started talking about my foot. I forgot it until someone mentioned it. "What's the matter with that foot? How did it get like that? Was it a birth injury or caused in a car accident?") "It should have been done long ago."

"Andrea doesn't object to that surely. She isn't a Christian Scientist is she?"

"Might as well be. It's God's will."

"Ah, the mark of Cain."

At the other meeting, later, in the motel in Salmon Arm, he seemed different. I couldn't even be sure if he was the same man. Now he had grey hair and a beard. I'd driven all night and planned to get back the same day, because I was on duty at the community centre. There were two of them this time. He was with a thin woman with circles under her eyes who smoked all the time.

"There's a definite resemblance to Simone," they said to each other but not to me. They never said "your mother" or "your aunt" but "Simone" and "Andrea." They explained about the money. "It isn't a huge amount as these things go, but it is a substantial amount and if invested wisely . . . " It seemed like a lot to me.

I wanted to say there were two of us. How could they be sure I was the one? When I brought up the subject, they didn't get it, said that the money was mine, to spend or share or do what I wanted to with it. That was the way Simone willed it. They didn't say to get my foot fixed, though the woman noticed, I could see that. He asked did I have any plans? I said I wanted to take some college courses. "Naturally," he said. "Good." "What are you interested in?" she said. "I like making things with my hands," I said. They smiled at that, liking the idea. "Would you like to take art courses," she said, "be a sculptor?" "No," I said, "I've been working at a dental clinic." "A dentist?" he said, with a look of surprise on his face. "No, a denturist," I said, "making false teeth." And their faces fell, the way yours did, Lucy, when I told you what I did. What I do. I'm very good at it and I take a lot of pride in my work. When I meet people in the drugstore, in the supermarket, or at church I always stare at their teeth. And if they have dentures and have a nice smile, I'm happy even if I didn't make the teeth myself. I think someone did a good job and changed their lives. You'd have been a lot better off, Lucy, with false teeth. They're healthier and more hygienic, and that chip on your front tooth looks awful.

What I do is an art, that's what it is. And I'm an artist in my own way, like a painter or a dancer.

The ending of life isn't easy. Much harder than the beginning, and that's bad enough. This is no worse than most. True, I seem to be alone and fairly helpless. But loneliness and pain usually go with death, especially for those of us who outlive everyone else.

All of them had harder deaths than me. I think most about Simone, wondering if she died instantly or if she lingered, perhaps lying in a dirty bed, the country in an uproar. Did they even have proper facilities, adequate medicines, trained staff? And Julia, coughing her last breath in that stable in the middle of nowhere, me running for help, screaming, and not finding it in time. And Max, living out his days in a warehouse for mindless shells of human beings. And the others too, some of whom I feel responsible for — poor abandoned Esther, sweet little Suzy, long-lost Lucia, and Jinny. That terrible diary of Monica's haunts me to the end.

Self-pity is the thing to fight, also despair, panic, and emptiness — the big void. I am still Lucy Heathcote and in command of my senses. More or less. I have this little gadget so that I can call for help and someone will come rushing to my side so that I don't die alone. Hired help at this stage is preferable to the kind that makes claims. The trouble is that anyone seeing this place might decide I shouldn't be here by myself, so I'll get taken to a warehouse.

I intended to arrange the ending myself, but I left it too late, so the most I can hope for now is to fall asleep, not wake up but drift peacefully into oblivion. Yet every day when I wake up, I'm happy that I survived the night. But I no longer want to hear movement below, the clumsy step on the stair, and a voice saying, "I'm sorry I was delayed, you didn't think, did you . . . ? Oh you poor old thing . . . " I heard enough about false teeth to last me a lifetime. I had a suspicion that you might be the other one, not the one Simone conceived. But you convinced me at last of your genetic heritage. It was when you said I didn't make the most of myself with my yellow teeth. It was your grandmother's voice exactly.

There's a lot of nonsense talked about dying. The main thing is that it's like being dragged out of the theatre before the end of the movie. You never know what happens next day, or next year, to the world, or to your children and their children. You have to leave because you have business elsewhere, you have a rendezvous, but the story goes on without you, and amazing things may happen, but you'll never know about them. Is it because I'm so curious that I've lived so long? I could never bear to leave before the end of a show.

Sam wanted me to one time. It was a movie we'd already seen, so I was supposed to know the ending. But I couldn't accept that it would be the same as last time, that everything was preordained. I thought there was a chance that the second time around it would all turn out better. I couldn't tear myself away, and he was furious. "I have to pick up the kids," he said. "Yes," I said, whispering in the theatre, "you go on. I'll get home alright." So he left, had to.

A good thing Simone didn't stick around for the ending and find out how her little love-child turned out. It's hard for women to be heroes, and martyrdom always beckons. Plenty of role models for that. But she should have found a better way for herself and the child. I can't say I want to know more myself, after that babbling about teeth. Not that I've anything against making teeth or fixing teeth, but it was the bit about art that finished me off. And not knowing the difference. How could I expect her to understand what I was trying to tell her? And such resentment! She didn't even stop to consider my deafness, realize that when she walked out of earshot I could only pick up the odd word. Simone.

I can't remember the name of the film just now. But it turned out badly again for everybody, exactly as it had the first time. And for me. I emerged from the dark theatre, the bright afternoon sunshine making me nearly as blind as I am now. I made my way to the bus stop and waited, alone, because the buses were infrequent and the next one wouldn't come for ages.

And then a car pulled up to the curb. It was Sam come to collect me, the girls in the back silent because he was in a rage and his rages were terrifying. I seem to remember that Simone was there, squeezed in the back seat between them and whispering, "Is your dad mad at your mom? Why is your dad mad?" And Suzy whispering, "Shush up, Simone," frightened, fearing an explosion.

It wasn't a happy moment, but it passed, and I'd give anything to have it back to live over again. At least we were all alive, and together, and there was the chance then that everything might have turned out differently. Perhaps the thing I cherish most in my whole life is something that Renny said.

"We were with you such a short time, Lucy, but it was the only time I knew what it was like to have a family, to go home and not be afraid of what I'd find there. Everyone needs that. It gave me a kind of permanent base, something to stand on. So in a sense you were the only mother I ever had."

And Sam — but that's another story, only there's no one to tell it to.

I've just remembered the name of the film. I knew it would come back to me because my memory still functions, though sporadically. It was *La Strada*. I can still hear the tune in my head. And I can feel Sam's arm, warm and heavy around my shoulder, before he took it away and said we had to leave. Now I've lost the tune. If I listen hard and don't try to sing it, it will all come back.